for:
Alice Anne Carroll, my grandmother
Emily Carroll Bell, my mother
Alice Carroll George Davidson, my daughter
Emily Anne Davidson, my granddaughter

How impossible to contend
Where I stop and you begin.

This One and Magic Life

This One and Magic Life

ANNE CARROLL GEORGE

AVON BOOKS  NEW YORK

This is a work of fiction. Names, characters, places and incidents either are the product of the author's imagination or are used fictitiously. Any resemblance to actual events, locales, organizations, or persons, living or dead, is entirely coincidental and beyond the intent of either the author or the publisher.

AVON BOOKS, INC.
1350 Avenue of the Americas
New York, New York 10019

Copyright © 1999 by Anne Carroll George
Interior design by Kellan Peck
ISBN: 0-380-97599-8

Library of Congress Cataloging in Publication Data:

George, Anne.
This one and magic life : a novel of a southern family /
Anne Carroll George. — 1st ed.
        p.   cm.
             I. Title.
PS3557.E469T48   1999   99-20896
        813'.54—dc21   CIP

First Avon Books Printing: September 1999

AVON TRADEMARK REG. U.S. PAT. OFF. AND IN OTHER COUNTRIES, MARCA
REGISTRADA, HECHO EN U.S.A.

Printed in the U.S.A.

FIRST EDITON

QPM   10   9   8   7   6   5   4   3   2   1

www.avonbooks.com

❧

Dance in the sunlight,
dance in the moonlight,
dance on through this do-si-do,
this one and magic life.

This One and Magic Life

Artie

THE BAY. IT DRAWS HER THESE LAST FEW NIGHTS OF HER DYING. She rises from her bed that has been placed downstairs, and, careful not to wake Mrs. Randolph, opens the front door and steps onto the porch.

She is weak, but the pain is distant, like a thunderstorm held at the horizon. She crosses the yard slowly and rests at the top of the steps that lead to the beach. The air is warm, moist, and still. She feels it settling around her. Then slowly she begins her descent. Sea oats brush against her hands as she clasps the railing.

She pulls off her nightgown, folds it on the last step, and crosses the narrow beach to the water. The sand is cool to her bare feet, but the water is warm and quiet as bathwater. She walks into it and sits down, then lies back, one arm beneath her head.

The moon is a cup spilling out stars. Was it Papa who had said that once? Or had she read it? It doesn't matter. She sees that it is true. Stars drop from the sky, burning, into the bay.

She could sleep here like a baby in its sea of amniotic fluid. Sometimes she thinks she remembers what that was like, floating with Donnie in Sarah's belly.

Sarah.

Artie closes her eyes and sees them all: Donnie, her other half, Carl, her husband, Bo, her love, Dolly, child of her heart, Hektor, Zeke Pardue, Papa, Mama.

Warp and woof of her life. But, on these last few nights of her dying, it is Sarah, her mother, that Artie longs for.

When she sits up, water pools in the bony conclaves of her body. She holds her palms together, fills them with water, and, bending, pours the water slowly over her head.

TWO

Mobile Bay

ALL DAY THERE IS A SLIGHT BREEZE FROM THE EAST. FLAGS ON the Harlow community pier stir, even ripple at times; washing dries on clotheslines strung between pecans and live oaks. Soon towels and sheets, stiff, smelling of soap, Mobile Bay, and August will be folded and put into linen closets. Out on the bay, brown pelicans skim the water.

And all day the people who live around the bay watch the water. They walk to the edge and dip their hands into the small warm waves that wash against the beach. They cup their hands around their eyes and look across the gray-green surface. Nothing. "But it's a full moon tonight," they agree. And they get their baskets and seines ready.

In Harlow, after dark, they put a watchman on the pier, but he is not needed. Even before his first shout of "Jubilee!" people are running to watch the fish slice the water's skin with their serrated, glistening fins, running to see the water whorl as the fish glide past each other, circling into the shallows toward the beach.

"Here they come!"

"Jubilee!"

"Would you look at that!"

"Jubilee! Jubilee!" sing the fishermen to the millions of moons in the bay.

"Jubilee! Jubilee!" Artie Sullivan hears. Then she clutches her sheet and dies.

Mrs. Randolph, the sitter, rushes to get buckets and a flashlight from the back porch so she can join the other Harlow residents who are already gathering fish, crabs, and shrimp that are silvering the beach like a wave. "Jubilee! Jubilee!" echoes across the bay.

"I knew it," Mrs. Randolph calls to the next-door neighbor who is running across the lawn carrying a net. "You could just tell the wind was right."

"Gumbo tomorrow!" the woman answers. "Come help me hold the net."

"Gumbo for everybody!" Mrs. Randolph hurries down the steep narrow path to the beach.

"Jubilee! Jubilee!" everyone sings before excited laughter becomes the silence of concentration, of choosing the choicest bounty. And even as they fill their buckets, more fish and crabs rise to the beach. Nets and buckets grow heavy.

"I never have understood why they do it," Mrs. Randolph says, picking crabs carefully from the net.

"Why they come to the beach? Something to do with the oxygen in the water." Both women suddenly remember how the beach will smell in a couple of days, how they will have to rake the fish carcasses into piles and pay the garbage men extra to carry the mess away. And the flies! Mrs. Randolph is thinking how impossible it is to get all the shells out of crabmeat. Even in the best restaurants you get shells. At a dear price, too.

By the time Mrs. Randolph returns to the house, slightly out of breath and with her neck aching, Artie is definitely dead.

For a moment, Mrs. Randolph is startled. But only for a moment. Then she straightens Artie's head on the pillow, goes to call Donnie and Father Carroll and find the crab boil.

THREE

Dream Catchers

DONNIE SULLIVAN IS HAVING AN ANXIETY DREAM WHEN MRS. Randolph calls. Ten strangers sit around a conference table looking at him expectantly. It's a board meeting, he realizes, and he has no idea what the meeting is about; his heart pounds. Still caught in his dream, he hears Mariel say hello from the other side of the bed.

"Yes," he hears her say. "Yes. Thank you, Mrs. Randolph." Mariel hangs up the phone, turns on the lamp, and sits up.

Donnie knows. "She's gone?"

Mariel nods. For a few minutes, neither moves. The air conditioner clicks on and the curtains stir.

"I'll make some coffee." Mariel pushes Meow off her chenille robe. The old cat yawns and stretches across Donnie's feet.

"Should we call Dolly now?"

"Let's let her sleep." Mariel starts out the door and then looks back. Donnie has turned on his side, his back toward her. She walks to the bed and touches his shoulder. "You okay? You want a Valium or something?"

"I'm fine. I think I'll call Hektor."

Mariel hesitates a moment and then leaves the room. Donnie reaches for the phone, but halfway through dialing Hektor's number in New Orleans, he forgets what the next digit is. He hangs up and tries again. "Hektor?" he says when he hears his brother's sleepy voice. "Artie's gone."

"What?" There is a long moment of silence. Donnie knows Hektor is pushing himself up, rubbing his eyes. "You said Sunday she was doing better, Donnie."

"She was, Hektor. I was out there last night."

"Well, damn Donnie. Artie died just like that?" Another long pause. "We should have been there with her."

Donnie rubs his own eyes. "I know."

"I'll be there as soon as I can."

"Okay."

Something else needs to be said. Donnie asks, "Hektor, do you remember getting bitten by a snake when you were real little?"

"No. Why?"

"I just wondered. Come as soon as you can, little brother." Donnie hangs up the phone and closes his eyes. Last night Artie had asked him if he remembered Hektor and the snake, and of course he had. He could still see the snake, brown with lighter rings of tan, could still hear Hektor crying. But he and Artie were crying louder because they didn't want to tell Mama they had been playing at the forbidden creek.

"Let's wait and see what happens," Artie had said finally. "If he gets sick, we'll tell Mama."

"Over fifty years ago," he had told Artie last night. "How old were we? Six?"

"Something like that. Old enough to know better."

And they had smiled at each other. Just last night.

Meow begins to knead the cotton blanket over Donnie's feet. "Stop that," he says, pushing the cat gently to the floor and getting up. The air seems heavy, as if he has to push against it. He walks to the window and lets up the shade. The moon is waning. The hour of the wolf, the time most people are born and die. And now Artie has died, his twin.

Across the bay, hundreds of small lights move in random patterns. For a minute, Donnie is puzzled. Then, "By damn, it's a jubilee," he says and leans his forehead against the cool glass.

Dolly Sullivan is awake when her parents decide not to call her. She is sitting at her kitchen table in her Atlanta apartment sampling a recipe she plans to call "Dolly's Chicken" for want of another name and trying to decide whether the curry powder and chutney are too exotic for what is basically a South Alabama recipe. Walt liked it, but what does he know? She takes another bite and holds it on her tongue. Definitely too exotic. Well, she won't include it in her low-fat cookbook. As for Walt, what on God's earth had made her think he would be interesting? His name? She's been a sucker for the name "Walt" since the eleventh grade when a hippie substitute stood on Mrs. Burris's desk and read Walt Whitman's "Song of Myself" to the startled students. He was there only one day, but he had made an impression. Well, tonight's Walt was neither Whitman nor interesting hippie. And she, Dolly, was twenty-seven years old and couldn't say "Go home" to a man who talked financial planning all night, brought a bottle of Gallo Rhine, and ate two huge breasts of Dolly's Chicken with chopped chutney. Then he wanted to spend the night. Ha! So much for venturing into the dating pool again. He was lucky to get coffee.

Dolly pushes her chair back and stretches. Her father laughed when she said she was writing a cookbook.

"Look at you," he said. "Think you could sell any cookbooks? You look like you never had a square meal in your life."

And her Aunt Artie had laughed at him saying, "With a body like hers, she'll sell a mint of them, Donnie." God. Artie.

Artemis and Adonis in Harlow, Alabama, with all the Shirleys and Joes. Their father's idea. But their mother could have put her foot down. Should have. Instead, she let him name the next one Hektor. Dolly isn't even sure who Hektor is in mythology, but she often wishes that she had known the couple who had the nerve to give their children such names.

She reaches into the cabinet for some aluminum foil, wraps the single remaining piece of chicken, and puts it into the almost empty refrigerator. She'll take it for lunch tomorrow. That Walt. What a waste.

She should have called Harlow tonight. Since Artie's been sick with lymphoma, she's called several times a week.

"I'm fine," Artie always says. "How's your work?"

"Fine," Dolly says. Both of them are lying and both of them know it. Dolly's dream of becoming a choreographer has dead-ended at the Atlanta Children's Theater, and Artie is dying. Each time Dolly has seen Artie this year, she has been smaller and more beautiful, almost silver. *If I turn out the light, she will shine in the dark,* Dolly thought the last time she was with Artie. And she had held Artie's hand lightly and dreamed of a dance so wild with leaps and whirls that only anger could sustain it. She would call it, she thought, "Capturing the Light."

She finishes clearing the table and goes into the bedroom. It's a small room almost filled by a king-sized brass bed that she and Bobby had splurged on when they first moved in together. Maybe it was the sight of this bed that had made Walt feel he might be welcome to stay the night.

Dolly walks across the bed. She's learned to do this; for a long time she walked around it. Drawing the draperies, she thinks how even the city has special pre-dawn sounds. Or silences.

Hektor Sullivan, president of Sullivan-Threadaway Imports, one of the largest importers of fruit from Central America, hangs up the phone after talking to his brother and stares at the ceiling. A presidential advisor on Latin America and sometime dabbler in politics where even he knows he has no business, Hektor is surprised at the overwhelming sadness that fills him. He has known since Easter that Artie's lymphoma was no longer in remission. Yet, somehow, he had not expected her to die. The whole thing is—he searches for the word—capricious. That's it. Capricious of her.

There is a strange sound in the room. Like small waves slapping the beach at Harlow. For a moment, Hektor is alarmed, and then he realizes it's his breathing, that with each outward breath there is a catch, a tiny groan. And when he wills the groans to stop, they don't but instead crawl through the air conditioner to ten-year-old May who runs to see if he is all right and who sees her father for the first time as a separate person. He is sitting on the edge of the bed; tears splash down his blue pajamas.

"It's your Aunt Artie," he says. May, sitting by him, holding his hand, already knows. "We have to go to

Mobile this morning. Can you help me get everything ready here?"

"Sure. I'm sorry, Papa."

She looks more Mayan every day, Hektor thinks, rubbing his freckled hand against her tanned arm. That black hair. Those eyes.

"Her Maya," the old woman had said. "Belong you and Ana. Ana dead."

And he had held out his arms and taken the baby and knew she was his, though he could not remember an Ana. And he had carried the baby to the bed and instinctively undressed her and counted her fingers and toes and admired the tiny whorls of her ears and sex. And when he took a washcloth and bathed her, she had opened her eyes and looked at him. It was an astounding experience.

"Bonding," his sister Artie had said when he tried to put it into words.

Whatever. Hektor only knew that if he couldn't have pulled strings to get May out of Honduras, he would have stayed there the rest of his life.

"She makes everything real," he confessed to Artie. And Artie hugged him and said, "I'm glad you didn't die, Hektor." Which seemed to him a strange thing to say.

"I'll make you some coffee." May stands by the bed, tall in her pink nightgown. Oh, god. Growing up.

"Fine," Hektor says. He opens the blinds; the sky is lightening. Outside Ruggy and Doc begin to bark loudly.

Wednesday.

Garbage day.

FOUR

Almond Pie

THE DEEP SOUTH IS STILL A MYSTERY. IT IS EVEN A MYSTERY TO those who live there. Live oaks trailing Spanish moss whisper and move around during the night. Sometimes they move next door. A mystery. But that's the way things are.

There are bays and bayous and runoff creeks that don't run but meander through swamp grass into deep woods where panthers and bears still live. Flowers no one has ever seen or cataloged bloom here; alligators and cottonmouths slide silently through the water.

It is here that Thomas Sullivan brings his bride, Sarah, in June 1927. Here to Harlow, Alabama, with Mobile Bay in front of them and the wild woods behind them. They come down the shell road in their new Model T that they paid $250 for yesterday in Mobile. Thomas has already changed one flat tire. They come to the water, to a narrow beach that magnolias and palmettos are trying to claim. If they turn left, they will have dinner at the Grand Hotel where guests are ferried in from Mobile. If they turn right, they will climb the only hill on Mobile Bay and look out over the water, dotted by sailboats. They will get out of the car and smell honeysuckle, magnolia, and the strong seminal odor of the bay.

"Let's see what's up there." Thomas points to his right. And that decision, of course, makes all the difference.

Two houses have already been built on the red clay bluff overlooking the water. Wooden steps lead from the front yard of each down to a pink strip of beach where a blue heron wades in a tidal pool. In the distance, the city of Mobile rises like a mirage.

Thomas, who is from Massachusetts, has never seen such exotic lushness. He equates it with Sarah who stands beside him in a peach-colored voile dress.

"Dear God!" he says, looking around, afraid he will miss something.

Sarah smiles at Thomas's reaction. Her front teeth are slightly crooked; freckles are scattered across her nose. She is beautiful.

"I want a house right here," Thomas says.

"Fine," Sarah agrees. She has been married five days. She takes Thomas's arm in both her hands. It is warm and hard. "But right now we'd better go to dinner. They'll run out of almond pie for sure."

And then Thomas Sullivan does something that delights his new wife. "Hold these," he says. He hands Sarah his glasses and then does cartwheels down the beach. And that is what Sarah will remember most about this day, the cartwheels and a boat with a vivid blue sail that draws a line across the horizon.

FIVE

Banana Republic Shirts

MARIEL CALLS HER DAUGHTER DOLLY ABOUT SEVEN O'CLOCK TO tell her her Aunt Artie is dead. Died in her sleep, peacefully, no pain, and Dolly should come as soon as she can. Oh, and be sure to bring something conservative to wear.

Dolly says she'll be there as soon as she can get a flight, buries her head in a pillow, and cries. Finally, exhausted, she gets up, goes into the bathroom, and takes some aspirin. That damn Walt. If it hadn't been for him, she would have talked to Artie last night. Tears flow again. She wets a washrag and sits on the side of the tub holding it against her eyes. Damn. Damn.

The alarm clock going off in the bedroom forces her up. She walks across the bed and turns the alarm off. Seven-thirty. Bobby will be up; he'll want to know about Artie. She dials his number, gets his answering machine, says, "Bobby, Artie's dead," and hangs up quickly. The call makes her chest feel tight. Or maybe it's the crying.

Dolly wipes her face again with the cool wet cloth.

There's a lot to be done here. Call Jim Nelson at the Children's Theater and tell him she won't be there for a few days to count the steps for the rabbits and robots. Call the airport.

First things first. She looks up U.S. Air's number and after listening to ten minutes of Vivaldi gets on a standby flight at noon.

Clothes. She ought to wear her silver cocktail dress, she thinks, opening her closet. Artie would have appreciated it. But she doesn't feel like facing her mother's lip-pursing. In the past, this has been brought on by such indiscretions as wearing flip-flops on the plane or carrying a tote bag with the logo MERLE NORMAN printed on it. Dolly pulls out everything black in her closet—a pair of jeans and a turtleneck sweater and a lot of leotards and tights. Nothing to wear to a funeral. Every woman in the world has a black dress but Dolly. Every single one. She blows her nose on the washrag and starts pulling out beige clothes and throwing them on the bed. Surely her mother can't complain about beige.

And then Dolly remembers the yellow gauze skirt that Artie had liked so well that she had painted her in it twice. She takes it from the closet; it must go with her to Mobile.

She wishes she could have spoken to her father, but her mother said he was asleep, that he had been awake most of the night.

"Is he okay?" Dolly asked.

"He knew it was coming."

Dolly wanted to say, "That doesn't mean he's okay." But she kept her mouth shut. She knows he's not. It was a stupid question; his twin is dead.

Artie is dead. Dolly begins to cry again, sitting in the middle of the beige pile of clothes, in the middle of the huge bed, crying for her Aunt Artie and her father. And for herself, holding her yellow gauze skirt like the security blanket her mother had packed away long ago.

Dolly makes the flight. She is seated in the last seat on the plane, the one whose back is the wall of the rest room, the one that doesn't have a window. Her seatmate is a well-dressed middle-aged black man who helps her put her tote bag in the luggage rack. As soon as he is seated, he takes out some forms and a calculator and becomes totally absorbed in his work. Dolly glances over and sees nothing but numbers that look important. When the plane takes off and the flight attendant comes along with drinks, Dolly asks for a vodka tonic which she handles nervously. She can just see herself wiping out this man's entire career with one spilled drink. She pulls down the tray and places the glass on it. The man looks up and smiles.

"My aunt died this morning," Dolly is startled to hear herself saying. "She lived in a little town out from Mobile named Harlow. She was an artist. A painter."

"I'm sorry." He looks like he means it.

Dolly nods yes. Her eyes hurt; her head hurts. She reaches over and drains the vodka tonic.

"Would you like another one of those?"

"Please." There is something about the man that reminds her of Reese Whitley. He's black, sure, but years younger and, God knows, Reese wouldn't be caught dead in a suit on an airplane. And with a briefcase? But there's something that reminds her. The eyes?

He hands her the second drink and smiles again. Whatever—she's glad he's there beside her. Even with the calculator which whines.

She sips her drink and wonders how Reese is holding up. Probably not too good. Artie's best friend since the day he showed up at her house. Father, child, housekeeper, yardman, psychiatrist, friend, pain in the butt.

"Who is that man hanging around out at Artie's?" Mariel had wanted to know when Reese first came. "Artie doesn't know him from Adam's house cat, and she sashays off and leaves him the run of the place. I swear, Donnie, he could haul off everything she owns. Find out who he is."

But if her father had ever investigated, Dolly never knew. It wouldn't have mattered anyway. Reese was permanent.

"Feeling any better?" asks the man. Old wisdom, Dolly thinks. Old wisdom in the eyes. That's it. And she turns to smile at him, but he is already studying his charts again.

"Yes," Dolly lies.

She has steeled herself for her mother meeting her and looking her up and down. She's chewing Certs as she walks up the ramp because of the vodka tonics, but, to her surprise, her Uncle Hektor and May are waiting for her. Both have on shorts and Banana Republic Hawaiian shirts which make her Merle Norman bag pale in comparison. Hektor holds out his arms and Dolly walks into them.

His hug engulfs her. Dolly is always surprised at how large he and her father both are and how they smell exactly alike. She feels dizzy, her nose pressed into a bright green palm tree that seems caught in a storm. Uncle Hektor is crying, Dolly realizes. Sobbing.

She and May lead him to a row of blue vinyl chairs and sit on either side of him, holding his hands, offering tissues and scowling at people who look their way.

Hektor shakes his head. "I almost called her last night. Something told me to call her but I got busy on some paperwork and first thing I knew it was after eleven."

"Me, too. I meant to call her, too."

"She loved you so much."

This does Dolly in. She burrows her face against Hektor's arm and cries for a long time, his hand pressed against her head.

Finally he pats her and straightens up. "Little girl, your mama would say we're making a spectacle of ourselves in a public place."

"Being common." Dolly is having trouble talking. "Where is Mama, anyway? I thought she'd be here."

"She went on out to Harlow."

People walking by appear blurry. Dolly blinks; May hands her another tissue.

"How's Papa?"

"Seems to be holding up okay. I talked to him in Harlow around ten. He said he thought you'd be on this flight. Hand me another one of those Kleenexes, May." Hektor mops the tears from his cheeks. "Damn. Anyway, he said he thought you'd be on this flight, and I told him we'd be coming through about this time and would pick you up."

"I'm glad you did."

May stands up and announces that she is going to go to the gift shop, maybe buy a Goo Goo Cluster.

Hektor hands her a dollar. "Don't talk to strangers." He and Dolly watch the child walk away.

"She's getting tall, Uncle Hektor."

Hektor sighs. "I know." They sit quietly for a moment. "You want anything to eat?"

"Not really. I had a couple of drinks on the plane. Probably shouldn't have."

"Sounds good to me."

"What happened? I thought she was getting along pretty well."

"We all thought she'd have more time." Hektor wipes the back of his hand across his cheek. "Donnie was out there last night and she seemed about the same. Then there was a jubilee, and when Mrs. Randolph came back from the beach, Artie was dead. Just like that."

"She died during a jubilee? She'd love that."

"Maybe she knew."

They manage to smile at each other.

"I'll go collect my suitcase," Dolly says.

"Can you carry it okay?"

"It's just a weekender."

"Well, here comes May. How about I go get the pickup and meet the two of you at the front door?"

"This is good," May says, holding out a half-eaten Goo Goo Cluster. "Y'all want a bite?"

At the baggage claim, the bags are circling the carousel. "It's a gray American Tourister," Dolly tells May. Packed with everything gray, black, and beige that she owns. Dolly sighs. She knows that all her life, even after her mother is dead and gone, she will hear Mariel's pronouncements on the proper way to dress.

She tries a pronouncement out to see what it's like. "Never wear patent leather shoes after five, May."

"Okay." May is watching the bags. "I think this one is yours." They grab for it and hit heads.

"Shit!" they both say, rubbing their heads while the bag continues for another lap.

"Are you okay?" Dolly asks.

"I'm fine." May feels to see if there is a bump on her head. "If it had been my knee, you know what Aunt Artie would have said?"

"She'd have said, 'It's okay. You've got another one.' "

"That's right."

"She told me the same thing. Once I rode my bicycle too close to the garage corner and hit my little toe some way. Anyway, the toenail was hanging on by a thread. It was awful. And Artie snipped the nail off and told me it was okay, that I had nine more. I remember it made me furious." And Artie had taken her, almost as big as Artie herself, and rocked her and sung, "Pony boy, pony boy, won't you be my pony boy. Giddyup, giddyup, giddyup, *whoa!*" with Dolly too large for Artie to let drop between her knees on the "whoa" and not mad anymore.

Now she rubs her hand across her eyes. "Here comes the bag again, May. You get it this time. It's not heavy."

Ordinarily Dolly loves the drive to Harlow. When she was in high school, the drama class had put on *Brigadoon* and she had thought something like this could happen in Harlow. Someone could wander in in a hundred years and the Christmas lights would still be strung across Main Street in August, and the same people would be sitting on the pier. Father Carroll would still be having early mass and the same seven women would be there, kneeling in the early sunlight which was broken by the stained glass windows, breathing the familiar incense.

She thinks this as they cross the causeway with the water level with the truck, small waves breaking over the crosstie retaining wall. The midday August sun hits the bay so hard it ricochets off the few fishing boats that dot the surface.

"Windy today," Uncle Hektor says. "Hot wind.

Hope nothing's developing in the gulf." This, too, will be the same in a hundred years.

And maybe when they reach Harlow, she'll wake up and Artie will be on the dune painting and Reese will be in the kitchen cooking one of his mystery meals.

Dolly is sitting between Hektor and May since the pickup has only two seat belts. In case of an accident, she'll be the one to go. Okay, she can accept that.

"Reese was real upset," Hektor is saying, "when we hired Mrs. Randolph, you know. Said he could take care of Artie."

"He could have."

"Your mama wouldn't even consider it."

"Why?" Dolly holds up her hand. "Don't answer that. My mama has a burr up her butt."

"She just didn't think it would be proper."

"What did Artie say?"

"She went along with Mariel, surprisingly. I don't think it was because of the impropriety, though. I think it was to spare Reese."

"Probably to keep him from putting a hex on Mama."

"There's a woman in New Orleans does that," May says in her high voice. "Takes warts off, too."

"I doubt Reese would stop with warts."

"Can he put voodoo spells on people?"

"Of course not, sweetie." Hektor reaches over and pats May's knee. "Dolly's just teasing you."

"Ha," Dolly says.

They have reached the main street of town. Baskets of red verbena hanging from street signs droop in the August heat. The Bienville Garden Club ladies will water them come late afternoon. Dolly counts five people walking down the sidewalk. Two of them are darting from air-conditioned cars into the air-conditioned drugstore. Two are walking toward the library, and one is a UPS man delivering a package to a new herbal shop which everyone knows will not make it here in Harlow two months. Herbs. Good Lord.

"Stop, Uncle Hektor. I want out," Dolly says suddenly as they reach the bay.

"You sick?" He puts on the brakes.

"I just want to sit in the park for a few minutes. I'll walk on up to the house."

"It's mighty hot."

"I'll stay in the shade. And I won't be long."

"Okay. May, hop out, honey, and let Dolly out."

"Hot as hell out here," May grumbles. Her father pretends he doesn't hear her.

Dolly slides out of the truck onto the bay road. If she turns left, she will end up at the Grand Hotel where they still serve almond pie. If she turns right, she will climb the small hill to the house her grandparents, Sarah and Thomas, built over sixty years ago and where her Aunt Artie died last night. But all Dolly wants is to cross the road and sit on one of the benches under the live oak trees. She wants to look across the bay to Mobile, to borrow time to come home.

The park is nothing more than a grassy ribbon between the road and the small beach. Dolly brushes tendrils of Spanish moss from a white wooden bench that has COMPLIMENTS, SERTOMA CLUB painted on the back and sits down. Heat curls around her, making her sleepy.

Along the beach, a few people are still strolling, carrying baskets, picking up what the bay had given the night before. Dolly watches them until they become a dream.

"Hey, Dolly."

Dolly comes awake with a start.

"Sorry," Kelly Stuart says, sitting on the bench beside her. "I didn't realize you were asleep."

"I wasn't quite. Just sort of drifting."

Kelly reaches over and touches Dolly's arm. "I was on my way to get some more crab boil and I thought it was you sitting here. You okay?"

"I'm fine." Dolly smiles at her childhood friend. The Stuarts have always lived next door to Artie, and Kelly, Dolly's age, was long days of summer, Kool-Aid, Barbie dolls, and later, boys. "I just thought I'd sit here a while before I went up the house."

"I hate it about Artie." Kelly pulls her dark hair back and holds it up; her neck is damp.

"Me, too."

They sit quietly for a few moments.

"These folks are crazy," Kelly says, "picking up fish in this heat. Look at that fool." She points. "I swear I think he's got on a white dinner jacket."

Dolly stretches. "Probably thinks he's still partying at the Grand Hotel."

"Some party."

As they watch, the man picks up a fish, still wriggling, and hands it to a little boy who rushes with it to his mother. She waves a thank you.

"Let me take you home," Kelly says, getting up. "All I've got to do is run by the store and pick up some crab boil." She rubs her shoulders. "I swear jubilees are nice but, Lord knows, they create a lot of work."

Dolly comes to her feet. For a moment she feels as if she is floating.

"Sure you're okay?" Kelly asks.

Dolly feels the ground solidify beneath her feet. "Fine."

They walk toward Kelly's car.

"What's the score with Bobby?" Kelly opens the

door and shoves some magazines to the floor so Dolly can sit down. "These are for the library."

"The divorce is final."

"You relieved?"

"I guess so." No, she isn't relieved. She is shackled with loss and hurt. "What about your wedding plans?" she asks as Kelly gets in the car.

"Next spring. We'd thought this fall, but Grandmama's not doing too good."

Dolly feels guilty that she has not inquired about old Mrs. Stuart whom she has known all her life and who has rheumatoid arthritis. "I'm sorry."

"Good days and bad days." Kelly starts the car, makes a U-turn, and heads up the hill.

"I thought you had to go to the store," Dolly says.

"I do. But you, my friend, are wilting. You need a big glass of water and some air-conditioning."

"A cool shower would be nice."

"Damn, that sounds good. And then you can come help me peel shrimp."

"Don't hold your breath."

Kelly pulls into the driveway behind Artie's house. Dolly sees her mother's car, her Uncle Hektor's truck, and a car she doesn't recognize parked beneath the pecan trees. And suddenly she understands why she had had Uncle Hektor put her out at the park, why she had lingered.

When she steps out of this car into the shafts of sunlight through the trees, she will have to accept that things are forever changed.

SIX

Shifting Gears

DONNIE SULLIVAN IS SITTING ON THE DUNE BEYOND ARTIE'S house thinking about life and death. He is telling himself that his twin is dead. He is telling himself that he is almost fifty-nine years old. Behind him is the house where he grew up; in front of him is the bay where his parents drowned. A few people still walk the beach picking up fish from the jubilee.

In his thoughts about life and death, Donnie Sullivan has concluded that everyone will die and that there may or may not be a heaven or hell. What he truly believes is that Artie is over the next dune painting one of the pictures that look so fuzzy and earn her so much money. She is happy doing that. She told him time went away when she was painting, that it was like the world shifted gears.

Damn, but she drove him crazy. He'd be talking to her about something important like her income tax and realize she wasn't listening at all but was off in her own world. And then she would turn right around and be totally practical about something. With Artie you never knew what to expect.

He thinks of the day the boat brought in the bodies of their parents, how he, Artie, and Hektor had watched the men throw the rope to the pier and lift the canvas-covered bodies. It was raining, the heavy mist of Mobile Bay that lingers sometimes after a thunderstorm and slides off everything. The three of them stood watching the yellow bundles, one larger than the other, being lowered from the deck. Had anyone said anything to them while the bodies were lying there or being placed in the ambulance? He can't remember. There was only Artie turning fiercely toward Hektor and him, her face and hair wet, her fists clenched.

"It isn't them," she said. "You know it can't be them. We fixed everything."

"No, we didn't," Hektor sobbed. "We just thought we did, Artie. That's Mama and that's Papa."

But Donnie had looked into the mist of the bay and had felt a weight lifted from him. What was going to happen had happened.

God, how long ago that had been. During the night the rain had become a thunderstorm again and he had gotten up to check the windows. In his parents' room the light was on, and Artie was pulling clothes from the closet, and throwing them into a pile on the floor. He stood watching her, and she saw him watching her.

I should have gone in and helped her, he thinks now. We should have gotten Hektor up and the three of us should have talked about what had happened. We owed that to each other. He runs his hands through his thinning hair. His scalp feels hot.

He has never lived in a world without Artie.

Reese, wizened and black, crosses the yard and sees Donnie thinking.

"Ha," he says.

SEVEN

Chowchow Pickles

"I CANNOT UNDERSTAND TO SAVE MY SOUL WHY NEIGHBORS bring food that has to be refrigerated. Can you, Mrs. Randolph?" Mariel Sullivan sits on her haunches before the refrigerator trying to find room for another bowl of shrimp Creole and another squash casserole. "I can't cram another thing in here."

Mrs. Randolph, Artie's sitter who is staying to help, comes and looks over Mariel's shoulder. "Half that second shelf is pickles been in there forever. We could just throw them out. Save the jars."

"Fine with me." Mariel begins handing jars to Mrs. Randolph. "Some of this stuff is so old, Donnie's mother could have put it up."

"I didn't think she did anything like canning."

Mariel hesitates. "Oh? I didn't know you knew her."

She rises to her knees and straightens her back. In one hand is chowchow, in the other, pear relish. In the jar of chowchow, clearly as if in a crystal ball, she sees sick Artie gasping out all the family secrets and fat Mrs.

Randolph lapping them up like cream. "Murder," Artie whispers from the pickle jar, her face a white blur.

"Let me write that down," Mrs. Randolph says.

"What?" Mariel says with a start.

"Let me write down Mrs. Bell brought that squash casserole. What I wish they'd do is put their names on a piece of adhesive tape and stick it to the bottom of the dish. Save a lot of trouble. We started doing that at our church." Mrs. Randolph takes a list from her pocket and looks for a pencil.

Mariel shuts the refrigerator and puts the pickles on the counter.

"Did Artie talk much about Mrs. Sullivan?" she asks hesitantly.

"Said she was a terrible cook. Didn't you know her?"

"Sure. I grew up here in Harlow." Mariel takes a sliver of ham from a tray and nibbles on it. "When I was a teenager, I'd help out when Mrs. Sullivan had parties."

"Folks still talk about what elegant parties she had."

"They were elegant. That's for sure."

"Don't eat with your fingers, dear," Sarah Sullivan says.

Mariel sighs and rinses her hands in the kitchen sink while her mother-in-law Sarah reads the cards on the food. "Mississippi mud cake. Artie's favorite. Be sure to get the thank-you notes in the mail within a week, Mariel."

Mariel, who goes to a Jungian analyst once a week, knows Sarah is only a shadow. Sarah, dead over forty years, does not know this. She looks Mariel up and down. "Of course, Artie could always eat anything she wanted and not gain an ounce."

"Artie must have taken after her mother. She was

gone a lot when I first married Earl and moved here from Selma, but everyone had stories to tell about her. And you know what? Even at the end you could tell how pretty she'd been." Mrs. Randolph fits another plastic-covered bowl of shrimp Creole into the refrigerator. "There."

Mariel looks down at her tan pants and beige shirt. Size ten. Shadow or no shadow, one of Sarah's favorite things to do is make Mariel feel insecure. Artie had done the same thing.

"Artie," Mariel tells Mrs. Randolph, "wasn't a thing like her mother. She wasn't like anybody else in the world."

Mrs. Randolph closes the refrigerator and smiles. She has not studied Jungian psychology, but the good Lord blessed her with common sense. She can spot jealousy in an instant.

The back door slams. "I'm here," Dolly calls. She stands in the wide hall that her grandmother Sarah had designed to pick up every breeze from Mobile Bay. The house smells familiarly of almonds, the potpourri that Artie ordered from California to fill the large Chinese bowl. Almonds. There is no smell of flowers or antiseptic or medicine. Just almonds. Dolly closes her eyes. Sarah, she thinks. Artie. And now me. If I stayed, what would I bring to this house? What would follow me into this house?

Mariel comes from the kitchen and kisses her. Dolly is five inches taller than her mother and has to lean down.

"We were scared you might not make that flight," Mariel says.

"Made it at the last minute." The two women check each other out. Beige.

"I see Uncle Hektor brought in my bags." Dolly

points to the American Tourister and the Merle Norman tote by the stairs.

"But I have your room at home all ready."

"I'm staying here. Where's Papa?"

"I saw him go out on the dunes while ago."

"I'll go find him." Dolly turns and bumps into May who is carrying Jerry, the cat. "Will you take my suitcase up for me, sweetie? Any room."

"Sure. Here, Aunt Mariel." May hands her Jerry.

May heads up the stairs and Dolly goes on out the door. For a moment, Mariel stands holding the cat, watching her tall graceful daughter run across the yard. "And hello to you, too, Dolly," she murmurs.

"Have you ever noticed how much she looks like me?" asks Sarah Sullivan's shadow. "And Artie, of course."

Mariel sighs and goes back to the kitchen.

He looks old, Dolly thinks, walking up the path toward her father.

He turns at that moment to see Dolly. She kneels beside him and holds him.

"I've counted fifteen barges," he says.

"Hello, Papa." Dolly smells the warmth of his skin, the shaving lotion.

"Traffic through here gets worse every year. There was a jubilee last night. Did you know that?"

"I heard."

Then they are silent, looking out at the bay.

EIGHT

Tomato Sandwiches

ON THE DAY THE STOCK MARKET CRASHED IN 1929, THOMAS Sullivan sat on the dune at Harlow, right where his son and granddaughter are sitting almost sixty years later, and watched his very pregnant wife, Sarah, waddle down the beach. Later, he would remember how happy he was on this day, how the sun was pleasantly warm, and how everything seemed to be golden, even Sarah in her yellow dress, bending awkwardly to examine something at the edge of the water. Sarah, sensing his interest, had looked up and waved. It was a picture he would carry with him the rest of his life, Sarah at the water's edge, one hand raised, the other resting on her huge stomach. Our child, he had thought, and literally felt his heart skip a beat. In two weeks he would know it was two children, a boy and a girl. And he would have learned about the stock market crash, how, as he sat in the sun, desperate men were jumping from buildings, their legacy financial chaos.

But for Thomas Sullivan, this October day was most memorable because it was the day they signed the final papers on the house at Harlow. Then they drove back to their apartment in Mobile, and Sarah fixed tomato sandwiches and iced tea and brought them to the screened porch.

"The house is perfect," she said. "That view, Thomas. Just think about it."

"We probably should have put in another bathroom."

Sarah put her hands over her ears. "Not one negative word about my house."

Thomas smiled. "I promise."

It was a day that would go down in the history books. The twins, entwined that day in Sarah's womb, would study it. So would their children and grandchildren. But Thomas would remember the day for goldenrod lining the shell road that led to the house, and Sarah looking up to wave, her blonde hair catching the sun, her hand pressed against her huge belly. It was a memory so magical, he kept it to himself. His gift.

NINE

Peach Cobbler

"PUSSY-WHIPPED," REESE WHITLEY MUTTERS. "ALL THE MEN IN this family pussy-whipped." He is running the vacuum over the already clean living room rug at Mariel's insistence, pausing every few minutes to wipe his nose on his shirtsleeve. He has been crying all day. Reese is so black, he is only visible when he moves into the late afternoon sunlight that strips the room.

Dolly loves Reese; she loves the mystery of Reese. For no one can remember when he became a member of the family. He wasn't there, and then he was, an integral part of Artie's life. At seven each morning, his '54 Studebaker rattles into the yard and the day begins. In the late afternoon, he rattles back to Harlow and Irene who towers over him and may or may not be his wife. No one knows how old Reese is or where he came from. His entire life is a mystery.

Donnie wonders if the United States government knows Reese Whitley exists. Artie says how can it not know; she's paid his Social Security twenty years. Who knows? When she first got sick, she wanted Reese to be given power of attorney, but Donnie reminded her that Reese was illiterate.

"Why'd you tell him that?" she asked Reese.

"Simplifies things," was his answer. Made sense to Artie who had walked outside twenty years ago, found Reese planting pansies, and never questioned her good luck.

"But where did he come from?" Even seven-year-old Dolly had wanted to know.

"Heaven."

The answer delighted Reese who was listening as usual. Now he sits on Artie's mother's Queen Anne chair and pushes the vacuum back and forth.

> *"Nobody knows de trouble I seen.*
> *Nobody knows but Jesus."*

Reese sings loudly and mournfully over the whine of the vacuum. He learned years ago the power of a Negro spiritual on the white conscience.

"I'll finish this, Reese. You go on home." Mrs. Randolph takes the vacuum. He goes out the back door. May, sitting on the steps, trying to comb an unwilling Jerry, the cat, with a flea comb, looks up and smiles.

"You going home, Reese?"

Reese wipes his nose on his sleeve. "Soon as I get drunk enough, May."

Hektor, upstairs in his old room, is learning that vodka and Valium will make you dream in color. He is amazed at this and intends to make a note of it when he wakes up.

He dreams he is on the pier and the sun is glinting on all the fish scales sloughed from the day's catch. His mother and father come hand-in-hand toward him. His father has on a blue seersucker suit and white shoes. His mother has on a pale blue dress with a white collar.

Hektor says, "You look beautiful as Easter eggs."

They seem pleased.

"As beautiful as words?" his mother asks.

"Of course."

"Both Easter eggs and words have to be handled carefully," Sarah says. "Refrigerated or they'll make you sick."

"Your mother and I are going for a sail," Thomas says.

"Please don't do that. This might be the day."

"Don't be silly," his mother says. "The sun is shining."

"Remember," his father says, "it's the search, not the finding. And the joy of the search."

"What do you mean?" But they are in the boat out on the bay.

"What do you mean?" Hektor screams. "And why are you so dressed up?"

"For my funeral," Artie says.

Awakened by May and told he is needed downstairs, Hektor still feels caught in the dream. A low red sun turns the living room golden. Across from him, seated on the sofa, his parents and Artie listen to Mr. Brock. Hektor closes his eyes.

"I can't believe it," his father says.

"Well, here it is in her own handwriting. I was afraid you might not know."

Know what? Hektor smoothes May's hair. She is sitting on the floor, her head against his knee. Know what?

"We can't do it, of course," his mother says.

Do what? His fingers slowly follow the ridge where

May's soft spot had been. He remembers seeing her pulse beating there. So fast it scared him.

"Hektor!"

"Ma'am?"

"For God's sake, Hektor. Wake up!" Mariel's voice has the shrillness of exhaustion in it.

"I'm sorry," Hektor says politely. Mariel begins to cry. Dolly pats her shoulder.

"Well, it was Miss Sullivan's wish. She was very specific about it. She wanted her ashes sprinkled in the bay." Mr. Brock leans back in the Queen Anne chair. "Though that may not be legal. I really haven't run into this before."

Her ashes? Hektor's fingers tighten on May's scalp. Artie wanted to be cremated?

"My mother is right. We can't do it," Dolly says.

Cremated? Hektor clears his throat and agrees. "Of course not."

"Well, legally I guess you don't have to, but it says right here," Mr. Brock pushes his glasses up on his nose and reads, " 'I request that my brother Adonis have my body cremated and that he broadcast my ashes onto the waters of Mobile Bay on the day he deems perfect.' "

"But that doesn't make a grain of sense," Mariel says, wiping her nose on a Kleenex. "Donnie and I have already picked out the casket, and I've already sent her yellow linen dress to the funeral parlor and told them we'd have viewing and the rosary tomorrow night and the funeral the next morning. Ordered the flowers."

"She wanted me to do what?" It's the first time Donnie has spoken.

"Have her cremated," Mr. Brock says again.

"No. The rest of it."

"Here." Mr. Brock hands Donnie the paper. Donnie

takes it to the window and reads it. The room is quiet except for Mariel's sniffling and the hum of the air conditioner. The sun touches the water.

Mr. Brock glances at his watch. He needs to get back to Mobile to feed his wife her supper. He is the only one she will eat for, opening her mouth like a little bird while he spoons in custard or pureed vegetables. "Don't leave me," he says, pushing food in until it runs down the sides of her mouth. "Don't leave me."

"I'm sorry I couldn't get here earlier today," he says, running his hand across his bald head, watching Donnie.

"It would have helped," Mariel says.

"My wife is very ill."

No one says anything.

"She's dying."

"I'm sorry," Dolly says.

Hektor sighs. Death. There is entirely too much of it. More all the time.

"I handled your grandparents' estate," Mr. Brock says to Dolly. "Got everything worked out without a hitch."

"That's nice."

The sun falls rapidly into the water. From the kitchen they hear voices, Mrs. Randolph and Kelly Stuart.

Donnie, looking at the sun, is thinking he should have known Artie would want cremation.

"Here, write it down," Mrs. Randolph says. "It'll work for any fruit, but peaches are best. You got to use butter, though. That's the secret. And a hot oven."

Donnie turns from the window. "We'll do what she wants." There is a collective sigh.

"Well," Mr. Brock says, "there's just one more problem. There's not a crematorium in Mobile. You'll have to take her to Birmingham or Tallahassee."

"Oh, my God," Mariel moans. She knows good and well that Artie knew about the crematorium. "You don't have to do this, Donnie. Everything's all set here." She turns to Dolly. "We took her yellow linen dress."

"Well," says Mr. Brock, "she'll have to wear something to Birmingham."

"Oh, my God!"

"I'll take her," Donnie says. "Thank you, Mr. Brock."

"You're welcome, Donnie. I'll go on and get the will probated. You know Dolly gets the house. Most everything else, too." Mr. Brock looks around for the straw hat he hasn't worn in twenty years.

"Yes. We're familiar with the will."

"Well, my condolences. She was a nice lady. And pretty." For a moment, Mr. Brock sees eighteen-year-old Artie in a peach-colored silk dress leaning over to sign some papers. "Call me when you get back."

"I will." Donnie walks to the door with the old lawyer. No one else gets up or says a word.

"At least eight peaches," says Mrs. Randolph in the kitchen, "and I like almond flavoring instead of vanilla."

"We can't do it," Hektor says finally.

"Tell Donnie." Mariel nods toward the door.

"Tell Donnie what?"

"That we can't have Artie cremated, Hektor!" Mariel cannot believe how stoned Hektor is. What in the world is he on? A lot more than the one Valium she had given him.

"We really can't. What would we do about a priest? Artie needs a priest. We can't bury her without a priest."

"She obviously didn't want to be buried," Dolly

says. She shivers. Artie nothing but ashes? She gets up and goes to the window where her father had stood reading the note. Out on the bay, a water-skier leaves a silver path. The earth is tilting toward the equinox, she realizes.

"Hektor," her father says, coming back into the room, "I need you to get me one of your company planes tomorrow morning."

"All right."

"Hektor," Mariel reminds him, "it's to take Artie to be cremated."

Hektor thinks for a minute. "I really don't think we should, Donnie."

Four faces, Hektor, May, Mariel, and Dolly, turn toward Donnie. They look like four moons in the encircling shadows.

"Hektor, she left me no choice."

"But what about a priest? We can't bury her without a Mass and you know what Father Carroll thinks of cremation."

"We're not burying her, Hektor," Donnie says. "And if you need a priest so you'll feel better, find one."

"Supper is ready and getting cold," calls Mrs. Randolph.

Everyone but Donnie moves toward the dining room. Dolly looks back and sees him at the window reading Artie's words again. Sometimes she forgets how large her father is. Now, outlined against the last light of the sun, he seems huge.

My brother Adonis.

The day he deems perfect.

Strange. Like some kind of code.

TEN

Shelling Peas

TYPICAL ARTIE THING, SPRINGING THE NEWS ON THEM THAT SHE wanted to be cremated. And having Mr. Brock tell them after she's dead so nobody could talk her out of it. Not that they could have anyway. Nobody could talk Artie out of anything she'd set her mind on.

Mariel leans her head against the coolness of the car window; her eyes hurt and there were watery rainbows all around the lights. The tires whine as they cross a bridge.

The depth of her sadness over Artie's death is a surprise. This was the woman who her husband loved better than anyone else in the world, the woman who had stolen her child, the woman who was so beautiful and talented that she made Mariel feel dumb as dirt. Artie painted seascapes that hung in museums; she, Mariel, cross-stitched pictures of mallards. Dumb as dirt.

She gazes at Donnie who is driving like a robot. She can't see the expression on his face, but he hasn't said a word since they left Harlow.

"You're really going to take her to Birmingham to be cremated tomorrow?" she asks.

"Guess I don't have a choice." They are on the stretch of road where, in the summertime, cars go rmmph rmmph over expanded concrete. They'll be in the Mobile city limits soon.

"I've been thinking." She lets the words hang in the air.

He doesn't reply.

"We could go on and have the funeral, Donnie. Just like we planned. No one would know the casket was empty but us. Not even Father Carroll."

At first he doesn't say anything. They pass the entrance to the battleship *Alabama*, anchored in the bay and lighted brightly for tourists. He says, "Hmmm."

Mariel isn't sure if that's a yes or a no. "Well, we could. Tell everybody Artie requested a closed casket, which you know she would have. Father Carroll incensed her last night or this morning. God, I'm losing track of time. Anyway, whenever Mrs. Randolph called him. He wouldn't question it."

He still doesn't say anything.

"Don't you think it would work?"

"Mariel, I don't think it matters."

"Sure it does, Donnie. People in Mobile don't get cremated. You know that."

"It's not a sin, Mariel. I read somewhere that in California half the people are cremated."

"That's California." She pauses. "Do you know anybody who was ever cremated?"

Donnie doesn't say anything. Of course he doesn't.

"And this way we wouldn't have to explain anything to anybody."

"We don't have to explain anything to anybody anyway."

Donnie looks over at Mariel. Under the streetlights, the lines in her face look etched. He reaches over and takes her hand. "Look, I don't care. Do what you want to," he says. "But I'm still taking her to Birmingham tomorrow to the crematorium."

"I'll work it out," Mariel promises, crossing her fingers for luck just like she had when she was a child.

They ride in silence, each lost in thought until they stop at a light and Donnie asks if Dolly has said anything about Bobby.

"She hasn't mentioned him. I don't know if she called him about Artie or not."

"Artie liked him a lot. I was out at the house when they called to say they were getting married. She made me open a bottle of champagne right by the phone so they could hear us celebrating."

"I liked him, too," Mariel says. "The whole thing's tragic." Then, "The light's green."

Dolly and May have built a fire on the beach with some cardboard boxes they found on the back porch. May is writing her name in the air with sparklers.

"M!" she shouts, running along the water's edge, her arms swooping. "A! Y!" And for a moment Dolly sees the name white against the darkness.

"Get some sparklers," she had called to May. "They're in the little drawer on the right of the sink. Let's go down to the beach a while." And she had thought, How well I know this house. Now she pushes some sticks May has found into the fire. They are wet and sizzle; they refuse to burn.

"It smells like old fish down here," May says, sticking her hands out for more sparklers. "Stinks."

"That's part of a jubilee. Tomorrow everybody will be cleaning the beaches. When Papa and Uncle Hektor were kids they used to rake people's beaches to make money. Kids still do it. They'll be knocking on our door in the morning."

"What about Artie?"

"You mean did she rake beaches for people? I never heard her say. Her mother might have thought it wasn't ladylike. She and I cleaned this beach, though, lots of times."

May sits down by the fire. Sparks of burning cardboard drift toward the dune.

"You stayed here a lot, didn't you?"

"Every summer. I couldn't wait for school to be out so I could come to Harlow. Probably hurt my folks' feelings I was so anxious. And we really didn't do anything much. Artie would paint all morning and Kelly Stuart and I would play. Her older brother built us a treehouse in the pecan tree. We loved that. And then in the afternoon when it would cool down, we'd swim or fish. Mrs. Stuart or Artie might bring us sandwiches to the beach for supper. Nothing, really. But I loved it." Dolly puts another piece of cardboard on the fire. The cardboard curls with a hissing sound. "I still think when you cross the causeway the light gets brighter. Clearer."

"But wasn't Aunt Artie gone a lot?"

"Not in the summer. Never in the summer." Dolly feels drained. She lies back and looks at the stars which are blurred, indistinct. "Reese would plant a big garden and we would put vegetables in the freezer. I think I was the champion pea sheller of Harlow."

"I helped her shell peas last summer," May says.

"Did she say, 'We're putting up nuts for the winter'?"

"Yep."

The cardboard catches and flames. It's the last

piece. "This is our Turning of the Earth bonfire," Dolly says. "Maybe it'll change our luck. God knows I could use a change."

May lights a sparkler and throws it in an arc toward the water. "Witches, be gone!"

Dolly feels the warm sand against her back. She thinks she's too tired to get up and go into the house. If she had a blanket, she'd stay right here, see the earliest chord of sun. She struggles up. "We have to go in, May. Let's put the fire out soon as this piece burns."

A few minutes later, they kick sand over the fire and start up the path.

"My sparklers," May says. She runs back to get them. Dolly, waiting, imagines she sees May jump three times over the embers of the fire.

Witches, be gone.

Tired as he is, Donnie can't sleep.

"You okay?" Mariel mumbles when he leaves the bed.

"I'm losing my mind," he mutters and walks out into the backyard, into air so heavy he can feel himself pushing against it.

This was the kind of August night when, before air-conditioning, as soon as his younger brother Hektor was asleep, he, Donnie, would fix their fan so it wouldn't oscillate but would blow only on him, not Hektor. It was the kind of still, sultry night that drew people from their houses to slightly cooler porches or to the damp sand of the beach.

One night, getting up to fix the fan, he had seen his mother coming from the beach. The lights were off, but as she crossed the yard, her white silk robe reflected the moonlight. He had gone to the window and watched her, wondering if she had been swimming, thinking she had no business swimming by herself at night. And then his father had stepped from the porch and held out his arms and Sarah had walked into his embrace. For a moment they held each other, and then they began to move in a slow dance, circling the yard lightly, unaware that their son was watching.

The next morning, their father said that their mother was sleeping in and they should be quiet. Donnie, Artie, and Hektor were sitting in the kitchen eating cereal and Thomas, their father, was on his way to work with his usual books and thermos of coffee, his glasses and thinning hair. He wasn't forty, but to his children he had looked like an old man, bent.

"I don't believe they were out there," Artie had said, slapping the cereal bowls onto the table. "It must have been a dream. They wouldn't have been out in the yard dancing in the middle of the night. Not Papa, anyway."

But Donnie knew what he had seen, and the memory stayed with him all his life like a blessing.

"She's crazy, you know." Later that day they were walking down the shell road carrying crab nets. "I hate everything about her."

"You shouldn't talk like that about Mama, Artie," Hektor said. "You really shouldn't."

"You don't think she's so bad because she doesn't stay on you and Donnie."

Donnie and Hektor both knew this was true.

"And Papa doesn't do a damn thing about it. Sits over there at the university. Comes home and dances with her. Shit."

"Most of the time she's fine, Artie," Donnie said.

"And some of the time she's nuts, and I'm the one catches it. Just once I'd like to do something to suit her."

They reached the community pier and took out the plastic bag with chicken entrails they would use for bait. "I wish these were her guts," Artie said, and Donnie felt like crying because Artie was hurting and because he loved all of them.

"But Artie—"

"Just shut up!" Artie leaned over the rail and dropped the crab net into the murky water, watching it sink slowly out of sight. "Just shut up!"

Now Donnie eases into the hammock and closes his eyes. Once more he sees Sarah walking into Thomas's embrace; once more they dance, light, young. How little we know our parents, Donnie thinks. How little we know each other.

He sleeps. When he wakes, stiff and uncomfortable, a brilliant Venus shines low in the morning sky.

Dolly can't sleep. She wanders the house. She looks at the picture above the mantel, a pier in moonlight with the figures of a man and woman standing apart. The man is looking at the woman, but her face is turned toward the water. It's not like most of Artie's work. "An early one and the light's messed up on the water," she had told Dolly and pointed out how the shadows were wrong. But Artie had liked it well enough to hang it over her mantel, and Dolly has always loved the picture, believing the figures are Artie and her husband Carl who was killed in Korea, killed before they ever had a life to live together, a marriage to weave.

Now Dolly turns on the light over the painting and studies it. She sees the shadows that Artie said were wrong, how they reach toward the pier, how the woman's hand is cupped, holding something that may be a shell, a suggestion of color.

"I came down to get a *Nancy Drew*."

Dolly jumps. She hasn't heard May come up behind her.

"I thought you were asleep."

"I tried. Some birds are fussing right outside my window. One of them keeps saying, 'Wee, wee' like the little piggy."

"They do that after jubilees; they get frantic and can't settle down." Dolly puts her arm around May and pulls her close. "You hungry? You want something to eat?"

"No. I'm full." May looks up at the picture. "That's Aunt Artie, isn't it?"

"I don't know, May. I've always assumed it was and that the man was Carl, her husband. But look at the way she's standing away from him. And the way he's looking at her."

"He's fixing to go get himself killed and she's mad at him about it."

Dolly kisses the top of May's head. Little girl sweat and shampoo. "You're too wise, little one."

"I know." May giggles.

"But not too wise for a *Nancy Drew*?"

"Nope. I love Aunt Artie's *Nancy Drew*s. I like the way they smell."

"Me, too. Do you know how to turn on the light under the steps?"

"Sure I do. Sometimes I just sit in there and read. Aunt Artie says she used to do that, too. Hide in the closet and read."

"I used to do that myself. I'm glad she saved them for us."

"Me, too. 'Night, Dolly."

" 'Night, sweetheart. Is your papa asleep?"

"He's snoring louder than the birds are yelling."

May goes toward the hall, and Dolly turns back to look at the picture. For the first time, she realizes that one of the shadows in the background may not be a shadow but a small boat. She rubs her hand over her eyes which are blurring. Sarah and Thomas. The figures could be her grandparents with Sarah already looking toward the boat that was waiting for them.

Dolly sighs. Or it could just be a pretty picture with the shadows messed up.

"I know what's in the lady's hand." May is beside her again.

"What?"

"A brass button."

Dolly sees that it's possible. "What makes you think that, May?"

"I asked Aunt Artie and she told me."

"Why a brass button?"

"Don't know. I didn't ask her." May hugs Dolly. " 'Night, again."

"Sleep tight."

May nods, holding up several books.

After she has gone, Dolly reaches up and covers the painted hand with her own. A brass button.

She feels disoriented, the room no longer as familiar. There is so much this house has to tell her. So much it will never tell her. Stories end.

She puts out the light and goes up the steps, past the room where Hektor is sleeping, past May's room where a light is on. The good scent of almonds follows her. She doesn't undress but lies across the bed looking out toward the pier, the moon-tipped water.

"Something is going to happen," she whispers.

In the Harlow jail, a drunk Reese is dreaming that Artie has bought a wagonload of sunflower seeds.

"Plant them, Reese," she says. "On the beach."

"But they won't grow there, Artie," he protests.

"But if they did, wouldn't it be pretty?"

"I'm too down in my back."

"Then I'll do it." Artie hovers above the beach, sprinkling sunflower seeds into furrows that open as the seeds fall.

"Why didn't you tell me you could do that?" Reese grumbles. "I dug up that garden for you every year."

Should have known. That woman could do anything she set her mind to.

ELEVEN

A Groom's Cake with Green Grapes

THE LAST THING SARAH HARVEY EVER THOUGHT SHE WOULD DO was marry a Yankee. Not that she had anything against them. They just usually didn't know how to act.

Thomas Sullivan was a perfect example of this. She was sitting on a bench and waiting for her date to arrive with some punch when she heard a deep voice with the most awful Yankee accent say, "You are the most beautiful creature I have ever seen in my life." She turned and there was Thomas, smiling at her, drunk. It was the only time she ever saw him drunk and the only time he ever said anything like that. But how was she to know?

Sarah, her sister Mary, and Emily Meadows had gone from Montgomery to Auburn University for the fraternity dances. The night she met Thomas was the third night of partying and she was exhausted.

"You should have seen me night before last," she

said, slipping out of her shoes and rubbing her aching feet against the carpet.

Thomas scooted around in front of her, knelt, and began to massage both her feet.

"Have you lost your mind?" She tried to pull her feet away, to put them back into her shoes.

"Absolutely."

"This little piggy went to market," her date, John Edgars, said. He had come up with two punch cups and, like Thomas, he was feeling no pain.

"Who is this person rubbing my feet, John?" Sarah asked.

"Sarah Harvey, may I present Dr. Thomas Sullivan."

"Please, God, let her be Catholic," Thomas said.

"I'm Catholic all right, but you're a Yankee."

The punch cups were leaning dangerously in John's hands. Sarah reached up and took them.

"That punch is spiked as a rail fence." John looked down at Thomas who was still working on Sarah's feet. "Thomas, are you a Yankee?"

"Of course not. I am a citizen of the universe."

"He's lying, Sarah. He's a Yankee. You want me and my brothers to ride him out of town on a rail? Hold him while you tar and feather him?"

Sarah giggled. "That's too kind."

"It was an accident of birth." Thomas squeezed Sarah's foot. "Something over which I had no control. Say I can live it down."

"There's no way you can live it down. We'll just have to live with it."

"Did you hear that, John?" Thomas tried to stand, but sank back on his knees. "Congratulate us."

"Congratulations. Now hand Sarah her shoes. We're going to go dance."

"Allow me, Cinderella." Thomas put each shoe on gently. "Notice they fit."

"Thank you." Sarah got up and went with John toward the dance floor. When she looked back, Thomas was already asleep, his head on the bench she had just vacated.

"He's a doctor?" she asked.

"Some kind." John grinned. "But not the kind he's going to need in the morning. A Ph.D. in Latin or something la-de-da."

But the next morning when Sarah and Mary came staggering down to breakfast, there was Thomas, his dark blond hair parted in the middle and slicked down. In the morning light, Sarah could see how green his eyes were and how the green was touched with little golden flecks. He held out a cup of coffee, just as she liked it, a teaspoon of sugar and a dash of cream. "For you, Sarah." He turned to Mary. "And how do you like yours, Mary?"

"The same." She pressed her fingertips against her forehead and watched Thomas walk across the room. "Who the hell is he, Sarah? And how does he know who we are?"

"Some kind of Yankee doctor. I met him last night. Maybe you did, too."

"It's possible." Mary slumped in a chair. "I'm getting too old for this."

Thomas was back with the coffee. "Toast? Oatmeal?" The sisters both shook their heads. "What time does our train leave this afternoon?" he asked.

Sarah took a big gulp of the coffee. It burned her tongue so bad her eyes watered. For days after, it hurt to eat.

Eight months later, they were married. Yankee persistence, Mary said.

Mama and Papa thought he was wonderful. So did the rest of the family though, at times, he drove Sarah crazy. She could never tell if he was teasing or not. Neither could anybody else, but they just assumed he was and laughed and winked at her and at each other when he would make some of his outrageous remarks. Like that first Sunday. Nothing would do but he must go home with the sisters though he had already said he was on his way to Mobile.

"I'll get the next train," he said and he got off the train and squeezed right into the Yellow Cab with them.

"Over three costs fifteen cents extra," the driver said.

"No problem."

"He's cute," Emily whispered. Sarah whispered back that she thought he was crazy.

They dropped Emily off on West Jeff Davis and then Thomas got in the backseat between Mary and Sarah. "Norman Bridge Road," Mary told the cab driver.

"Fifteen cents more."

"You ladies live in the country?" Thomas found some more change.

"Our father is a contractor," Sarah explained. "He builds houses and we move into them until he sells them."

"That sounds like fun. I've lived in the same house all my life."

"And where is that?" Mary asked.

"Salem, Massachusetts."

"I knew you were a Yankee," the cab driver said. "I could tell in a minute."

"No more," Thomas said. "Last night I discovered what I have always been in my heart—a Southerner.

When I marry this young lady here, I will be granted all the rights and privileges that go with that title."

"It don't work that way," the cab driver said. Mary and Sarah both giggled.

"Scoff if you want, ladies, but that's the way it'll be. Mint juleps on the veranda. The whole bit."

When they got home, Mary didn't even wait to help with the bags. "Hey, Mama," she yelled into the hall. "Come meet Colonel Thomas Sullivan who says he's going to marry Sarah and turn Southern."

Thomas went to meet the family, a big grin on his face. But Sarah went around the back and sat in the old porch swing. She wasn't sure what was happening, but whatever it was, she'd lost control over it. It gave her the same feeling as a dream she would have sometimes. She would be at a party and wouldn't know a soul. And she would realize she was at the wrong party. One she hadn't been invited to.

And she sat in the swing for a long time listening to the laughter from inside. And then Thomas came out and walked around the house toward her. It was late afternoon and the shadows of the pecan limbs were like bars between them. He stopped and looked at her and neither of them said a word. Who are you? Sarah thought. Who are you, Thomas Sullivan? And then she got up and went to him, holding out her hand, stepping over the shadows as if she might trip on them.

Years later she would tell her three children how it was that she married Thomas Sullivan, moved to Mobile and then around to the bay. "Tell us, Mama. Tell us how you and Papa fell in love and got married," the children would beg. And Sarah would say, "Close your eyes and I will tell you." And she would start with the dance at Auburn and Thomas following her home.

They liked that part best of all, their serious father acting silly.

As for the truth of the story, how could Sarah tell the children that were half hers and half Thomas's that marriage was something that just happened? That walking down the aisle of St. Jude's that June with her sisters and brothers waiting for her at the front and Mama smiling but already crying, she could hardly remember Thomas. She could feel Papa's heart beating in the hand that held her arm, or maybe it was her heart. She couldn't tell. And the bouquet of gardenias they had gone to the cemetery that morning to pick were the sweetest she had ever smelled. She wanted to bury her face in them they looked so cool. But if you touch a gardenia, it will turn brown.

"Speak to the Sullivans," Papa whispered as they got to the front pew. And Sarah nodded and smiled at the couple who were Thomas's parents, who had come all the way down from Massachusetts to see their only child married. They were very old, both dressed in dark clothes, and with sweating flushed faces. Mrs. Sullivan had been so exhausted from the trip, she had had to go right to bed when they got to the Harvey's. "Death's stalking that woman," Idabelle said, taking her some tea and aspirin. " 'Bout to catch her, too." And it was true. In six months they both were gone. But they had made it to their child's wedding. It was the only time Sarah ever saw them.

"It was hot," she would tell the children. "One of the hottest June days ever in Montgomery. When Father told your papa and me to hold hands, our hands slid right apart they were so wet."

Artie, Donnie, and Hektor would giggle and hit at each other. "Tell us about the food," Donnie always demanded. And Sarah would lay a banquet before them of a bride's cake with yellow flowers and a groom's cake, chocolate with chocolate icing, decorated with green grapes.

"That's the one I want," Donnie said. "And punch and cheese straws and strawberries you dip in sugar."

"Tell us about all the presents."

"Crystal and silver goblets and trays, and the good china," Sarah would list for Artie.

"And you and Papa promised to love, honor, and obey?"

"Of course." But the truth was that Sarah couldn't remember a word of the ceremony. When Mary married Bo Hardeman several months later, Sarah was frightened to hear the vows she and Thomas had taken. The whole event had been like a big game you play with parties and presents and new clothes. And then everyone was following them to Union Station and Sarah was leaving home with Thomas. Going to live a life in Mobile with someone she hadn't even known a year before. She had a gardenia corsage pinned to the lapel of her pink linen suit and she held it to her face and cried. Even if it did turn brown. Thomas sat beside her on the drawing room seat which would soon be turned into a bed and tried to hug her. But she put her face against the window and watched the late afternoon sun winding up the Alabama River, turning it golden. She wouldn't look away or let Thomas open the window until the train crossed the bridge and there was nothing but pine trees pressing close to the tracks.

TWELVE

Space Genes

MARIEL SULLIVAN GETS THE *MOBILE REGISTER* OUT OF THE
azaleas where the boy has thrown it. Opening it, she
sees a picture of Artie, her sister-in-law, taken when
she was around thirty. The headline reads NOTED LOCAL
ARTIST SUCCUMBS. Mariel, still in her robe, sits down on
the steps to read it.

> Artemis Eleanor Sullivan, 58, of Harlow died yesterday
> following a long illness. Miss Sullivan, whose works are
> represented in museums and galleries worldwide, was
> a lifelong resident of the Mobile area. Daughter of the
> late Thomas and Sarah Sullivan and widow of the late
> Carl Jenkins, also of Harlow, Miss Sullivan was best
> known for her "Seascapes with People" in which she
> is credited with capturing light in the most inimitable
> way since van Gogh. Several of her works are on
> permanent display in the Mobile Museum of Art and
> a retrospective of her work has already been planned
> there for next year.
>
> Miss Sullivan is survived by two brothers, Donald

J. Sullivan (Mariel) of Mobile and Hektor R. Sullivan of
New Orleans, as well as two nieces, Dorothy Sullivan
and May Sullivan. Private services will be held in Harlow on Friday. The family requests that any memorials
be made to the Mobile Museum of Art or to the
American Cancer Society.

Van Gogh? Artie and van Gogh? Lord! Mariel folds
the paper and rests her chin on her knees. The calico
cat rubs against her. At least Donnie will be pleased at
the "Donald." That's easier to live with than "Adonis."
Whatever became of Adonis in the Greek myths, anyway? Did he live to be old with a potbelly and thinning
hair? She has always meant to look it up, the whole
story, not just what it says in the dictionary: "A beautiful youth loved by Aphrodite."

At least he wasn't a parenthesis. She rubs her hand
over the purring cat. She notices the skin at her wrists,
loose, wrinkling; freckles are enlarging into liver spots.
Artie looks up at her, thirty again.

"Hell," Mariel grumbles. She gets up and goes inside where the phone is ringing. She takes it off the
hook and goes to take a shower. Half an hour later,
she's on her way to Harlow. She's tired and there's this
whole day to get through before the funeral tomorrow.
If they are having one. If her husband and Hektor can
agree. She wonders if Donnie is in Harlow or at his
office. She woke around dawn and saw him in the hammock. Then she went back to sleep. He was gone the
next time she woke up.

Mariel could wring Artie's neck for causing all
these problems. No funeral and wanting to be cremated! Hektor, she could tell, was as appalled as she
was. She hopes he's sober today; she needs his help.
Dolly won't do anything. Dolly will be sitting on the

bluff idle when Gabriel blows his horn. Mariel has spent half her life explaining to teachers, who complained that Dolly was a smart child who didn't pay attention, that spaciness was a Sullivan gene. And those teachers swearing such a thing as absentmindedness (they had smiled at "spaciness") couldn't be inherited. But Mariel knows better; she's lived with the Sullivan family for over thirty years. Hektor, once, driving from New Orleans on the interstate, had completely missed Mobile and was almost to Pensacola when he (as Artie put it) came to himself. Everyone else had thought it funny. Donnie and Dolly would forget to eat if Mariel didn't put the food on the table and call them. "Supper?" they would ask, like she'd said something weird. It drove her crazy the way they'd look around as if they'd just found themselves in a strange place. Mariel knows this was the look Dolly gave her teachers: a polite, well-liked child—just spacey.

"They got it from Thomas," Sarah Sullivan's shadow says. "It's what drove me crazy."

Mariel turns on a tape; Beethoven's Sixth is much more soothing than Sarah's voice which she understands is in her subconscious. God knows her analyst has told her that enough. But it doesn't help.

Mariel turns the volume up and tries to relax. No good; she needs a cigarette in the worst way and she hasn't smoked in twenty years.

She hasn't planned to, but when she gets to the road that leads to her mother's house, she turns in. The road is rutted, and blackberry bushes threaten to scratch the car on both sides. Someone (Mariel wouldn't put it past her mother) has been dumping garbage at one spot. Plastic bags have split open and a trail of debris leads into the woods. She makes a mental note to call the sheriff's office again about the littering.

Let them catch her mother who's probably the one doing most of it. Serve her right. It would cost 500 dollars, though. Mariel sighs and thinks she'd better ask Reese if he'll go up there and help her for a spell. Her mother would be delighted at that; Naomi thought Reese was handed down. They would fry fish and watch television and the trash cleanup would take days. Well, it had to be done.

Mariel comes around a slight curve and pulls into her mother's backyard. Naomi Cates lives in what some enthusiastic real estate person might describe as a beach bungalow. The beach part is true, the bungalow imaginative. A square of concrete blocks, the house consists of a living room across the front, a bedroom, bath, and kitchen across the back. A screened porch overlooking the bay is much larger than the house itself and it's here that Naomi lives except in the coldest winter weather. Here are her couch and television and, to Mariel's dismay, her freezer, washer and dryer. Naomi Cates is well aware of her daughter's disapproval. At eighty, she doesn't give a damn. She eats when she wants to, sleeps when she's sleepy. After raising six children and putting up with an alcoholic husband for forty years, Naomi Cates is, in a word, happy. She comes out the back door to greet Mariel in some yellow boxer shorts one of her grandsons had left after a visit. Her legs are stick-thin and tanned; varicose veins wind up them like a road map.

Mariel gets out of the car and hugs her mother. At one time she had been only a couple of inches taller than Naomi. Now she looks down into thinning white hair, sees the pink of scalp

"Well, this is a surprise," Naomi says. "Why aren't you over at Artie's?"

"I'm on my way. I just wanted to check on you."

"Well, I'm fine. Come on in and I'll get us some coffee."

Three concrete steps lead up to the back door. She needs a rail to hold on to, Mariel thinks, following her mother. What if she should fall down the steps out here by herself?

"Are you wearing your pager?" she asks.

"Right here." Naomi pulls what looks like a small transistor radio on a cord from beneath her tee shirt. For the first time Mariel notices the shirt. Emblazoned on it is HAIL MAUI FULL OF GRASS and what looks like a cross between a palm and a marijuana plant.

"Where did you get that shirt, Mama?"

"Teddy. He brought it back from Hawaii. It's wild, isn't it?"

"Don't let Father Carroll see it."

"He already has. Laughed till he cried. You know how he always cries when he laughs. Like Dolly. When she gets really tickled at something she just blubbers." Naomi pours water into two cups and puts them in a small microwave on the counter.

"Have you checked your batteries lately?"

"What batteries?"

"In the pager."

"They're fine, Mariel. Slip, slide, or twinge and every rescue squad in Mobile and Baldwin County will be beating on my door. Quit worrying about me."

"But I do. You're so isolated out here."

"Thank God." The microwave dings and Naomi takes the cups out and spoons instant coffee into them. "Here's the sugar."

Mariel should refuse. Instead she takes two teaspoonfuls as well as a generous amount of milk. "Cookie?" her mother asks. Mariel shakes her head no. At least she has some willpower.

"Let's go out on the porch." Naomi takes a handful of cookies and leads the way. "Your brother Jacob called yesterday. I told him about Artie. He said he used to be in love with her when they were in high school. I never knew that, did you?"

"I couldn't keep up with everybody." Mariel can't keep up with Dolly. She can't imagine what it was like for her mother with six children to feed and dress and try to teach some social graces to. Especially with so little help from their father.

Her mother laughs. "Neither could I. I remember that terrible crush Elizabeth had on Pete Spencer and that's about all."

"I remember that one, too. She nearly drove us crazy. I wonder whatever happened to him."

"I'll bet your sister knows." Naomi bites into a cookie. "Here," she says, pushing some magazines from the couch with her elbow. "Sit here."

Mariel sinks into the soft pillows. A ceiling fan cools her face. She closes her eyes and thinks she has never been so tired in her life. She wants to stay here and let her mother take care of her, her alone; she wants to be her mother's child. She doesn't want her mother to be eighty years old and frail. She doesn't want to worry about her falling or having a heart attack.

"How's Donnie doing?" Naomi asks.

"Okay, I guess. He seems to be all right."

"And Dolly?"

"I guess she's okay, too. She stayed out at Artie's last night. I'm surprised she's not over here to see you yet. She's getting the house, you know."

"I figured she would. I wonder what she'll do."

"I have no idea."

"She's a good girl."

"She's not a girl, Mama. She's twenty-seven years old and doesn't have a clue what she's going to do with her life. And she won't even talk about Bobby. All she'll say is that the marriage just didn't work out. Well, my Lord, Mama, how could it? The man was hooked on every pharmaceutical known to mankind. I mean I'm talking Elvis here, Mama. And Dolly knew it when she married him. That's what I can't understand. Why latch on to someone who's headed down the toilet?"

"People do it all the time, Mariel. They think they can rescue them."

"I guess so. And like I was telling Donnie last night, in spite of his problems, Bobby is one of the most likable people in the world."

"And it took strength for Dolly to put him out. Think of it that way, Mariel."

"And dumbness to have let him in. Those Sullivan genes. No common sense."

Naomi reaches for another cookie. "Well, they've done pretty good. Look at Artie, famous all over the world, and Hektor, rich as Croesus. Donnie's always done fine, too."

"Hektor's pure luck. And speaking of being stoned out of your skull, you should have seen him last night."

"Drunk?"

"I don't know what he was on. Probably something exotic his company is importing from Latin America." Mariel moves a *Family Circle* magazine on a wicker table and places her cup on it carefully. "Sometimes I think he has better sense than Donnie, though. At least you can reason with him."

"Donnie is a very sensible man," Naomi says. "You know that."

"He's taking Artie to Birmingham to be cremated."

"Lord!"

Mariel is pleased at the expression she has caused on her mother's face. "I told you, Mama, the Sullivans don't have any sense. Artie wants to be cremated. Mr. Brock came out from Mobile yesterday afternoon with that neat little piece of news. Of course by that time we already had everything planned. The announcement's already in the paper this morning about the funeral. Everything."

"What are you going to do?"

"I don't know. First I thought we'd just go on and have the funeral and then Donnie could take her to Birmingham. But he wants to go today like there was some hurry. And then I thought, Well, nobody would know the casket was empty. We could just go on and have it anyway." Mariel looks out at the bay. "I don't know. It doesn't matter anyway."

Naomi sees the deep circles under Mariel's eyes. "Pull your shoes and stockings off," she says, "and let's walk down to the beach. I got it cleaned up from the jubilee yesterday."

Mariel is alarmed. "You shouldn't be down raking that beach, Mama."

"I waited till it was cool. Did you see that sunset last night?"

"We would have sent somebody."

"Mariel, you worry too much. Reckon it's a Cates gene?"

Mariel bursts into tears. "Those damn Sullivans. None of them with a grain of sense."

Naomi holds her middle-aged child. "Shhh," she says. "Come on, dry your eyes now. Of course Artie ought to have a funeral. Let's figure out just what all we need to do."

THIRTEEN

Artie on Her Fifteenth Birthday

MAMA'S RUN AWAY AGAIN. I KNEW IT AS SOON AS I WOKE UP this morning. The house had that too quiet feeling. I got up and looked in their room and, sure enough, the bed hadn't been slept in. I went in and woke up Donnie and Hektor and told them.

Hektor said, "Maybe they're just walking on the beach." And I said, "Sure, Hektor. And maybe pigs can fly."

But he and Donnie had to get up and go check their room themselves. And then they went downstairs and out on the porch with Hektor calling, "Mama! Papa!" loud as he could.

I went in my room and started dressing for school. Might as well. Wasn't anything we could do about it. In a few minutes the boys were back upstairs.

"Maybe they just went to get some bread or something," I heard Hektor say.

"Maybe they did. Go on, get dressed now. We have to get you some breakfast before the bus gets here." Then Donnie was banging on my door. "Artie!"

"Come on in."

Donnie had slept in an old bathing suit for some reason. His hair was sticking up in spikes.

"Did you hear anything last night?" he asked.

"Nope." I leaned closer to the mirror and started putting on the mascara Mama had forbidden me to wear.

"You think she's really gone?"

"Sure. Happy birthday, Donnie."

"Well, hell. Where do you think Papa is?"

"Out looking for her, of course. He'll probably be back in a little while."

Donnie sat down on the bed. He was so skinny you could count the ribs down his back. "I'm not going with him again," he said.

"Me neither. Let her stay."

"Let her stay."

"Willie Mae takes care of us, anyway."

"We can take care of ourselves. Hektor, too."

"That's the truth."

"Donnie!" Hektor called.

Donnie got up and went toward the door. "I wonder where she is," he said.

"Who knows. She'll turn up."

"Maybe one day she won't."

"She will, Donnie. You know she will. Papa'll find her and she'll come sashaying in like the queen who never did anything wrong."

"She's sick, Artie."

"I know." I had gotten some of Mama's mascara in my eyes and it was making them water. Well, hell, why not use it? It was my birthday. "Go help Hektor get ready for school. I'll get us some breakfast."

Where had she said she was going last night? A meeting at the church? That was it. That was where

Papa had taken her after supper. She had said she would get a ride home. Well, she had gotten a ride, all right. Only not home.

Had she planned it or had it been a spur of the moment thing? Sitting in the meeting, had she suddenly thought *I don't want to be here* and left, getting into the first car that stopped? Or had she met some man earlier and gone with him? It had happened both ways before. This time it seemed without warning, though. I thought about supper last night. Mama had been okay. Hektor had knocked over his milk and Papa had jumped up to wipe it up but Mama had said, "I'll get it." And she had put her napkin over it to keep it from spreading and then had gotten a dishrag and wiped it up. She hadn't even seemed upset. Maybe not upset enough I realized now.

I fixed three bowls of cornflakes for us. Willie Mae would be in later and would cook supper before she left. So there really wasn't anything to worry about. Donnie, Hektor, and I would be just fine. Willie Mae might even remember and bake us a cake.

They came down and we ate. We heard the bus coming just as we finished. "Get your books, Hektor," I said.

That was when he put his head down on the table and began to cry like a baby instead of a ten-year-old. "I want Mama and Papa."

The bus horn was blowing. "For God's sake, Hektor. Shut up," Donnie said. "We've got to go."

Hektor looked up. Tears rolled down his round face that looked so much like Papa's. "You go," he said. "I'm gonna wait on them."

Donnie and I looked at each other. "I'll stay with him," he said.

"We'll all stay," I decided. I ran outside to tell Mr.

Barganier that we wouldn't be riding today, that Mama was taking us all to the doctor for checkups.

Carl Jenkins stuck his head out of the window while Mr. Barganier was turning around in our driveway. "You sick?" I shook my head no. "Tell Donnie I'll be over this afternoon."

There were whoops and catcalls from the bus. Eric Palmer stuck his head out and yelled, "You be sure and tell Donnie, Artie! He won't want to miss Carl!"

I just grinned. I knew who Carl was coming to see. He had liked me since we were in the third grade. Last year when the boys were playing football, Carl had been knocked into the goalpost and hit his head. He was knocked out for a minute. And when he came to, he was saying, "Artie. Artie." Coach Giles teased me about it. Said he thought he was going to have to come and get me. It made me feel good.

We put on our bathing suits and went to the beach. It was October and the water was still warm. We built a sandcastle, something we hadn't done in a long time.

Sometime during the morning, Willie Mae came to the top of the bluff and yelled down wanting to know what we were doing home. "Playing hookey!" Donnie answered. "It's our birthday!"

"Well, you better come get shirts or you're gonna be sick. Out of school for real."

We went traipsing up to the house. We knew Willie Mae was going to ask where Mama and Papa were, but she just said, "Shame on you not going to school. Gonna grow up dumb as fence posts."

"I'm hungry," Hektor said. Willie Mae fixed us sandwiches and we took them to the beach and sat in the shadow of Buck Stuart's sailboat to eat them.

"I wish Mama wasn't crazy," Hektor said, his mouth full of peanut butter. It came out "cwazy."

"Well, she isn't, always," Donnie said. "Think of the nice parties she has. And how pretty the flowers always are."

"Ha!" I said.

"Well, she's not!" Donnie glared at me. "You just don't give her any credit."

I held out my arm toward him. The sun had turned the scar just above my elbow a jagged red. "You mean I don't give the devil her due?"

"That was an accident!"

"Throwing a knife is an accident?"

"She didn't mean to hurt you."

Nobody was going to win this argument. We had it all the time. Donnie always took up for Mama.

"She's sick, anyway," he said.

That was always the last line of the argument. We crumpled up the wax paper our sandwiches had been wrapped in and stuck it in Buck's boat.

"Let's walk to the hotel," Donnie said. And that's what we did. A slight breeze blew across the water. Our lips tasted salty when we ran our tongues around them. We drank for a long time from the fountain by the pier.

"There's Mrs. Cates," Donnie said. We saw her coming from one of the guest cottages, her arms full of sheets and towels. She spied us.

"What are you doing here?" she called. "There's a thing called school, you know."

"Maybe it's a holiday," Donnie said.

"And maybe you kids are playing hookey." She smiled. "Well, I didn't see you. Okay?"

"Okay." We watched her go on down the walk, carrying her bundle.

"I'm hungry again," Hektor said. "And I have to go to the bathroom."

"Well, you can go to the bathroom here," Donnie said. "But we don't have any money."

"I want some almond pie."

"Too bad." Donnie disappeared into the bathhouse with Hektor. I sat on a bench and watched two swimmers go back and forth the length of the pool. Back and forth. They couldn't be enjoying themselves.

And then I heard our mother's laugh. I thought for a minute that I was hearing things. And then I heard it again. It was coming from the cottage next to the one Mrs. Cates had just come from. I got up and walked toward it. And then I stopped. I turned around and saw that Hektor and Donnie had come out of the bathroom and were blinking in the light, looking for me.

"Here I am," I said. "Let's go home. Let's walk down the road. It's closer."

When we got home, Papa was there. And in the afternoon, Carl came. He and I sat in the swing and he showed me the schoolwork I had missed that day. But I wasn't paying much attention. All I could think of was that I knew where Mama was and I ought to tell Papa. But I didn't. Willie Mae had made us a birthday cake and was fixing meat loaf and mashed potatoes for supper; Papa was reading in his study. Hektor had fallen asleep on the front porch and Donnie was listening to the radio. Everything was peaceful. It was enough to drive you crazy.

The trouble was never knowing which Mama we were going to get. She might sit in her room for days, just sit there looking out of the window or looking at the same page of a book. She wasn't crazy like not knowing where she was. She would speak to us and even ask how school was. But it was like she was a stranger. A very formal stranger. And then we would hear her singing in the kitchen. She would hug us and plan shopping trips to Mobile and have parties, shrimp boils and cocktail parties and seated dinners. Sometimes she would tell Papa and sometimes she wouldn't. He would come in from work and there would be a houseful of people, most of whom he didn't know. Willie Mae wouldn't help with the parties and after Mama threw the knife at me, I wouldn't either. So she would get some of the Cates kids or someone from the hotel who wasn't working that day.

The way I got cut with the knife really was an accident. At least, it was an accident that my arm was in the way. It wasn't an accident she threw it. She was slicing a roast and I was peeling shrimp at the sink.

"Goddamn dull knife!" And she threw it at the sink. I felt it slice my arm, but the funny thing was it didn't hurt. And it didn't bleed for about a minute. Mama and I stood there and looked at each other, surprised. And then the blood just spurted. She grabbed a dishrag and wrapped it around my arm. "Willie Mae!" she called. Willie Mae came to the door. "We have to go to Daphne to the clinic. Would you please put this food in the icebox?" That was when I looked down at the dishrag and saw it already getting red. And I fainted. The only time in my life. Willie Mae caught me just as I went down. She hollered for Donnie and he ran next door to get Mrs. Stuart to drive us to Daphne. But Papa drove up just then so he and Donnie took me to the clinic. Papa cried all the way there and back. Donnie cried, too. But I didn't. "Hush," I said. "Y'all hush. I'm okay." And I was. Even when the doctor stitched me up, it didn't hurt. It was like I was somewhere else. "Hush, Papa. Please hush."

Maybe the worst times are when she goes away, though. Papa always goes looking for her. Takes us with him, too. Someone will call and say they've seen her in New Orleans or Jackson and off we'll go. Of course he sat us down a long time ago and explained manic depression to us. "She's hurting as much or more than we are," he said. But most of the time I find that hard to believe.

She's with a man at the hotel, probably Zeke Pardue. She was with a man in New Orleans and Jackson, too. Probably Zeke Pardue at least part of the time. Papa knows it. Donnie and I know it. Maybe Hektor doesn't, but he's the only one. Even Carl knows it. I've told him. Sweet Carl. He says, "It's okay, Artie." But it's not. It never will be. She never even said she was sorry about my arm. And today's my birthday. And Donnie's.

FOURTEEN

Armadillos

AUGUST MORNINGS, DAWN POUNCES EARLY AND HEAVILY ON
Harlow. The air smells like coffee, bacon, tea olive
bushes, and tidal pools. The fishing boats have already
gone out; the automatic sprinklers at the Grand Hotel
have shut off. By the time the first rays of the sun hit
the water, most of the three thousand residents of the
town have a start on their day. Nine women and two
men attend six o'clock mass after which Father Carroll
sits down with a bowl of cereal to watch *Today*. War,
murder, and mayhem. Father Carroll spoons in cornflakes and watches them drag dead Bosnians away. Or
are they Rwandans? Laotians? Kurds? Or maybe there
was a blackout in New York. He should have listened
closer. Well, he'll pray for them all. He finishes his
breakfast, takes his Lanoxin, Lopressor, and a vitamin,
and hits the remote. Time to go to work.

Dolly awakens with a sense of loss. She has slept
in her clothes and has a headache.

"My God," she says when she looks in the mirror.

She takes three aspirin and a shower. Her scalp feels sore as the water hits it. She may be getting sick.

"Telephone, Dolly. It's your mama," she hears May calling as she steps from the shower. Dolly puts on her pink seersucker robe and goes into Artie's room. She sits on Artie's bed and answers the phone.

"Hey, honey," Mariel says. "Now regardless of what you hear, we are on schedule. Rosary tonight. Funeral tomorrow at ten."

"Okay," Dolly says.

"Just act like nothing has happened."

"All right."

"You all right? You sound funny."

"I have a headache."

"Well, I'm at Mama's. I'll be over there after while. Don't let Mrs. Randolph leave any food out. I read an article about salmonella last week. Just what we need."

"I won't."

"Well, I'll talk to you later. Bye. Take some aspirin."

"Bye, Mama." Dolly wonders vaguely what her mother was talking about. She looks out Artie's window. She counts eighteen sailboats. May comes in bringing her a cup of coffee.

Downstairs in the living room, Reese is granting an interview to a reporter from *People* magazine. Reese has been out of jail two hours.

"Well, I really wanted to talk to a member of the family," the reporter says, placing a small tape recorder on the coffee table.

"Anything you want to know, I can tell you. I been her faithful retainer for twenty years."

"Her what?"

"Her faithful retainer."

The man smiles and Reese narrows his eyes.

"It's just that I haven't heard that expression in a long time." The man reaches over and turns on the tape. "Is that what she called you?"

"She called me Reese."

"And what did you call her?"

"Artie. Her real name was Artemis but nobody called her that." Reese leans forward on the Queen Anne chair and looks at the recorder. "Is that thing getting everything I say?"

"Absolutely."

"Well, she was a fine lady and a great painter and the world is a fairer place for her having been here."

"A fairer place?"

"Yes."

The reporter clears his throat. "Mr. Whitley, are you sure there is no member of the family I can talk to?"

"I'm sure. They too bereaved anyway. Would you like a Coca-Cola?"

"No. Thank you."

"Well, I'm going to get me one. I don't feel good this morning." Reese groans as he gets out of the chair and goes toward the kitchen.

The reporter looks around. What he had been hoping for was to talk to Hektor Sullivan. That would have been the story. One of the richest men in the world talking about his famous, beautiful sister.

Reese comes back in, rubbing his knuckle against the coldness and wetness of a Coke bottle. "You sure you don't want one?"

"No, thank you." The reporter reaches over and turns the tape on again. "Now, Mr. Whitley, about Mrs. Sullivan's husband."

"He was Greek. Killed in Korea."

The reporter checks his notes. "Carl Jenkins was Greek?"

Reese takes a long drink of Coke and hiccups. "Sure he was Greek. Dived for sponges in the bay."

"I didn't know there were sponges in Mobile Bay," says the reporter.

"I didn't either," says Reese. Both men are silent for a moment. May walks by, looks in, and waves. "Hey, May," Reese says. "That's May," he tells the reporter.

"A niece?"

"Probably."

The reporter turns off the recorder and stands up. "Thank you, Mr. Whitley, for your time."

"You welcome." Reese walks to the door with the man and stands there smiling. "You write a good story now."

Hektor, on his way to Bay Chapel East, swerves to avoid an armadillo. He has already seen three squashed ones. Where had they all come from?

He thinks he really should go to Birmingham with Donnie. They could talk on the plane. It would be good for both of them. There's something he needs to do for Artie, though. Something important.

As he turns into the Bay Chapel East driveway, he realizes he has forgotten the money Mariel requested. She is sitting on a concrete bench on a green canopied walk looking old, anxious. She gets up and comes across the parking lot.

"What's going on? Reckon they'll take Visa?" he asks, getting out of the pickup stiffly. Every muscle in his body seems to have tightened up during the short drive.

"We're going to have the funeral."

"But Donnie is going to Birmingham."

"I know he is." They reach the bench and sit down. "And tomorrow we're going to have a closed casket funeral."

Hektor understands instantly. He sees ancient Father Carroll wafting incense over an empty casket. He hears Father Carroll's shaky voice petitioning that Artie's soul be allowed into heaven. Interesting. "Does Donnie know what you're doing?" he asks.

Mariel nods yes. She is not the frantic woman Hektor had expected from her earlier phone call. She seems quiet, thoughtful.

"And the money?"

"Another casket. Generous tips."

Hektor rubs his stiff neck and stretches. It is hot under the canopy. "I've got to go to the bank unless they'll take Visa. I don't even have a check with me."

"Okay. You want to see Artie first?"

"Yes," he lies.

The funeral parlor doors are wooden, massive. Hektor opens them for Mariel and follows her into the darkness and coolness of the lobby; it's like diving into the bay. Hektor feels he is swimming toward the man seated at the desk who rises, smiling.

Mariel introduces them. "Mr. Griffin, my brother-in-law, Hektor Sullivan."

The undertaker has an unexpectedly warm smile and hearty handshake. "Mr. Sullivan. My father buried your parents."

"Oh?" Hektor remembers little of his parents' funeral. And right now he is having to remember to breathe.

"Yes. I remember it because it happened the very first week I worked here and, of course, it was unusual, too. I looked it up so we could have comparable arrangements for your sister. For instance, they were buried in our number two hundred metal caskets, gray, both of them. They still make that same casket so that's the one Mrs. Sullivan selected. I think you'll be pleased."

"Thank you."

"Now, if you'll come this way."

Hektor and Mariel follow Mr. Griffin down the hall.

"In here. I'll leave you two alone. My sympathies, Mr. Sullivan."

Hektor nods. He steps into a small sitting room decorated in blues and mauves. To his left is an alcove and a casket almost hidden by flowers.

"We asked for no flowers, but people are sending them anyway." Mariel puts her purse in a chair and walks around looking at the cards on the floral arrangements. Hektor sits in the chair nearest the door.

"Here's one from Carl's sister. I forgot to call her, too. I need to do that."

"Mariel," Hektor asks, "why are we doing this?"

"Hektor, the least we can do is bury the dead decently. And I'll tell you this, it's what your mother would have wanted."

His mother would have wanted them to bury an empty casket? It occurs to Hektor that Mariel may be as unhinged as his mother had been. It occurs to Hektor that all of them are.

"I'm going to see if Mr. Griffin has finished all the arrangements." Mariel picks up her purse and searches through the compartments. "I'll be back in a minute."

"Ask him about the credit card."

Hektor sits in the chair. He smells carnations and lilies and formaldehyde. He does not get up and go into the alcove where Artie is lying in her yellow linen dress, a smile on her face. Hektor has seen death in the jungles of Central America, on the streets of New Orleans, and on Mobile Bay. And now he has a small epiphany.

"Artie, we're all armadillos," he whispers toward the alcove.

FIFTEEN

Our Glorious Dead

DOLLY, SECOND CUP OF COFFEE IN HER HAND, SITS AT THE TOP of the steps and watches the cleanup crews on the beach with their rakes and shovels. How strange and exciting jubilees are, she thinks. All you have to do is stand there and hold out your bucket and the fish jump in. "Manna from the sea," the Chamber of Commerce brochures describe the phenomenon. Well, even manna has to be cleaned up.

Light reflecting on the water is not good for her headache. She puts her head on her knees and watches a line of ants trying to move a dead June bug. What am I going to do? she thinks. What am I going to do?

Mrs. Randolph sticks her head out the door and asks Dolly if she wants a blueberry muffin, still hot.

Dolly shakes her head no. "I think I'm going to walk up to my grandmother's. But thank you."

"Well, wait a minute and you can take her some." Mrs. Randolph returns in a few minutes holding out a warm aluminum foil package. "Here. Mrs. Cates loves blueberry muffins. I'll take that cup if you're through with your coffee. You feeling okay? You look a little peaked."

"Got a headache this morning. Maybe I can run it off. Thanks for the muffins." Dolly gets up, swaps the empty cup for the aluminum foil package, and goes around to the front of the house to the road. She remembers when this road wasn't paved, when it was a shell road; the shells are still there, their shapes discernible through black asphalt.

She has jogged about ten minutes when a car slows down beside her. "Hey. How's it going?" Kelly Stuart asks.

"I'm okay." Dolly jogs in place. "Need to work off a headache. I didn't get much sleep last night."

"Well, don't go too far in this heat. I'll talk to you later."

After Kelly drives off, Dolly realizes she should have hitched a ride home or have Kelly take her to Nomie's. She feels dizzy and sick; she needs to rest a while in some shade.

Just ahead of her is the path that leads to the Confederate cemetery. Most people don't know it's back there in the woods, but the Daughters of the Confederacy keep the grass cut between the many small obelisks. It's cool and shady in there, and Dolly walks up the path and under the wrought iron archway that proclaims OUR GLORIOUS CONFEDERATE DEAD.

There is a concrete bench which seems to be a favorite roosting place of seagulls, with proof of their visits. Nothing recent, Dolly ascertains, stretching out on the bench, feeling the world reel around her.

The concrete is cool, and the Spanish moss on the gnarled live oaks moves gently in the breeze from the bay. Dolly turns on her side, her folded hands under her face, and thinks how peaceful this place is. And how simple. These glorious Confederates went to war, got shot or bayoneted, died, and were buried in the ground. Not a single one of them asked to be cremated.

Dolly closes her eyes. She wishes she had a drink of water. And then she sleeps.

"Lord, child," she hears her Nomie's voice saying. "Here you are on this bird-pooped concrete bench sound asleep. Are you all right?" Dolly feels Nomie's cool hand against her forehead, feels her bangs brushed back.

"I called down at Artie's and Mrs. Randolph said you were on the way to my house, but she didn't think you felt very good. So when you didn't show up, I came looking."

Dolly sits up and feels dizzy. She grabs the bench with both hands to steady herself.

"Here," Naomi says, taking her by the shoulders. "Lie back down and put your head in my lap."

Dolly does what her grandmother says. As long as she holds her head perfectly still and her eyes closed, the world quits tilting. "Hey, Nomie," she says.

"Hey, sweetheart. You think it's the heat getting to you?"

"Maybe. I haven't had much sleep in the last couple of nights."

"It's no wonder." Naomi rubs Dolly's head. "Think you could handle a drink of water?"

"Lord, yes!"

"Then raise your head just a little. I've got this fancy foam thermos your mama ordered for me from some catalog. Hooks on my belt in case of old age instant dehydration, I guess. But damned if it hasn't come in handy. Doesn't weigh an ounce."

The water tastes wonderful to Dolly.

"Not too much," Naomi cautions. "Our glorious Confederate dead just hate to be puked on."

Dolly smiles and puts her head back on Naomi's lap. Naomi pours a little of the water onto her fingers and rubs them across Dolly's forehead and wrists.

"Your mama was out to the house earlier," she says. "All worried about Artie's funeral. Or lack of one."

"She called me and said she was going to have one." Dolly is beginning to feel almost comfortable.

"Won't hurt a thing. Long as she can work it out. Donnie's still taking Artie to Birmingham, though, so I guess they'll be burying an empty casket." Naomi resumed stroking Dolly's hair. "Did you know Artie wanted to be cremated?"

"No. And I don't know why Mama's so upset about it. Like it's something to be ashamed of."

"Well, your mama's always been the only one of my children who thought everything should be done the same way all the time, that things should stay constant. And that's a burden. You know it, Dolly? Stockings are plain gonna get runs in them on your way to church."

Dolly smiles. "Mama always carries an extra pair in her purse."

"Hush. You know what I mean."

They are quiet for a few minutes. Dolly is about to doze off again when Naomi says, "You reckon any of these boys thought they'd end up in a cemetery in Harlow, Alabama?"

The word "boys" startles Dolly. For the first time, she realizes that was what most of them were—boys, some of them probably no older than fifteen. And there was nothing glorious about their deaths.

"Some of them are Yankees, you know," Naomi

continues. "The Grand Hotel was a hospital and they brought them here when they died."

"It's peaceful here."

"Yes, it is."

"Nomie, can I have another drink of water?" Dolly sits up slowly. The world is not reeling as it had been. When she reaches for the thermos, she notices Naomi's tee shirt. "Hail Maui full of grass?"

"A present from your cousin Teddy."

"It's a good one." Dolly drinks slowly.

"Lie back down a few more minutes. You may have some fever." Naomi is thinking, as she frequently does, how glad she is that Dolly has Thomas Sullivan's mouth and the cleft in his chin. She wishes she could tell this granddaughter they share how when Thomas Sullivan would walk into church, it was all the blessing she needed.

Instead she says, "The first time I kissed was in this cemetery."

"Really, Nomie? Was it Grandpa Will?"

"Nope. A boy named Harvey Musgrove. I knew good and well what he was fixing to do, saying let's come in here, and I cooperated fully. I think I nearly scared him to death."

"How old were you?"

"Fifteen, I guess. I married Will when I was eighteen."

Dolly lies back down and puts her head on her grandmother's lap again.

"Nomie, Bobby and I aren't together anymore. We haven't been for months." Dolly can't bring herself to say the word "divorced" to her grandmother.

"I know, honey. Your mama told me."

"Did she tell you why?"

"She told me. You think you'll be able to work things out?"

"I don't think so." Dolly closes her eyes. "And it's not that I don't love him, Nomie." Tears roll down her cheeks.

"Lots of fish in the sea besides Bobby Hamrick, sugar." Naomi says this quietly. She knows Dolly won't believe it.

"That's what Artie said. But you know, Nomie, things just aren't as complicated here in Harlow. You meet someone and you fall in love and marry and you make a life together."

Dear God, Thomas, Naomi thinks. Our granddaughter hasn't got a lick of sense.

SIXTEEN

A Circle Humming

IT'S A LITTLE AFTER NOON, AND DONNIE IS GETTING READY TO leave as Mariel walks in from the funeral parlor.

"It's all done," she announces.

"You got everything settled?"

"I think so. I just explained it all to Mr. Griffin and he said he'd see to everything. They're taking Artie to the airport now."

"Did he charge a bundle?"

"Hektor gave him some money. I don't know how much." Mariel sits on the bed and watches Donnie tie his tie. He has on his new gray suit. "Are you angry?"

"Of course not. I told you it was fine." Donnie reaches for his keys, his change.

"Your voice sounds angry."

"Well, I'm not."

"Have you had anything to eat?"

"I had some toast and coffee."

"You want me to fix you something?"

"No, thanks." He leans toward the mirror and straightens his tie. Mariel looks in the mirror. She thinks if she looks hard enough she will see the twenty-eight-year-old Donnie that she married. She knows he is encapsulated inside her husband. Sometimes she catches a glimpse of him and catches her breath.

"Hektor liked the idea of a funeral."

"Good."

"Don't we need to talk about this, Donnie?"

"Nothing to say." Donnie leans over and kisses her cheek. "I'll see you tonight."

Mariel watches him leave the room. She goes to the window and watches his car drive away, even waves, but he doesn't see her. She remembers a dream she had last night that woke her up. She and Donnie and Artie were in a small boat and a huge wave came and hovered over them. Looking up, she could see shadows coursing through the water. Screaming, she threw herself toward Donnie, but he and Artie were laughing and pointing at the wave. Mariel woke up drenched with sweat and wrote the dream down immediately for her analyst. After all these years, she knows how her analyst will interpret it, but Mariel still likes to recount her dreams. She likes the way her analyst makes sense of them. The shadows in the water looked like porpoises, but of course they had more meaning. Mariel is a good dreamer. Her analyst is always pleased with what she brings her.

Now she thinks she'd better get her clothes together for the rosary and head back to Harlow. How simple Artie could have made things. But she never did.

Donnie sees Mariel in the window but doesn't wave back. He knows he should have, but somehow he feels too distant, too uninvolved. He drives carefully down the familiar tree-lined streets and thinks if it doesn't rain today he'll have to turn the sprinklers on in his yard tonight. He thinks if he went all over the world that he would instantly know Mobile. The air is a blanket that smells like the bay, and the treefrogs sing even at the airport. He could hear them when he was getting off a plane and would know he was in Mobile because of that buzzing, moaning sound.

"Listen to those tree frogs," his mother would say. "Y'all go touch the trees and make them hush." And he and Artie and Hektor would run around the yard touching the pines and live oaks, and the noise would stop instantly. But in a few minutes, the tree frogs would begin again. First one place, then another, until a circle of humming rose and fell like waves. It said summer and home.

Now he enters the interstate politely and stays in the right lane. Sunlight glints on the bay and on a long barge heading toward the river. A few sailboats glide across the water. Once again, Donnie is glad this is home. His father was fond of saying, "Everything is here." Now everything is not here, and Donnie feels stiff with grief, wounded.

He turns on his right turn signal and exits to the airport. The Sullivan-Threadaway jet is in the area where large companies keep their planes. Donnie circles behind the hangars and finds a parking place. Heat shimmers in waves about the black asphalt and hits him as he opens the door.

"Uncle Donnie!" May waves to him from the door of the small waiting room for private plane owners. "We're in here."

Donnie had half-expected Hektor to show up. But to bring May! He can't believe Hektor would subject her to this.

"He's talking to the pilot," May says. Donnie brushes by her. He sees Hektor behind the counter with a tall man, a man so bald his head looks shaved. The two are bent over a map spread out on a table; the man is marking something on it with a pen.

"Hektor," Donnie says, "I told you I wanted to do this by myself. I don't want you to go, and I certainly don't think May should go."

Hektor looks up in surprise. He hadn't heard Donnie come in. The man with the pen turns away, not wanting to get involved.

"We're not going with you, Donnie," Hektor says. "We're going to Mississippi. I just came by to see that everything's okay."

Donnie's anger rushes away and for a moment nothing takes its place. He stands there silently, waiting for an emotion which eventually turns out to be emptiness.

"Wait, Jimmy," Hektor says to the bald man who is leaving. "This is Jimmy Tucker, your pilot, Donnie."

Jimmy turns and the two men shake hands. "Donnie and I've met before, Hektor," Jimmy reminds him. "I flew him and your sister to Rochester last year." He turns back to Donnie. "I was so sorry to hear she had passed away."

Donnie remembers a pilot with hair, not someone with light glinting from his head. "Thank you," he says.

"I'll just go and check everything out. You come on whenever you're ready."

"Thanks, Jimmy," Hektor says. The tall man nods, picks up the map they had been studying, and leaves. Hektor takes Donnie's arm and leads him to a row of connected orange fiberglass chairs. "Sit down a minute and I'll tell you what May and I are going to do. Let me go check on her, though."

"She's okay. She's right outside," Donnie says. The

two large men fold their bodies into the uncomfortable chairs.

Hektor clears his throat. "Well, what I said about May and me going to Mississippi. We're going for a priest."

"For what? I thought you and Mariel had it all arranged. Did Father Carroll find out the casket's empty?" Donnie doesn't know where the sarcasm came from. God, he's tired.

Hektor ignores the sarcasm. "We need a priest for Artie, even if she is cremated. I've been thinking about it. You know as well as I do that she has to have a funeral mass, just like you and I'll have to have one."

"Look, Hektor. If you think you can find a priest to say a mass over Artie's ashes after another priest thinks he's buried her body, forget it. It doesn't matter anyway."

"It matters to me, Donnie."

Donnie suddenly sees a fourteen-year-old altar boy holding the chalice for the priest's blessing. He remembers the expression on Hektor's face, rapt, nourished by the mysteries, believing in redemption.

"Why Mississippi?" he asks.

"There's a group of people who live up the bayou not far from Pascagoula. One of them's a priest."

Donnie knows what's coming. "And this group of people. Do they speak English?"

"Not much."

There is so much Donnie wants to say. What he says is, "Don't get yourself in a passel of trouble with the feds, little brother.

Hektor grins. "You sound like Mama," he says. " 'You boys are going to get in a passel of trouble.' "

"We did, too."

"All of us." The brothers sit quietly for a moment.

"But we had a hell of a lot of fun part of the time."

"That's for sure." Hektor looks at his watch. "How did we get on this, anyway? Listen, the plane's ready. Artie's already on it. And Patty James will be helping Jimmy out. I asked for her especially. Married and three kids, but just looking at her gets the old juices going. You can do a little daydreaming. Anyway," Hektor stands, "we both need to get going if we're going to get back tonight. You're sure you're okay?"

Donnie gets up slowly. "I'm fine." They come together in an embrace so hard it hurts their ribs and startles them both.

"God, Donnie!" Hektor says and rushes out the door calling for May. By the time Donnie gets outside, Hektor and May are almost to the pickup. May turns, sees him, and waves.

Jimmy Tucker sticks his head in the door. "We're ready, Mr. Sullivan, when you are." Donnie follows him to the plane. He has been wondering where they would put the casket. Now he sees it's in the aisle in what Artie called the living room when they had gone to Mayo last year on this same plane. Donnie eases by it and sits in a blue leather chair. It's hard for him to realize that such luxury as this plane belongs to Hektor who drives pickups that junkyards would refuse.

"Buckle up, Mr. Sullivan," says a female voice. Donnie snaps his seat belt and places his hands on Artie's casket. The engines whine and the plane vibrates. "Here we go, Mr. Sullivan," says the voice. Donnie leans back and waits for the thrust of the jets.

Five minutes later, they are over the bay and he can see Harlow. He should have called Dolly this morning. He wonders what she will do about the house and everything else. At twenty-seven, she's not going to make it as a dancer. Not much of a future choreographing for kids. Artie had lucked into a good deal with her painting. She could work when she wanted to.

He smiles a little. He had made the mistake once of telling Artie he thought she was lucky; it made her furious.

"Screw you, Donnie Sullivan," she said. "I work like hell and I'm a goddamned good artist."

Patty James comes in from the cockpit. Instead of the uniform Donnie had expected, she's wearing jeans and a beige silk shirt. In her thirties and redheaded, she is, as Hektor had said, decidedly attractive.

"Let me make you a drink, Mr. Sullivan," she says. "Almost anything you want. And we have some sandwich fixings. I'm going to make Jimmy and me one. Have you had any lunch?"

Donnie shakes his head. "Nothing to eat, thanks. I'd like a vodka tonic, though."

"Sure." Patty eases around the casket and goes to what Donnie knows is a complete kitchen and bar. He hears bottles opening and ice rattling. In a moment she's back with his drink. "Here you go." The drink comes in a glass with the Sullivan-Threadaway Imports logo on it. The napkin has the same logo, a tree that appears to be an apple tree with a bunch of bananas hanging from it. Artie had declared it a wonderful logo the first time she saw it, the ultimate of artistic license.

"You're sure you don't want anything to eat?" Patty James asks. "Some snacks?"

"I'm positive."

Patty sits on the arm of the chair across from Donnie. The fabric of her jeans presses against her thigh and makes a wonderfully curved line. Donnie admires this as he would any finely crafted work of art. No juices. God, he is tired. He takes a large swallow of his drink.

"Mr. Sullivan, I just want you to know how sorry I am about your sister. I've admired her work for a long time, and I was on several flights with her. She was a wonderful lady."

"Thank you."

"I kept that article that was in *Time* a couple of years ago that had all the pictures of her paintings, and she signed it for me and did a little pencil sketch around the edges. I have it framed in my bedroom." Patty stands up and pats the casket self-consciously. "Anyway, I just wanted you to know. She touched a lot of lives."

"Yes, she did. Thank you."

Patty nods and goes back to the kitchen again. In a few minutes she comes by with some sandwiches and disappears into the cockpit. Donnie nurses his drink and looks out at the green that is South Alabama. Farm ponds reflect the sun; a school bus sits motionless on the interstate.

Donnie wants to open the casket and talk to Artie, hold her hand. He needs to tell her that he, Donnie, is not sophisticated enough for cremation. He needs to ask her why she wanted this when all he wants is to put her in her yellow dress by Mama and Papa or by Carl's marker and take her flowers on their birthday and be buried beside her someday. He places two fingers against the cold gray metal. That wouldn't be bad, up there in Myrtlewood, Artie. Maybe Hektor would come, too, and Mariel, of course, and eventually Dolly and her children. Surely she'll have some kids. Maybe May and her family, too.

He leans over close to the casket. "Artie," he whispers, "why in hell are you making me do this? Is there something here I'm supposed to understand that I'm missing? Is it Mama? Zeke Pardue?"

The air conditioner is too low; Donnie is freezing. He gets up and goes to fix another vodka tonic. On the counter in the little galley is a jar of beer nuts. He takes a handful with his drink and goes back to his seat. He is shaking so hard the ice cubes in his drink rattle against the banana tree on the glass.

On *One Life to Live,* Vicky Buchanan is having brain surgery to rid her of the evil Nicky Smith who is her alter ego and who pops out at crucial times in Vicky's life to go to bars and pick up men and generally cavort in a manner unseemly for the ladylike Victoria.

"Goodbye, Vicky. You'll miss me," says Nicky, rising from the body on the operating table and wafting across the room. A last toss of her rakish red wig and she is out the door.

"I'm gonna miss her," says Reese. "She got Vicky in a lot of trouble." He, Dolly, and Mrs. Randolph are sitting at the kitchen table eating lunch and watching TV. Reese and Mrs. Randolph are glad to have Dolly in the chair that has been empty for weeks. They were just sitting down as Dolly came in, and they insisted that she join them. "Just drink some iced tea, anyway," Mrs. Randolph said when Dolly hesitated. "Make you feel better," Reese added, pushing the chair out.

"That Nicky was no good." Mrs. Randolph points a fork toward the TV. "You watch this?" she asks Dolly.

Dolly shakes her head no. "Well, when I was down here, I'd watch it sometimes with Artie."

"Artie did like her stories," Reese says.

"Well, Nicky was all in Vicky's mind," Mrs. Randolph explains the story line, "because she was abused as a child."

"Her very own daddy. Off in the head." Reese takes another helping of potato salad. "You know, I knew a man once thought he was a chicken part of the time, sort of perched on his steps and crowed. Never bothered a soul and nobody paid him much mind. Got run over by a train, though. Number Six on its way to Montgomery. Real slow train, too. Makes you wonder."

Dolly and Mrs. Randolph think about this for a minute. Dolly sees the man perched on the track crowing at the oncoming Number Six.

"The mind can do strange things," Mrs. Randolph says. "My brother Rudy was out in the field one day baling hay and not a cloud in the sky and bam! A streak of lightning came out of nowhere and knocked him down. Near about electrocuted him, but it turned out all right. Anybody want anything else?" Mrs. Randolph gets up from the table.

"Not a cloud in the sky?" Reese asks.

"Not a one. My papa was with him and had to beat him on the chest."

"Where did the lightning come from?" Dolly wants to know.

"God knows. Bless Rudy's heart, though. He was the first of us children to go. Got it in his mind that if he went outside, lightning would hit him again. We all told him that was crazy. Finally talked him into going out."

Dolly is intrigued. "And lightning hit him again?"

"Of course not. A bee stung him, though, and he went into some kind of shock. Died before we could get him to the hospital. He was my favorite brother, too. I don't make any bones about it." Mrs. Randolph begins to rinse the dishes. "Eat that fruit salad, Dolly. You need something in your stomach. You're skinny as a rail."

Dolly is having trouble with one strawberry going down.

"I knew a man got hit by lightning twice," Reese says. "Both his arms looked like a zipper running up them."

Mrs. Randolph sits back down. She's rubbing Jergen's lotion on her hands. "Well, some people are just plain magnets, aren't they?"

Reese agrees. "God's truth."

On TV Vicky is waking from surgery. She reaches toward her husband who offers her a huge strawberry. Dolly knows she needs to go rest.

SEVENTEEN

Daylilies

AFTER YOU CROSS THE MISSISSIPPI LINE, ANY EXIT ALONG I-10 will take you into bayou country. It stretches the width of the state, swampy, fertile. Hektor turns just past Pascagoula and heads inland through swamp grass almost as high as the truck. He crosses dozens of small bridges that span dark, unmoving streams. Beside him, May concentrates on the bottle of Dr Pepper into which she has poured a package of peanuts. Every time she turns it up, Hektor holds his breath. He has only seen the Heimlich maneuver on TV. Besides, by the time he stopped the car and got her out, it might be too late. "Please be careful," he says. May smiles at him, puts her thumb over the bottle top, and shakes it. Foam and peanuts bubble up; she clamps her mouth over the bottle. Her cheeks swell like small balloons.

"Quit that," Hektor says.

May burps and chews.

"A lot of flying saucers land in here," Hektor says.

May looks at the grass, the stunted palms. "Why?"

"I don't know. You just see it all the time in the

paper. Two fishermen from Pascagoula said they got carried for a ride."

May looks at Hektor. "You don't believe that, do you, Papa?"

"No. But I think the men believed it. Something happened to them out here that scared them nearly to death. I saw them on TV still shaking." Hektor remembers how big the men's eyes were, how they stuttered. "Never put any foreign substances in your body, May. Promise me."

"I promise." May shakes the Dr Pepper again. Hektor sighs.

They are entering an area of thin pine trees that lean away from the prevailing wind off the gulf. Not for the first time, Hektor thinks of the people who paved this road. There must be cottonmouth moccasins in here as big as boa constrictors. And alligators and mosquitoes and leeches that would grab you like they did Humphrey Bogart. He still wonders how they filmed that. If a flying saucer did land here it wouldn't stand a chance.

"There are some cars up there," May says. "Maybe it's a wreck or something."

Hektor pulls to a stop behind a rusty Chevy pickup and gets out to see why the road is blocked. A woman is sitting in the cab crocheting. Hektor nods hello.

"It's a gator," she says.

"What?"

"A gator. Asleep on the road. Managed to get in both lanes. He don't want to, but they're trying to get him to move."

"How?"

"Very carefully." The woman and Hektor both laugh appreciatively. She wipes sweat from her forehead with the back of her arm. The little round crochet piece dangles for a moment in the air. She holds it out for Hektor to see. "A bedspread," she explains. "Our youngest is getting married."

"That's pretty," Hektor says. "Well, let me go see what's happening."

He starts away and then turns back. "Who's marrying her?" he asks.

"A boy from down Gautier. Nice boy. Just got out of the Navy."

"No. I mean the priest."

"You mean the preacher? Brother Edwards from Ruhama Baptist. That's where we go. Why? You need a preacher?"

"I'm looking for a priest who lives around here somewhere. You know one?"

"Maybe you mean Father Audubon. They say he used to be one. They call him that because he likes birds."

"Do you know where I can find him?"

"No. Bouchet at the store could probably tell you, though."

"Thanks. Where's the store?"

"Down the road. We'll get there after while, I guess." She wipes her forehead again.

"Thanks." Hektor walks back to his pickup. "It's an alligator across the road," he tells May. "Come on, let's go see what's happening."

"Hey, that's great." May jumps from the truck and starts running toward the front of the line of parked cars.

"Wait," Hektor calls. But May doesn't slow down. She pushes through the small crowd and disappears. "Lord God," Hektor hears her say.

"Excuse me." He wedges between two men and grabs May's arm. On the road before them is the largest alligator Hektor has ever seen. It stretches at least ten feet across the middle of the road. Dead, Hektor thinks. But even as he is thinking this, the alligator moves its tail slightly. Twelve people move backward as one. Hektor snatches May back so hard she is airborne.

"Don't you ever do that again!" he hisses.

"What?"

What? Put yourself in danger? Leave me?

"Say 'Lord God' like that. And get so close to an alligator."

"I just wanted to see him."

"So did Captain Hook."

"What?"

Hektor sighs. He is raising a culturally illiterate child who won't test well and who will never make it into a good college and it's his fault.

"That gator's Big Ben," the skinny redheaded man beside him says. "He does this ever now and then. We just wait till his nap's over usually. Yell at him some."

"How long does he usually sleep?" Hektor asks.

"Differs."

"I thought Big Ben was a bear," May says.

"That's Gentle Ben."

"Big Ben's a clock, though."

"Right. Goes tic toc because it swallowed Captain Hook's arm."

"Whose arm, Papa?"

"I'm not sure." Hektor turns to the man next to him. "You want me to call the Highway Patrol or something? There's a phone in my truck."

"Won't do any good. But I sure would like to call my wife and tell her why I'm late."

"Sure. It's that blue pickup."

"How does it work?"

"I'll come get it for you." Hektor turns to May.

"Move an inch and I'll send what's left of you to the reform school."

"What's the reform school?"

"You don't want to know."

"You're not going to send me to the zoo to shovel elephant doo?"

"Same thing." Hektor leaves a grinning May and accompanies the man to the pickup. While the phone is doing its roaming bit, he thinks this is a perfect example of irony, space age technology to inform someone an alligator has the road blocked.

"Honey?" the man says when the satellite cooperates. "I'm down by Big Swamp. Ben's got the road blocked again." He listens a moment and hangs up.

"She says I'm lying." He looks sadly at the phone in his hand. "Can I call somebody else?"

"Sure." Hektor shows the man how and goes back to join the crowd gathered around Big Ben. The crocheting woman is sitting in a frayed aluminum chair in a patch of shade.

"Hot," she says, but to Hektor she looks cool and peaceful, her fingers moving like little flashes of light. He thinks of his mother and Artie and Dolly, none of whom he has ever seen crochet.

"Could you show my daughter how to do that?" he asks.

"She can come watch me if she wants."

"Why?" May asks when Hektor tells her the lady is going to teach her to crochet.

"Because it's a good thing to know how to do if you get stopped on the road by an alligator."

May shakes her head no.

"Or waiting at an airport, or watching TV. It's something every lady should know how to do. You could make us a tablecloth."

"Why?"

"Because they're pretty. And idle hands are the devil's workshop. Take my word for it." He turns her around. "Now get over there."

May looks at Big Ben who has not moved an inch and decides to go see what the lady is doing.

An hour later, when the sheriff arrives, she is asleep, her head against the woman's thigh. The man in Hektor's pickup, still using the phone, spots the flashing lights first. "Here they come," he calls.

The group, which has grown much larger, parts for two uniformed men, one of whom carries an electric cattle prod.

"Y'all move way back," he says. The crowd obeys. "Sorry, Ben," he says, "but you gotta nap somewhere else." He lightly touches the alligator's tail with the prod and Ben comes to life, swishing his tail toward the running sheriff and then waddling slowly to the side of the road, down the bank, and into the swamp.

Everyone claps and laughs. The sheriff grins and holds up the prod. "These things are illegal, you know. Just for emergencies. I'd say that's what we had here."

Hektor wonders if it would take them over an hour to answer a real emergency but he thinks he already knows. He goes over to the sheriff, however, and thanks him and introduces himself. "I'm looking for Father Audubon," he says. "Do you know where I can find him?"

"Probably fishing. You know where Hurricane Lake is?"

"No."

"Well, it's a right big lake. You won't have any trouble finding it. Turn left up the road at Bouchet's store. When you get there somebody will know where he is."

"Thanks."

"Sure." The sheriff points the cattle prod at a small boy who screeches delightedly and runs.

May, groggy with sleep, is waiting in the truck. "He didn't hurt Ben, did he, Papa?"

"No, honey. Just startled him and woke him up. It got him out of the road, didn't it?"

May yawns. "He was so big."

Hektor yawns, too. "Did you learn how to crochet?"

"No, but the lady was real nice. Her name is Annie Dolores. Isn't that a pretty name? Mrs. Dolores. She's sixty-six and her daughter who's getting married's name is Delnora. She was a change-of-life baby. Do you like that name, Papa? Delnora Dolores? She works for Gulf Power and she's gonna have six bridesmaids. They're gonna wear blue dotted swiss. Mrs. Dolores says she's so glad dotted swiss has come back. Delnora's dress is peau de soie, though. Do you know what that is, Papa? And her veil is the same one Mrs. Dolores and her other two daughters wore. She's been married forty-eight years and says that's why she has high blood pressure. She has to take eight pills a day. That's a lot, isn't it, Papa?"

Hektor marvels at his girl child. He feels her words flowing over him like warm rain. Women, he thinks, picking up her small hand and kissing it. Bless their hearts.

The road to Hurricane Lake is not paved. There are deep mud holes that people have gone around so much they have worn down a new roadbed. Spanish moss brushes the windshield.

"I think Spanish moss is pretty," May says.

"One time Artie and Donnie and I decided we would pick it and sell it to florists to put in hanging baskets."

"Did you make any money?"

"We got red bugs. That stuff is covered in them. I had them the worst because they made me go up the trees. Mama soaked all of us in salty water. Didn't do a bit of good. They were all up under my arms. My legs."

"But did you make any money?"

"We wouldn't go near the stuff. We left it out in the backyard. I think maybe mama used some of it after it dried."

"I would have used a rake and not climbed up the tree," May says.

"Good thinking." They come around a curve and see the lake before them. The road ends at a boat dock; the water is unusually blue.

"Hey, neat." May jumps out as soon as the truck stops and runs out onto a small pier.

"Wait, May!" Hektor scrambles from the pickup and hurries after her. If she fell in, he would panic; they would both drown while he was trying to get her out. Things happen. He knows.

"You wouldn't panic, Hektor." It's Artie's voice, clear as if she were walking beside him.

"Yes, I would. I know what drowned people look like."

"What, Papa?" May is smiling at him.

"I said you could drown in this lake. It looks deep."

May looks back at the water. "There's lots of boats. Reckon which one is Father Audubon's?"

"I have no idea. I guess we'll just have to wait for him to come in."

"But that could take all day and I'm starving."

"There are some boiled peanuts in the truck."

"They make me thirsty."

"There's some water in the thermos."

But May shrugs and sits down on the pier. A tiny lizard darts across the piling in front of her. The sky is bright blue, not hazy like it will be later in the fall, and the dark green of the pines is punctuated with the lighter green of willows. For the first time, Hektor wishes he could paint what he sees, the child, the lake, the day. He wants Artie to see this and put it on canvas so he can keep it. But he wants even the light breeze that stirs the water, and the earthy, fishy smell that rises from the bank. Not even Artie could do that. He sighs and sits down beside May.

"Aunt Artie would like it here," she says.

"That's just what I was thinking."

"I guess she's in heaven."

"I guess so."

"Reckon what it's like?"

"Nice. Peaceful."

May nods. "That's what they say."

Hektor thinks of all the things he was taught in Sunday school about heaven. Artie and Donnie had said it sounded boring. Well, maybe she could get something going. Or come back as somebody terrific if that's an alternative. Who knows? Hektor isn't sure what he believes about the afterlife except you shouldn't take chances.

A small boat is coming toward the pier. A man waves at them.

"Are you Father Audubon?" Hektor calls.

"He's over there." The man points in a general direction toward several boats. "You want me to get him for you?"

"I'd appreciate it."

"They're not biting anyway." He turns the boat around and chugs toward the other fisherman. Tiny waves slap against the pilings of the pier. Hektor and May hear him shout, "Hey, Audubon!" They hear an answering "What?" and in a few minutes the man Hektor assumes is the priest is pulling his boat up beside the pier.

"You want me?" he asks, throwing the rope to Hektor and cutting his motor.

"Hektor Sullivan, and this is my daughter May."

"May," the man says, shaking hands with her, too. "Yep, I'm Father Audubon. Beats hell out of Delmore Ricketts, doesn't it?" He pulls off his straw fishing hat and runs his fingers through thinning red hair. In his late forties he is a small man with the freckles that go with his hair. He has on a stained blue many-pocketed mechanic's outfit that seems to be two sizes too large with the cuffs turned up several times. "Bye, Bud. Thanks," he calls to the man who had gone to get him and who is pulling out of the parking area, boat attached to an old Buick.

"Y'all wanted me?"

"We need a priest," Hektor says. "I heard about you."

"Where abouts?"

"Mobile."

"Lots of priests in Mobile."

"My sister died, Father." Hektor isn't sure that's the proper way to address him, but he decides it won't hurt. "We need someone to say mass for us."

"Like I said, there's lots of priests in Mobile."

"She's cremated, Father."

"Oh." Delmore Ricketts concentrates on sticking the toe of his shoes between two boards on the pier.

"She wants her ashes scattered on the bay."

"Is that legal?"

Hektor is losing his patience. "I don't know

whether it is or not. All we want you to do is whatever you do when you put people in the ground. Can you do that? There's money in it for you."

"I figured there was. You know I'm out of favor with the Church, though, don't you, Mr. Sullivan?"

"Yes."

"You want to know why?"

"No."

"Good." Delmore Ricketts looks out over the lake. "There's not a damn thing biting today."

"Well, will you do it?"

"Sure. I was just wondering why you wanted me to."

"I don't know." It was the truth. Why did he need this man to say some words and waft incense around over Artie's ashes? And yet he did. Artie did.

"Okay. When do you want me?"

"I'm not sure. My brother's in Birmingham now at the crematorium. Probably in the morning. You could go back with us now if you'd like. I can bring you back or you can follow us."

"I'll follow you. Tell you what. I need to go by the house and get cleaned up and get my priest stuff."

"Priest stuff?"

"Priest stuff." Delmore Ricketts looks at Hektor with narrowed eyes. "You sure you want me to do this? You know you could easily find a priest to hold a special service."

"I'm sure."

"Then wait for me at Bouchet's. I'll be there in a little while. Help me get this boat out, too."

An hour later they leave Bouchet's, the back of the truck loaded with daylilies they have bought from Mrs. Bouchet while they were waiting, three dollars a shovelful. They are followed by Father Audubon Ricketts in a 1957 Chevrolet, red fins flaring defiantly.

"He doesn't act a bit like a priest," May says, looking back. "You reckon he really is?"

Hektor sighs. "I don't think it really matters, honey."

EIGHTEEN

Northern Lights

IN BIRMINGHAM, IN THE MEN'S ROOM OF THE MORTUARY, DON-
nie runs hot water over his hands. He is still freezing.
The skinny kid who met them at the airport with the
hearse had the goddamn air conditioner as low as he
could get it.

"Stuck," he said when Donnie complained. But
Donnie knew he was lying, pissed because the casket
wasn't what he'd expected and he hadn't brought the
right kind of rig to get it off the plane.

"Thought this was a cremation," the kid had said,
eyeing the gray metal that took up the center aisle of
the plane. "This is a burial casket."

"What's the difference?" Donnie never should have
asked.

"Cremation casket's made out of wood usually and
the bottom drops out."

"What?"

Patty James stepped up and took Donnie's arm.
"Come on, Mr. Sullivan. Sit in the cockpit. Jimmy and
I'll take care of this.

"Asshole," she mouthed to the mortuary guy. He shrugged.

Donnie hadn't seen that, nor did he know how the casket was finally put into the hearse. He sat in the cockpit, studied the instrument panel, and tried not to think until Patty came, patted his shoulder, and told him everything was ready. Then there was the freezing ride across town.

"Bear Bryant's buried over there." The kid pointed to a large cemetery across the street as they turned into the mortuary driveway and circled around the back. "You ought to go over and check it out. Just follow the red line. Something to do while you're waiting."

"How long will I be waiting?"

"Depends."

"Two, two and a half hours," a middle-aged man in an office told Donnie. This man was dressed in a dark suit and was sitting behind an elegant desk on which were spread the papers Donnie had to sign. "I think you'll find our waiting room very comfortable, Mr. Sullivan. And if there's anything we can get for you or do for you . . . Or is there somewhere you'd like to go? We can call you a cab."

Donnie shook his head. "I guess I'll stay here."

The man pushed a brochure across the desk. "You'll want to look at this, Mr. Sullivan. We have most of these urns in stock, but we can order anything you select, of course. Takes just a few days. Free delivery, of course."

Donnie took the brochure simply because it was in the air between him and—he looked at the sign on the desk—Mr. Powell.

"And of course," Mr. Powell continued, "there'll be some refund on the casket. But we'll work that out with the gentleman at Bay Chapel. Okay?"

"Where's the men's room?" Donnie asked.

When he enters the waiting room, a young couple is sitting on a sofa holding hands. Donnie walks past them and outside where he sits on the steps in the sun. Across the busy street, the cemetery looks cool and peaceful with its large oaks and magnolias. No live oaks or Spanish moss like Myrtlewood. Was it his mother who had told him that Spanish moss didn't grow north of Montgomery?

The hearse comes from behind the building and enters the traffic. He knows where it's going, and he begins to cry. Damn it, Artie. We could at least have talked about this. He reaches into his pocket for a tissue and pulls out a wet paper towel which is such a ludicrous thing to find in his pocket that he smiles.

We should have talked more, Artie. Talked more about things that mattered. And things that happened. And Hektor, too, Artie. We all should have forgiven ourselves, forgiven each other.

Donnie wipes his face with the paper towel which he then wads up along with the brochure advertising urns. He's getting a cramp in his leg sitting on this short step. Hell. Mariel keeps telling him he ought to take calcium. "Just chew up a couple of Tums at bedtime, Donnie, or drink a glass of milk and you won't wake up with those leg cramps."

He walks up and down the sidewalk and then remembers what the hearse driver had said about Bear Bryant. Follow the yellow brick road? He goes to the corner where there is a streetlight which provides a chance for him to survive crossing six lanes of heavy traffic, and darts across into the open cemetery gates and blessed coolness. At some point his chill has vanished; now he's sweating.

He sees instantly what the driver had been talking

about. Yellow, red, and blue lines are painted on the roads that lead from the gate where an old black man holding a broom is sitting on the step of a round guardhouse.

"Hey," he says to Donnie. "You looking for the Bear?"

Donnie nods yes.

"Down the red line."

"Thanks." Donnie turns left onto the road with the red stripe. In the distance, he sees cars and a group gathered for a funeral. Some of these mourners will stop by to give the Bear their regards on their way out of the cemetery, but right now, Donnie has the grave to himself. It was easy to find. At the end of the red line were two large arrows pointing to the grave. Plus, it was the only one with red and white shakers stuck in the ground and a football balloon anchored by a plush red elephant sitting above the marker. The marker itself said simply PAUL WILLIAM BRYANT, SR., SEPT. 11, 1913. JAN. 26, 1983.

There should have been more. "Bear" should be on the marker and the number 323 for his football victories. Those sweet, sweet Saturday afternoons.

Donnie picks up what he thinks is a piece of trash and sees that it's a note that says "I love you, Bear." When he bends to replace it, he realizes he is crying again. His tears fall on the thick green grass.

An elderly couple coming down the red line see Donnie crying. They understand. The man tiptoes over and places a pack of Chesterfield Kings on the grave, and then they leave. Donnie wipes his eyes and follows them back down the red stripe.

Too late, he realizes. Too late. There was so much he should have told Artie. He should have told her that when he studied *Our Town* at the university, he had decided that if he could be like Emily and come back, that he would choose the summer of 1943 when they were fourteen and Hektor was ten. Mama had spent the spring in a hospital in Georgia and was staying a few weeks with Grandmama in Montgomery. Because there were so few students at the college, Papa was off for the summer. He went to see Mama and then came back to work on his book, a textbook on Greek mythology he had been working on as long as Donnie could remember. Some of the neighbors got together and planted a big Victory garden. But mostly, they had hung around, the three children pretty much on their own.

Papa was too old to go to the war, Donnie and his friends too young. At night they would sit in Papa's office and listen to the news while he moved red pins around on the map of the world on his wall. Stalingrad. Okinawa.

Donnie understood later that it was hormones kicking in, but it seemed that summer that his sense of smell was working overtime. The gardenias that bloomed in late May by the side of the house would wake him during the night, sweet and strong, a presence in the room. The sharpness of the tomatoes in the garden. The smell of the wood they cut for stakes. The creosoty, fishy odor of the pier. He was walking around in a world of smells he had never noticed before.

It was the summer Artie began to paint, too. She talked Mr. Harmon at the grocery into letting her have some of the white paper he wrapped meat in, and she would work for hours using leftover house paint and crayons and anything she could find. They should have talked. Maybe it had been her summer of colors like it was his of smells. She bought a Tangee lipstick, which she used every day until Mama got back.

One night during that summer, Papa had awakened them. "Come outside. Leave the lights out." They had first thought it was a jubilee, but it was too quiet. Half-asleep, they followed him out to the dune.

"Look," he said.

On the horizon were pale waves of light, pink and greenish white arcing into the sky and then falling, seemingly, into the bay.

"It's the northern lights," Papa explained. "The aurora borealis. Real unusual display."

"What's doing it?" Hektor asked.

"The sun. Solar winds. They're electrically charged and when they hit the earth's magnetic field they glow like this. You seldom see them this bright and this far south, though, because the particles are drawn toward the poles."

Hektor pressed against their father. "Is it safe?"

Thomas hugged his son. "Safe and beautiful, Hektor. The only thing it may mess up is the radio. We'll have more static."

Artie reached for Donnie's hand. "Look at that. It's the most beautiful thing I've ever seen."

Donnie had thought so, too. He went inside and got a quilt for them to lie on, the four of them. No one had said, "I wish Mama (or Sarah) were here." Not even Hektor or Papa.

Since then, Donnie has seen the northern lights several times over Mobile Bay, but never again with the intensity of that night. The intensity of that summer.

There were tomato sandwiches and iced tea every night for supper, and they would sit on the porch and eat. And it would stay light so long, and the bay looked like you could walk on it. But they never again believed the world ended at the bay after that summer.

And now, a lifetime later, the old black man waves Donnie through the gate with his broom. "Come back to see us."

Donnie turns to him. "My sister is being cremated. My twin."

"Oh, do Jesus, I'm mighty sorry."

"Yes." For a moment the two men look at each other and then Donnie goes through the gate, waits for the light, and walks back to the mortuary. There he washes his face again and sinks down into a sofa.

"Mr. Sullivan." A slight young man with acne is standing over him. "We're ready. We just need you to sign that you've received the remains."

Donnie sits up, wiping his mouth. He has drooled on the sofa; he's disoriented by the depth of his sleep.

"Would you like some water?" the young mortician asks. Donnie nods yes. The man disappears for a second and returns with a little paper cone of water. Donnie drinks it gratefully.

"You okay?"

"I was just sound asleep."

"I understand. I was sorry to disturb you, but I know you want to get home."

"Sure." Donnie gets up.

"This won't take but a second."

Donnie follows the young man to an office.

"Here you go," the mortician says, handing Donnie a plastic bag and pushing a piece of paper across the desk. "Sign right here."

Adonis J. Sullivan he writes on the next-of-kin line trying to keep the pen firm. The bag in his left hand is ridiculously light. He imagines it still feels warm, which in fact is not his imagination, but what does he know? This is what happens with a rush job when you have to use a freezer instead of the usual cooler.

"You're sure you don't want an urn?" The young man is doing his job.

"No."

"Well, that'll be it, then. Thank you, Mr. Sullivan, and please accept our sympathy."

"Yes. Thank you. Could you call me a cab, please?"

"Of course."

Donnie has never fainted in his life, but he thinks he may at any moment. Walking back through the waiting room he sees furnishings and people through a cloud. Outside, he sinks down gratefully on the sunlit steps again, puts his head between his knees, and closes his eyes. In a few minutes, feeling better, he opens them and is looking right into the plastic bag. In it is a small container, the kind you burp. It could be full of applesauce or a morning's shell collection. It's the most matter-of-fact object Donnie has ever seen. It's not Artie. When the cab comes, Donnie picks the bag up easily and heads home.

NINETEEN

A White Dinner Jacket

NAOMI CATES, MARIEL'S MOTHER, KNOWS THE DEVIL HAS BEEN buried up Logan Creek some forty-odd years. Tropical depressions and hurricanes have done their work; he's coming apart. A whole leg bone, no longer connected to a thighbone, washed into the bay during Hurricane Frederick. But so did a lot of other bones. What's one more?

His white dinner jacket, now the color of red clay, is amazingly intact. If one looks carefully, the label on the left-hand side under the breast pocket is legible: Loveman, Joseph, and Loeb, Birmingham, Alabama.

The creek is widening, becoming deeper. Another hurricane and the devil may be gone. Good riddance.

Naomi Cates knows this; Donnie and Hektor Sullivan know this; Artie Sullivan knew this. Artie, Donnie, and Hektor buried the devil up Logan Creek. They have never known Naomi knew.

TWENTY

Naomi Cates and the
Space-Time Continuum

I REMEMBER NIGHTS I COULDN'T SLEEP BECAUSE THE BABY HAD gotten so big. I hated it when I got that pregnant. You can pull one leg up and sort of lie on your side and sometimes it works for a while and you sleep. But mostly you just lie there, dozing, listening to the sounds of birds rustling in the trees right outside the window, calling out sometimes in their sleep. And inside, the children doing the same, turning, mumbling. You'd think that hard as they play, they'd sleep like the dead, but they didn't. Sometimes during the night, they'd begin to move, drifting like ghosts through the dark hot house. In the morning I might find Jacob asleep on the front porch and Mariel at the foot of our bed. Steve would be in Jacob's place and Elizabeth in Mariel's. "Fruit basket, turn over," I'd say each morning when I'd open my eyes and see none of my children where they started out the night before. They didn't remember moving, either. One morning we couldn't find Harry and I thought, Oh, my Lord, he's been kidnapped like the Lindbergh baby, which was a dumb thought since we didn't have a dime a kidnapper would want. He could have wandered into the woods, though, and we were really scared for a while, hollering "Harry!" all around the house, even out at the chicken coop. And finally here he came, crawling out from under the girls' bed, rubbing his eyes. Don't ask me how he got out of his crib and under there.

The only one I could depend on sleeping and not moving was Will. Soon as he thought the children were asleep, he said, "Naomi." And I'd follow him into the bedroom and pull off my clothes and he'd get on top of me. Sometimes, if he'd had too much to drink, he'd go to sleep without doing anything. And I'd just push him off and cover him up. But sometimes he'd pump up and down for a long time saying "Oh, God. Oh, God" over and over until I was scared he was going to wake up the children and I'd reach down and pull the quilt up over our heads to muffle the sounds. It made him sweat, I'll say that. Then he'd say, "Jesus!" and it was over. He'd roll over and next thing I hear is a snore. I'd get up and put on my nightgown and tiptoe among the sleeping children out to the back porch where we keep a washpan.

It's funny, but it was one of my favorite times. After I bathed, I'd sit on the back steps and let the night air dry me. Summer nights I could hear the music from the Grand Hotel down the bay. I always told myself one night I'd walk down there and just watch the people dancing out in the pavilion on Julep Point. It's not far, but I never have. Which doesn't mean I won't some night.

But one night, just before Toy was born, even after I'd gone inside and gotten into bed beside Will, I could still hear the music. A full moon had come up and the tree frogs were humming. But suddenly they would all stop like they do, and there would be the music. Will snoring, children stirring, tree frogs, birds rustling, the baby inside me moving. And a mile away people dancing under a full moon.

I lay there a long time; maybe I slept. Maybe the moon in my face was too bright. Whatever. All I know is that suddenly everything was still. Too still. I looked at the Big Ben on the nightstand. Twelve o'clock. We were caught between yesterday and today.

And then I felt the baby kick, and Will sighed and turned in his sleep. The Big Ben gave a loud click. But I had the strangest feeling that I was still caught. There are times between, I thought. And if I had to explain what I meant to anybody, they would have thought I was crazy. But I knew I was right. There are spaces between breaths, when one year becomes another or one second another. Between the clock's tick and the second's hand. There are all these spaces, these times. Like when a person dies. There has to be time between being there and not being there.

Well, it knocked me out of sleeping the rest of the night. All I did was lie there and think about spaces between things and what did it mean. At first light when I picked my way among my sleeping children and went out to the yard, I felt like I had learned something. I wasn't sure what. All I knew was that while I waited for the sun to show first orange, I wriggled my toes in the sand and thought. Spaces. Spaces.

And now Artie is gone, caught in the space between one breath and the other while I kept breathing, old woman breathing that hardly moved the sheets. I heard the shout of "Jubilee" and thought the touch on my cheek was a memory.

Lord knows, there are enough memories. Live this long and they run out of your ears, disappear. And the ones still in your head you can't trust.

But I trust the memory of the beach that morning, me going to work late because I'd been up all night with sick children, seeing what Artie, Donnie, and Hektor saw lying in that tidal pool, and watching what they did. And I didn't say a word. Never will.

Why should I?

I loved Thomas Sullivan. Simple as that. Many's the day I'd time my walk home from the Grand Hotel and dawdle at the shell road until I saw his car coming. Then I'd hike my heels like I was in a hurry and he'd stop.

"Come on, Naomi. I'll give you a ride home."

And I'd slide in that car that smelled of Prince Albert tobacco and something lemony and be happy.

It broke my heart to see the way Sarah treated him. And the way she treated those children and not a one of them being able to forgive themselves all these years.

If Thomas had said, "Naomi, I'm going to keep driving," I'd have said, "Fine," and gone with him. Gone hightailing right on down the road with that good, sweet man and the smell of Prince Albert and lemons. But he didn't.

The strange thing, though, is how it's not Thomas in my dreams but Will. He comes in the door with rabbits he's shot or fish he's caught and he smiles at me over the heads of our children. Him with all that dark curly hair.

Well, it's all dreams anyway. And dreams don't make a grain of sense. And sometimes I don't know if I'm beginning or ending. Or if any of us are. And that's all right.

Artie, it's time for *One Life to Live.*

Go with God.

TWENTY-ONE

Barbie Dolls

WHEN DOLLY AWAKENS FROM HER NAP, HER HEADACHE HAS
come back in full force, and her whole body is stiff.
She rolls over and pulls the drapery back. The light on
the water is like a blow. God, she thinks, I'm really
sick. She groans and sits up. Her stomach heaves; she
makes it to the bathroom just in time.

"Dolly?" Her mother's voice. "You okay in there?"

Okay? Another spasm of retching grabs her. Her
mother opens the door and comes in. She holds Dolly's
head like she did when Dolly was a child. "It's all
right," she says. "It's all right." She wets a washrag and
holds it against Dolly's forehead, against her throat.
The nausea begins to subside. Mariel leads Dolly back
to the bed and folds the cloth against her forehead.

"Wait here," she says. "I'm going to take your
temperature."

Dolly sinks back against the pillow. She is content
to let her mother take over. She opens her mouth obediently when Mariel returns with the thermometer. She
holds her mother's hand. It's cool and familiar.

"Almost a hundred and one," Mariel says. "I'm going to call Dave Horton."

Dolly doesn't argue. She feels limp, drained. She hears her mother in the hall dialing, talking. Talking to Dave Horton's office. Dave Horton who is a doctor now, who had helped Dolly cut up a pig in biology when they were in high school. She dozes, incorporating the hum of the air conditioner and the sound of her mother's voice into a high school lab.

"It's simple," Dave says. "The aorta is right here. See?"

"They said to come in. They'll work you in as soon as they can," Mariel says. "Those shorts you have on are fine. Here, let me brush your hair."

"I'll do it," Dolly says. "I need to brush my teeth, too."

Under the fluorescent light in the bathroom, she looks terrible. She sees what she'll look like as an old, old woman. The reflection waves, blurs. She closes her eyes and holds on to the sink. When the room quits revolving, she combs her hair and brushes her teeth. At this rate, they can put me in the casket, she thinks, and Father Carroll won't be working for nothing.

Her mother is sitting on the bed when she comes out. She looks worried. "Anything hurt you besides your head?" Mariel asks. "Your neck isn't stiff or anything?"

"No, Mama. Just my head."

"Well, maybe we won't have to wait too long. Dave's been here less than a year, but his practice is already growing by leaps and bounds. He took over Dr. Garret's practice, you know. Looked after Artie the last few months after the specialists had done all they could do." Mariel pushes some sandals toward Dolly who is wandering around the bed. "What are you doing?"

"Looking for my purse."

"In the chair. You don't need it, though."

"Insurance card." Dolly is amazed at how willing she is to surrender totally to her mother's care. She gets her billfold from her bag, slides her feet into her sandals, and they go down the stairs.

"I'm taking Dolly to the doctor," Mariel calls into the kitchen.

Reese sticks his head around the door. "You sick, Dolly?"

Dolly tries to smile. "If I'm lucky, Dave Horton won't recognize me."

"Puke on him if he don't."

"If Donnie calls, Reese, will you tell him to come on out here? We need to be at the funeral home by at least six."

"I'll tell him. Wait a second." He steps into the hall bathroom and hands Dolly a towel. "You might need this."

"Thanks." Dolly holds his gnarled hand against her cheek for a moment.

Reese watches the car pull away. How many times he had driven Artie down that same road to the doctor. He starts to go back into the house but changes his mind and goes to sit on the dune instead. He waves at a barge; a man standing on the deck waves back.

The Harlow Medical Arts Building is a small brick building that houses Harlow's one dentist and one doctor. At one time Dr. Garret had delivered babies here and done minor surgery in a small operating room. Three rooms had been available for overnight stays. Insurance costs had put an end to that, though, and those rooms are now examining rooms or are used for storage.

The waiting room, Dolly realizes, has not changed

since she was a child and Artie had to bring her here frequently. She rubs the small scar over her eye, the result of tying a rope to a hammer and trying to throw it over the limb of a pecan tree. By the time she got to Artie, she had had a handful of blood, and Artie had almost fainted. "Don't ask me how or why, but she hit herself in the head with a hammer," Artie had told Dr. Garret, handing Dolly over to him. And he took her in and stitched her up and gave her a sucker. And the time she stuck a needle in her knee, the infected cut from a catfish fin, the minor fevers, bumps, scrapes. The patience Artie had had with her.

There are only two other people in the waiting room, an old man and woman who seem to be together. Dolly sinks into a chair still holding her towel while Mariel takes her insurance card and goes to sign her in.

I want to have children, Dolly realizes. Bring them in here for their shots, have their height measured on the Mickey Mouse wall chart, hold them against me. She looks at her mother filling out the form. Mariel has put on her glasses and is holding the insurance card away from her, trying to make out the numbers.

"Just a few minutes," Mariel says, coming to sit by Dolly. Dolly reaches over and takes her hand.

Mariel wants to say, "I love you, Dolly." She wants to say, "I'm sorry for everything," but she doesn't know exactly what she's sorry for. Mariel wants to apologize to her grown child for something, a whole sea of vague failures. Instead she holds Dolly's hand, feeling how hot it is, and worries. She feels a pulse beating. She doesn't know if it's hers or Dolly's.

"Dolly?" A woman in a nurse's uniform is standing over them. "Billie Joiner. We used to live down from your Aunt Artie."

"Barbie dolls," Dolly says. "You had dozens of them."

Billie grins. "I still have them. Saving them for my daughter. So far I have two boys. My husband says I get one more chance. Say you're feeling puny?"

"To say the least."

"Well, come on lie down. It'll be a few minutes before Dr. Horton can see you, but at least you'll be more comfortable." She leads Dolly into one of the examining rooms, takes her blood pressure and temperature.

"I was so sorry to hear about your Aunt Artie," she says. "We got very fond of her in here. She really fought, you know."

"Thank you."

"One of her paintings is in the waiting room. I don't know if you noticed it or not. She gave it to Dr. Horton just a couple of months ago. She kept on with her painting regardless of how bad she felt. We're gonna miss her." Billie looks at the thermometer. "You're running a hotbox, aren't you?"

"I feel crummy."

"Well, Dr. Horton will be in in just a few minutes. Just lie back. I'll turn off the top light for you."

"Thanks." Dolly turns on her side. She is still clutching the towel Reese gave her. It smells like almond sachet. She dozes lightly.

"Dolly?" Dave Horton says. "You don't have to sit up yet, but I'm going to turn on the light."

"Okay."

Dave rolls a stool over to the examining table and sits down. "Anything hurting besides your head? Billie says you're nauseated."

"All generic symptoms," Dolly says. "I felt real

tired last night and again this morning and my head hurt, but I thought it was from crying."

"Grief doesn't cause fever. Why don't you sit up now and let's see what's going on."

Dolly would have recognized Dave Horton anywhere. A few lines around his eyes are the only traces of the eleven years that have passed. His hair is black and curly, his skin tanned. And she looks such a mess. She groans and puts her face into her hands. Her pale hair hangs forward limply.

Dave feels the glands in her neck, listens to her heart, has her cough. He has Billie come in and take some blood. And all the while he is talking about Artie, about Harlow, about high school in Mobile. Dolly says very little. She's impressed with Dave's authority and sense of competence.

"You helped me cut up my pig in biology," she finally says.

Dave laughs. "You think I should have been a surgeon?"

"No. It's just that I've never been to a doctor before who wasn't older than me. It's strange."

"I'm older than you. Two years. I was a lab assistant my senior year."

"Doctors should be old, though. You know what I mean."

"Fortunately everyone doesn't feel like that."

Dolly is afraid she has hurt his feelings.

"Before you know it, we'll be the age of the presidents. How does that strike you?" He's washing his hands, drying them on a paper towel.

"As scary. I wouldn't want anyone I know to be president. Just like I don't want to see the pilot of the plane I'm on. I like to think there are some people who aren't ordinary human beings."

Dave laughs again, a deep chuckle. Dolly likes the sound of it. "Remember Sonny Thurman? He's a commercial pilot now, so I always look to see who's flying the plane I'm on. I draw the line with Sonny. He used to get lost coming to school."

"Sounds like my Uncle Hektor," Dolly says. "He drove right by Mobile on the interstate one time." Laughing hurts her head. She presses her fingers into her forehead.

"I think what you have here is a rip-roaring sinus infection," Dave says. "We'll know more in a minute when Billie gets your white count, but I think it was probably already coming on and the plane trip and the crying aggravated it. You just rest here, and if that's what it is, Billie will give you a couple of shots. One's an antibiotic and the other's an antihistamine. You're not allergic to anything, are you?"

"No."

"Good."

"Dave, Artie's visitation is tonight."

"You still nauseated?"

"That's passed off."

"Well, I'm going to give you something to take the fever down. You go home and take it easy and then play it by ear. You might feel like going for a little while." Dave pats her shoulder. "It's good seeing you, Dolly. We all thought the world of Artie, you know."

"Thanks. It's good seeing you, too." As he turns to leave, she asks, "Dave, why Harlow?"

He grins. "Because they keep their Christmas lights up all year."

Mariel is looking at a *People* magazine when Dolly comes into the waiting room. "Elizabeth Taylor is getting fat again," she says, putting the magazine on the table. "Well?"

"Sinus. I got two shots."

"Well, we'll take you right home and put you to bed." Mariel takes off her glasses and collects her purse. "How did you like Dave Horton? He's a handsome man, isn't he?"

"He's very nice. Too bad he's getting married next month." Dolly doesn't know why she does her mother this way. All the way home, she pretends she is dozing.

Mariel knows Dolly's not asleep. She also knows Dave Horton isn't getting married next month. But Dolly's half Sullivan and, Lord knows, Mariel has never been able to figure the Sullivans out.

"Do you think Artie's still grieving for Carl?" she asked Donnie once. And he had said, "I doubt it." But Mariel wasn't sure. After all, Artie had never remarried. She had never seemed to be seriously interested in any other man, though a lot of them had wandered through her life. Only once had Mariel been suspicious that Artie might be in love and nothing had come of that.

"Maybe she's subconsciously looking for a father," Mariel told Donnie after a series of visits to Harlow by several older men from exotic places such as Mexico City and New York. Men who were obviously smitten by Artie and obviously made to feel welcome.

"She knows where our father is if she wants to find him," Donnie replied. "Right up there in Myrtlewood."

"But she could still feel an empty psychological space, Donnie. Artie doesn't think the drowning was an accident and you know it."

"Shit, Mariel. If Artie told you that, she's putting you on. She knows good and damn well what happened."

"I'm just saying what Artie might feel."

Donnie had put down the ham sandwich he was eating and looked across the kitchen table. He had the two deep lines between his eyebrows that Mariel hated to see appear.

"Mariel, Papa explained manic depression to us as children. Of course, we knew about her bad spells without anyone telling us. We lived with the kindest, most loving woman in the world or with someone we didn't even recognize as our mother. But she was definitely not a murderer. If anybody was going to do anybody in, it would have been our father going after our mother. Which, of course, didn't happen, though, God knows, he had enough cause. It was nothing more murderous than a thunderstorm that turned the boat over."

And Mariel had slipped this conversation into her DONNIE file which went back many years to the Christmas party where she had recognized Donnie immediately and he hadn't any idea who she was.

She had once read that in every couple's relationship, one was the lover and one the receiver. She's always known which she is. Her father, Will Cates, in spite of his alcoholism, had been the lover. Maybe he loved everything too much. Thomas Sullivan was a lover. Carl Jenkins was a lover. Artie would definitely have been a receiver. And what about Dolly? Mariel glances over at her daughter and realizes she doesn't know. She hopes a receiver. Mariel turns onto the shell road.

Dolly doesn't stir. How much she looks like Donnie, Mariel thinks. She wonders how he is doing in Birmingham. She wishes he had wanted her to go with him.

Artie's studio is a large room above the garage. There are windows on three sides as well as a skylight. Finished and unfinished canvases are propped against the fourth wall. On an easel is the painting Artie was working on, a woman on the beach with her hair blowing. Her back is to the water and she is reaching out her toe to touch a large fish skeleton that has almost a cartoonish grin on its face. The sky above the woman is blue; near the horizon is an ominous cloud with a waterspout twisting from it.

Mariel looks at it carefully. She tries hard to see the way Artie painted the light that is considered so unusual. It looks like all the rest of Artie's paintings, though, rather ethereal, pretty. She knows this is a damning word, but damn it, it's pretty, the symbolic dark cloud notwithstanding. She looks around at the other works. They all look similar. What made them worth thousands of dollars?

The smell of turpentine is strong in the room. Brushes are neatly arranged on a worktable. Tubes and cans of paint line shelves under the windows. Mariel picks up one of the brushes and idly brushes it against the tabletop. "Artie," she says, "you're really dead."

Artie laughs and comes from behind the stacked pictures. "Yep. Guess I am. How clever you are, Mariel."

"Don't get smart-ass with me, Artie. I always let you get away with too much of that." Mariel walks around the studio, touching the pictures. Artie perches on a stool.

"Have you seen your mama?" Mariel can't resist the dig.

"Your child's grandmother? Watch it, Mariel."

"You're not going to make me mad anymore. You can't. You're in Birmingham being cremated."

"And Donnie's with me. That makes you mad, doesn't it?"

"Well, the whole thing's damn inconvenient. I

should have expected it, though. You always did like to dramatize things."

Mariel picks up a picture of a man and woman pushing a sailboat into the water. "These things are worth a lot of money, aren't they?"

"With a little wise investing, Dolly will never have to work a day in her life."

"Dolly will work. She's not lazy."

"I know. She's like me."

"You go to hell!"

"Sure you want that?"

"No," Mariel admits. She looks at the picture on the easel, an unfinished one that Artie had been working on before she got too weak to paint. She must have felt terrible while she was doing this, but it is as light, as ethereal as the others propped against the walls. It's the usual beach scene, but there is a single figure on this one, a woman walking toward a setting sun.

Mariel shivers. The woman on the canvas seems so small, lost in a world of sky and water. And she is alone.

Mariel suddenly feels very sad. She sees Artie in her Harlow High cheerleading outfit, the head cheerleader, jumping higher than anyone else, flirting, laughing, throwing kisses from a red convertible, the Homecoming Queen, so cute, so pretty.

"Everybody thought you were wonderful, Artie."

"No, Mariel. No, they didn't."

"I did," Mariel confesses. She touches two fingers to the lone figure in the painting.

Reese, coming up the steps to tell Mariel Donnie has called, could have sworn he heard Artie's voice. Downright ghosty. He opens the door and looks in cautiously, is relieved to see only Mariel standing before the easel.

"Donnie called. He said to tell you he's home and he'll be out after while."

"Thanks." Mariel looks around the studio. "She's gone, Reese."

"I know." He doesn't tell Mariel that he had seen Artie just this morning sitting under the pecan tree.

"And I'm so tired." Mariel rubs her neck. "I'm going to go call Father Carroll and the funeral home."

"What for?"

"She didn't want a funeral, Reese. Donnie's done what she wanted."

"Bless her heart."

"Yes." Mariel turns out the lights and follows Reese down the steps.

When he finally answers the phone, Father Carroll is either drunk or asleep. Probably both, Mariel thinks.

"What?" he asks. "What?"

"No funeral, Father. It's Artie's request. We were going to go on and do it anyway, but I decided it just wasn't worth the trouble."

"What?"

"It's not what Artie wanted, Father."

"The funeral?"

"Right."

"You're not having a funeral for Artie?"

Mariel speaks slowly. "There is not going to be a funeral, Father. Artie didn't want one."

"But why?"

"I have no idea. But I hope you'll accept our apologies for the trouble we've put you to.

"But the rosary is tonight and the funeral in the morning."

"It *was*, Father. No more."

"I don't understand."

"Neither do I, but I've decided to quit fighting it. If Artie didn't want a funeral, so be it. If Donnie doesn't want one, so be it."

"You don't even want a prayer at the graveside?"

"No, Father. But thank you."

"Mariel, are you all right?"

Mariel can imagine the puzzled, worried expression on Father Carroll's lined face. She feels a twinge of tenderness for the old priest.

"I'm fine, Father. And like I said, we thank you for everything."

"I'm coming out there."

"Please don't, Father."

"I'll be there as soon as I can." The phone goes dead. Mariel stands in the hall and stares at the bay for a few minutes. Then she goes to check on Dolly who is asleep with her mouth open so wide that Mariel can see the silver of fillings. The Sullivan teeth.

TWENTY-TWO

Christmas Lights

DELMORE RICKETTS IS SITTING BETWEEN HEKTOR AND MAY IN Hektor's truck. His red '57 Chevy had made it almost to I-10 before it became enveloped in a cloud of smoke that looked terminal. Hektor had jumped from his pickup with a fire extinguisher thinking Father Audubon was about to be as cremated as Artie. The priest, however, had crawled out, coughing, cursing. "Points. Goddamn points."

Given the amount of smoke, Hektor was highly suspicious of the diagnosis, but he didn't want to say anything, just stood there with the extinguisher on ready. Father Audubon opened the hood to a cloud of steam. "She's about shot," he admitted.

Hektor thought the "about" was putting it mildly. "Junkyard shot" was more like it.

"I keep her for sentimental reasons. She was my first car." Father Audubon shook his head sadly. "First time I got laid was in this car. In the trunk."

"The trunk?"

"It's huge."

"But the trunk? You couldn't have been very comfortable."

"Mr. Sullivan, I ask you, do you remember thinking of comfort?"

"No."

"Right." Father Audubon put the hood back down. "First time," he sighed, "last time."

"Well, maybe we can get it fixed. There's a gas station at the Pascagoula exit that has wreckers. We'll send them to get it."

Delmore Ricketts brightened. "Do you really think she can be fixed?"

"Most probably. This is a classic, you know. They may have to order some parts, but I'll bet they can get them. Cars like this are worth saving."

"Yes, indeed." Father Delmore Ricketts Audubon fanned smoke away with his fishing hat. "I hate to leave her here, though."

"I'm sure nobody will bother her. Probably everybody out here knows it's your car anyway."

"Of course they do. I hadn't thought of that."

At the service station, Hektor explained to the kid leaning against the wrecker where the car was and that they couldn't miss it, that it was a red '57 Chevy, tow it in, and do whatever needed to be done to fix it. He also slipped a fifty into the kid's hand which elicited a promise of immediate action.

"Be gentle with her," Father Audubon said.

"You got it."

Hektor said they would check on it the next day. The grinning boy was already getting into the wrecker as they walked to the pickup.

"Seems like a nice young man," Father Audubon said.

"Eager," Hektor agreed. When they got to the truck, he explained about the two seat belts and that Father

Audubon would have to ride in the middle. "We'll grab you if we have a wreck," he assured the priest.

Fortunately the problem doesn't come up. May goes to sleep before they reach Pascagoula, leaning awkwardly against Father Audubon's shoulder.

"Bless her heart," he says, moving his arm so her head will be cushioned more. And then to Hektor, "Tell me about your sister."

"She was my older sister. She and my brother Donnie were twins. She's had lymphoma for almost two years. Her name is Artie. Artemis, really. She's an artist. Pretty well-known."

"Artemis Sullivan? She painted those beautiful beach scenes?"

"Yes. You know who she is? How about that."

"I can't believe it. I actually met her once in San Francisco. A showing at a gallery. I really believe she was the most beautiful woman I've ever seen. And that accent! My God! She called me Fahthah Ricketts. Said she was the ahhtist. You wouldn't believe what a hit she was. I hadn't heard that many Deep South accents at the time, you understand, but, even so, when she walked into the room, something happened. Something exotic and yet wholesome and sweet. You know?"

"I suppose so." Hektor does not know. He sees Artie with scraped knees and a runny nose. He sees Artie and his mother fussing, Artie dry-eyed at Carl's memorial service.

Most of all, he sees Artie on the beach looking first at Donnie and then at him declaring, "Each of us has to do it. We have to do this together."

"Actually, she was a very complicated woman, Father."

"Aren't they all. And just call me Del."

"Sure, if you'll drop the Mr. Sullivan. It's Hektor."

"Your parents had it in for you, too, didn't they?"

"Well, it beats Adonis. That's my brother's name."

"Adonis, Artemis, Hektor. Somebody was into Greek myths."

"My father." Hektor passes a truck loaded with watermelons. "Are you from San Francisco?"

"Just north of there, on the coast. There's a huge bird sanctuary up there where I grew up. They used to pay me to count the birds when I was a kid. Now I automatically look around and count them. I guess Audubon isn't a bad nickname, though. You wouldn't believe some of the birds I've seen down here and recorded."

"How did you get here, anyway?"

"The civil rights marches. The issues looked cut and dried in San Francisco. Trouble was when I got here, I could see everybody's side. Theoretically, I guess that's what priests should do. Practically, it doesn't work that way. And in the meantime, I'd discovered the swamps and bayous. Anyway, I stayed. Everybody seems to have forgiven me. Except the Church. We sort of lost contact."

"Don't you think some of the issues were cut and dried?"

"Of course. It was just that the issues kept getting mixed up with the people. I tended to lose track. Can you understand that?"

Hektor is not sure he can.

"We all have a lot to regret," he says. They have crossed Jubilee Parkway and are entering Harlow's main business street.

"Christmas lights!" Father Audubon exclaims. "They leave them up all year in my hometown, too. The day after Thanksgiving, they have a parade and turn the lights on. Do they do that here?"

"Sure do."

"Santa Claus came in on a sleigh last year with real reindeer," says May, who has awakened. "Something scared them and they ran away and Santa Claus jumped out of the sleigh."

"Sounds like a smart man to me."

"We spend every Christmas here. One year Mary dropped the baby Jesus at the pageant. It was just a doll, good thing, but Joseph and the Wise Men got to laughing so hard that Mary picked up the doll and started hitting them with it. That was about the most fun one we've had." May giggles, remembering. "She knocked one of them down. Aunt Artie said it was like Paul on the road to Damascus. She had to tell me what it meant, and the Wise Man wasn't really blinded, but he was felled."

"Felled?" Hektor laughs.

"Like Paul. You know, Papa."

"That sounds like a wonderful Christmas pageant," Father Audubon says.

"They're all good. Last year one of the shepherds fainted and knocked over the stable."

"You must go through a lot of pageant directors."

"No. Mrs. Aleta Forehand has been doing them as long as I can remember," Hektor says. "I was a Wise Man for several years. The only thing I remember happening unusual was one of the angels throwing up."

"Mrs. Forehand says she's earned her place in heaven," May says.

Delmore Ricketts takes off his fishing hat and runs his hand through his thinning red hair. "And to think I could have stayed in a church."

"It's a fun place." May points to a white wooden church with a red door. "That's it there."

"It's the biggest one in town. The Greek one is next.

It's pretty, too." May turns in her seat to wave at a woman on a bicycle. "Kelly Stuart," she says. "She lives next door to Aunt Artie. I think Papa ought to marry her."

"She's too young for me, sweetheart."

"Well, Aunt Artie says you missed your chance anyway."

They come to a stop sign; Hektor turns right toward the beach.

"But we are up high," Father Audubon exclaims as he sees the water. "This is like the white cliffs of Dover. I thought everything around here was flat."

"No. We have to climb down to the beach. Most people have steps. Our house does."

"Are they just high dunes or what?"

"Mostly high dunes," Hektor explains. "There's a lot of limestone, though, so it's not just sand and clay. It gives you one heck of a view. We had a jubilee here night before last. Have you heard about them?"

"When all the fish and crabs come up on the beach for apparently no reason?"

"I'm sure there's a reason. We just don't know what it is. But it's not like a red tide that kills the fish and makes them inedible. These suckers come dancing up healthy as can be to shake hands. And right along here is the only place in the world that it happens. Everybody grabs nets and buckets and loads up their freezers. Before freezers, you had to cook everything right away and everybody would party. Jubilees are like hitting the jackpot at Las Vegas. All for free."

"I'd like to see one."

"Well, I'm afraid you're just going to get the aftermath. It takes a few days for the beach to get cleaned even though we rake it and bury all the stuff that's washed up. It's worth it, though. What do we do, May, when somebody yells 'Jubilee'?"

"Have a fit. Go running to the beach. Aunt Artie said it's good as Christmas," she explains to Father Audubon.

They pull into Artie's driveway and park beside Mariel's car.

"What a pretty house," Father Audubon says. Mariel is sitting on the back steps, her face in her hands. She looks up as the truck pulls in.

"That's my sister-in-law," Hektor says. "I'm just going to introduce you as a friend until I get a chance to explain."

"Explain what?" May asks.

"That he's Father Audubon. We'll just say he's our friend Delmore Ricketts for the time being. Okay, honey?"

"Sure. It's the truth, isn't it?"

"Absolutely," Delmore Ricketts says. "That's all anyone ever need know, Hektor."

"Well, we'll see. I'm pretty sure I want the family to know. I think it would make everybody feel better. But we don't want to mess up Mariel's plans."

"Absolutely not." Audubon has no idea what plans Hektor is talking about.

"Hey, Aunt Mariel," May calls, getting out of the pickup. "We got held up by an alligator on the road. We brought you some daylilies, though."

"Fine. I was getting worried about you." The explanation has totally missed Mariel who is wondering who Delmore Ricketts is. Probably some hitchhiker Hektor has picked up.

The two men walk to the back steps. "Mariel," Hektor says, "this is Delmore Ricketts, a friend of mine from Pascagoula. He was a friend of Artie's, too."

Mariel stands up. "Mr. Ricketts." She holds out her hand.

Delmore Rickett's hand is surprisingly warm and strong. "I was so sorry, Mrs. Sullivan, to hear of your loss."

"Thank you. Won't you come in? Would you like some tea or Coke? Beer?"

"A beer would be great," Hektor says. "Come on, Del. I'll get us one."

Mariel sits back down on the steps. "Who's that man, May?" she asks as the men disappear into the kitchen.

"Delmore Ricketts."

"But who is he?"

"I don't think I'm supposed to tell. I can give you a clue, though. He likes birds."

"What do you mean, 'He likes birds'?"

"He just does. He grew up in California where there were a lot of them."

Mariel decides she's too tired to pursue this. She closes her eyes and leans against the bannister.

"You should have seen that alligator," May says. "He was so big, he was across both lanes of the road and they called him Big Ben. We had to wait forever."

Mariel opens her eyes. "Where? Which road?"

"In Mississippi. Not far from Bouchet's store."

"You've been to Mississippi?"

"Yes ma'am. That's where we got the daylilies. Papa said we could plant some here and you could have some and we could plant some at home."

"Sounds like you got a lot of daylilies." Mariel smiles fondly at the child. May's going to be beautiful, she thinks, with those dark eyes and black hair. Hektor is going to have his hands full and soon.

"We did. They were three dollars a clump."

"Well, I'll certainly plant mine soon as I can so they'll bloom next spring. Thank you."

"You're welcome."

"You want a Coke?"

"No'm. I'm full to the gills with Dr Pepper and boiled peanuts."

Mariel holds the child against her. "That's a good feeling, isn't it? Being full to the gills with peanuts and Dr Pepper."

"Yes ma'am," May agrees.

The car Mariel has been waiting for turns into the driveway.

"There's Father Carroll," May says.

Mariel stands up. "Do me a favor, May. Run see if you can find the cat. I haven't seen him since I've been here and I need to talk to Father Carroll about Aunt Artie's funeral. Okay?"

"Sure." May waves to the priest on her way around the house.

Father Carroll has been the priest at Harlow for as long as Mariel can remember. He had confirmed her, confessed her, married her and Donnie. For a while, when she was a child, she had been confused, thinking him God. He would loom before her in his robes with his incense and bells and body of Christ with its papery taste, and she was sure he knew every bad thing she did. For a while, she had even had him confused with Santa Claus. It's hard to reconcile that majestic presence with the frail old man who walks across the yard toward her now.

She rises and goes to meet him. He holds out his arms and she goes into them, feeling his thinness. Oh, God, she thinks, dissolving into tears, I knew I'd do this.

Father Carroll pats her on the back. "It's okay. We all loved her. It's okay."

"No, it's not," Mariel sobs.

"Well, let's go talk about your decision. And I think a good shot of whiskey wouldn't do you any harm." Father Carroll hands her a handkerchief. She wipes the lapel of his coat and then holds the handkerchief against her face. "Is Mrs. Randolph still here?" he asks.

Mariel nods.

"Well, I'm going to get you something to drink. Don't you want to come inside where it's cooler?"

"I think we'd better talk out here. Hektor's got company, and Dolly's sick. Maybe we could sit in your car."

"Sure." He climbs the three steps slowly, painfully. "Where's Donnie?"

"Mobile. He'll be out after while."

"Well, you just sit down a minute. I'll be right back."

Mariel watches him disappear into the darkness of the back hall. She realizes that this is the way he will disappear from her life one day soon. And the way her mother will disappear. And Donnie. Just step into a shadow and be gone. Just like that.

She cries harder into the already wet handkerchief. "Artie," she says, "I wish you had wanted to be buried in your casket in your yellow dress. We wouldn't have let anybody see you, and you would have been at Myrtlewood."

"I wanted purification by fire."

"Whatever. Dead's dead, Artie." Mariel wipes her eyes. "And did you see that sweet old man? I guess we're going to have you a funeral."

Father Carroll comes out with two glasses. "Let's go see if the car is still cool," he says. "I need you to explain about the funeral."

Mariel holds the handkerchief against the already sweating glass. "There's nothing to explain, Father. I shouldn't have called you. It's just that Artie requested no funeral, and for a while, we considered going along with it. But we've decided we can't." God, how can she be doing this!

"I'm glad, Mariel. Artie probably wasn't thinking clearly when she made that request. She was so sick for so long. You and Donnie are doing the wise thing."

"Yes," Mariel says. Donnie? The wise thing? She takes a large swig from the drink. It's pure bourbon; she chokes. Snot, tears, and spit all hit Father Carroll's handkerchief.

He pats her on the back and opens the car door for her. "There's something psychologically necessary about a funeral," he says. He goes around to the other side, gets in, and continues. "It's like putting a period at the end of a sentence."

"You think of life as a sentence?" Mariel takes a cautious sip of the drink.

"In some ways, yes."

"Like a prison sentence?"

"For some people I think it is. Of their own making, of course. What I meant, though, was the clean page, the writing we put upon it."

Mariel looks across the yard toward the bay. "How well did you know my in-laws?" she asks.

"Very well. Their dying was one of the greatest tragedies I've had to deal with. They were more than parishioners; they were personal friends. I was especially close to Thomas. What a chess player he was." Father Carroll chuckles. "Poker, too. Fortunately he put his winnings back in the pot."

Mariel sighs. "I remember how beautiful Sarah Sullivan always looked in church. The hats she'd wear.

She could even kneel better than anyone else. You know what I mean? Delicately. Thank God, Dolly's got some of her gracefulness."

"Sarah wasn't perfect."

"I know that now. But at the time . . ." Mariel takes another drink. "I helped out here sometimes when they had parties. People from the university and even the governor once." Mariel smiles. "He took off his shoes, the governor did. Lost them under the table. Sarah Sullivan just laughed and said, 'Everybody feel around for the governor's shoes.' She was a perfectionist in some ways, though. If there was a spot on the crystal or the dessert fork wasn't headed in the right direction, we caught it. I didn't even know there was such a thing as a dessert fork."

"They aren't important," Father Carroll says.

"Mrs. Sullivan thought so."

"Maybe. I'm not sure."

"Artie didn't, though." Mariel starts to cry again. "I don't know what she thought was important."

"Love. Family. Her painting." Father Carroll sees Artie at her first communion. The wafer from his hand. At her wedding. Shining.

"She was one of the cleverest people I've ever known. Witty, irreverent, of course. I've been trying to pin down what to say about her tomorrow." He pauses. "We *are* having a funeral tomorrow?" Mariel nods yes. "And I almost want to say she was like mercury. You know when you break a thermometer and try to hold it, how fast it is, how it'll break apart and come back together, and you can never quite grasp it. I'm not sure everyone would understand, though, since they don't put mercury in thermometers anymore."

Mariel turns up her drink and finishes it. "You think Artie was like mercury."

You know what I mean. I remember Thomas Sullivan telling me one time that he thought Artie was a lot like her mother. At the time I couldn't see it, but I've come to think he was right. They both were like quicksilver, beautiful, strong, and fluid." He turns to look at Mariel. "Don't you think the metaphor would work tomorrow?"

"Isn't mercury poisonous?"

"In certain compounds. I'm sure nobody would think about that aspect, though."

Mariel runs her finger around the top of her glass and makes the crystal hum. Whmmm, whmmm, the noise gets louder. "Think about this for a minute, Father. If it were me you were burying tomorrow, what metaphor would you use?"

Father Carroll smiles. "I wouldn't need any metaphors for you, Mariel. I'd simply say you were a lovely woman, mother, and wife."

"That's what I thought. We'll see you at seven, Father." Mariel opens the door and gets out.

The old priest is puzzled. "Did I say anything wrong?"

"Of course not. That's exactly what I am, Mrs. Adonis J. Sullivan, the mother of Dorothy Artemis Sullivan. And I'm fifty-seven years old, Father."

"What's wrong with that?"

"Something."

"Well, we all get old, Mariel, if we're lucky."

"Thanks, Father. We'll see you at seven." She starts across the yard, turns, and calls back. "You wouldn't by any chance say I'm mercurial then?"

He doesn't hear her.

In the back hall, Mariel runs into Hektor. "Father Carroll is just leaving," she says, "if you want to catch him."

"Nothing's wrong, is it?"

"I called and told him we weren't having a funeral for Artie."

"You did?"

"I changed my mind, though. Let him bury an empty coffin. Serves him right. Throw incense and holy water around."

"Why? What happened?"

"Nothing. He said he was sure Artie requested no funeral because she wasn't thinking right. And I said, Okay, go ahead." She pauses. "He said funerals are psychologically necessary."

"I think he's right."

"We'll give you a big one, Hektor." Mariel starts into the kitchen with the glasses. "By the way, who's your friend?"

"He's a priest."

"I thought so. He looks like one."

Hektor thinks of Delmore Ricketts and his fishing hat. "He does not."

"Does, too. Priests always look alike."

"How's that?"

"Holier than thou. I'm beginning to think Artie was right. Don't give me a funeral either, Hektor."

"Okay."

"Promise."

"Promise."

"Don't cremate me, though. That's going too far."

"What's in those glasses, Mariel?"

"Straight bourbon. And there's going to be more. Want to join me?"

Hektor remembers the dream he'd had the night before of Thomas and Sarah going sailing.

"I think I'll pass."

TWENTY-THREE

Four Women

DONNIE HAS GONE HOME TO SHOWER AND SHAVE BEFORE GOING out to Harlow. He places Artie's ashes on the kitchen table, but that bothers him. He takes them into the bedroom and puts them on the dresser. This also bothers him. He finally puts them on the mantel in the den under one of her paintings, a woman climbing the dunes to a house which is obviously the one at Harlow. The picture has hung here for years, part of the furnishings. But now he looks at it carefully. Sea oats at the top of the dunes are bent over in a strong northerly wind. February, Donnie knows. When the woman gets to the top of that dune, it will be freezing. And it's around three o'clock because the shadows are beginning to lengthen. Behind the woman, though it's not in the picture, the bay is shimmering, rippling.

Would Artie have painted like this if Carl had lived? He tries to imagine Carl and Artie growing old together, having children. Would her talent have gone into creating a family? Probably, he thinks, considering the time she spent with Dolly and how close they were. If she had had children, painting might have been just a pleasant diversion. But she would have been happy. He knows that. His twin would have been happy with big sweet Carl Jenkins.

"You know Carl, Donnie. You know everything's going to be fine. Just look over toward Harlow any night and you'll see us sitting on the screened porch having a couple of beers and listening to the music from the hotel. Maybe we'll even get in a couple of slow dances. Then we'll go upstairs and make babies."

That was Artie in her wedding dress reassuring him. And he, Donnie, was jealous. It wasn't the fact of Carl, and, God knows, he was happy that Artie was happy. It was the assimilation. Artie was changed, and that was hurtful. Twins, he thinks. Twins. It's so damn complicated.

And then Carl was gone and Artie was another person. This one Donnie understood better, though. And wherever she was, whatever she was doing, he knew she needed him. He was never again on the outside.

He wonders if Hektor remembers the first time Carl had shown up at the house. It was Valentine's Day and he and Artie were thirteen. It was Hektor who had answered the knock on the back door.

"Is Artie home?" Donnie heard Carl say. And then Hektor's amazed "Is *that* for Artie?" *That* had been a heart-shaped box of candy. He had been almost as impressed as Hektor. His own idea of a Valentine at the time had been an envelope with a rubber band twisted around a popsicle stick so when the envelope was opened, it would rattle viciously. "Rattlesnake!" he would yell, managing to get some violent reactions.

But Artie had accepted the candy graciously, and she and Carl had walked down to the beach. He and Hektor were picking out all the chocolate-covered nut pieces when their mother caught them and made them put the box up. After that, it seemed Carl was always there. He and Artie had married the week they graduated from high school. He, Donnie, had walked down the aisle with her, had been the nervous one. Then he had gone off to the university while Hektor had continued to live with Artie and Carl. And then the Korean War had come along.

Donnie touches the woman in the painting. Who are you? Four women, he thinks. Artie, Mama, Mariel, and Dolly are at the center of my life and I don't understand a damn thing about any of them. Hektor is just plain old Hektor, and Papa was certainly easier to know than Mama. Suddenly, as if someone had flipped a slide, he sees his father sitting at his desk. His head is in his hands, and the desk lamp is casting an elongated shadow that spills from the desktop to the floor. Donnie sighs. Maybe we never really understand anybody, not even ourselves. Or our motivations.

Mama. We killed for you.

It's four-thirty. He should be getting ready to go to Harlow for the rosary. Maybe Mariel is going to pull this thing off after all. What he can't figure out is why it's so important to her. What really puzzles him is that he senses somehow that it's because of him.

"Screw it all," he says out loud and goes to take a shower.

Clothes are thrown across the unmade bed and the chair. This is so unusual, it worries him. He pushes a dress aside and calls Artie's number. Reese answers.

"Reese? Is Mariel around?"

"Somewhere."

"May I speak to her, please?"

"I'll see can I find her. Dolly's sick."

Donnie feels the parent's instant rush of fright.

"What's wrong with her?"

"The doctor says a sinus infection. Mariel took her to the doctor."

"Well, will you see if you can find Mariel for me?"

"Sure." Reese pauses. "You back from Birmingham?"

"Yes."

"Okay. I'll get Mariel."

Donnie waits for what seems to him a long time before Mariel answers the phone.

"Donnie? Reese says you're back." It's a formal voice, slow and polite.

"It only took a couple of hours. Reese says Dolly's sick. What did the doctor say?"

"She has a sinus infection. He gave her a couple of shots and she's asleep. I don't know if she'll feel like going tonight or not."

"Is Hektor there?"

"He brought some guy with him."

"Well, I'll be there around six."

"Fine."

"Mariel, are you all right? You sound funny."

"I'm fine, Donnie. I'll see you at six."

The phone goes dead. Donnie puts it in the cradle. Well, hell. What has he done now? He grabs clean underwear from the drawer and hurries to the shower.

Women. He doesn't understand a one of them.

TWENTY-FOUR

Sarah Sullivan Explains to the Devil, 1940

WHEN I WAS A CHILD, MY MOTHER KEPT A SILVER-FRAMED PHO-tograph of her and her two sisters on her dresser. The picture fascinated me. I would sneak in her room and take it, hiding it in the pocket of the pinafore she made me wear. Then I would take it to the attic or, if it were summer, down to the creek where I'd take it out and examine it.

It wasn't an unusual picture. Just three young ladies posing in a photographer's studio. One sister was seated; the other two were standing, each with a hand on the back of the chair. On the gray mat it said S. Lindbergh, Lynchburg.

They look alike, my mother and her sisters. They each have on suits with fitted jackets and long skirts that appear to be gathered more toward the back. My Aunt Daisy is seated, my mother stands to the left, my Aunt Annie to the right. Not one of them is smiling. Their heads are held high, unnaturally high, as if the ruffles on their blouses are starched and scratching their chins. They all seem to be in their late teens, though my mother was twenty-two when the picture was made, and engaged to marry my father. The other two were older.

I never knew what it was about that picture that fascinated me so. I only knew I could take it out and look at it, and it would be May, 1890, and I would be there with them, literally.

"Be still, now," the photographer says, and the three sisters try to quit giggling. "I mean it!" His voice is stifled under a mantle of black canvas. For a second, they look toward him seriously. He snaps the picture with a small explosion. Each girl shrieks. The smell of sulfur is loud in the room. "Let's try one more," he says.

Later they walk down the street. It's early afternoon on a perfect day in Virginia. They stop at Carter's Jewelry to admire Jenny's china and silver patterns again. Daisy and Annie, too, have selected theirs, though that July, Daisy will prick her finger cutting roses for a party and die two weeks later from blood poisoning.

But they don't know that, any more than they know I'm walking with them. They go into the tea shop and order a lemonade. They know they are pretty; they see the admiring glances of the other women. They fold their fingers daintily around the icy glasses and lift the lemonade to their mouths.

This is true. I could hear the swish of their petticoats as they walked down the street.

"Jenny O'Farrell Harvey. Sounds wonderful, doesn't it?" my mother says to Daisy and Annie as they lean over the rail of the bridge they have to cross on their way home.

"Wonderful," they both agree.

I climb on the rail. "I'm here. Look at me."

But they keep looking into the creek, watching the way the water divides around small stones.

One day when Mama switched me hard for fighting with my brother Johnny and then sassing her, I went in her room, got the picture, and took it to the creek like I usually did. But that day it didn't say anything to me. The three faces just stared at me, frozen in that second in 1890. So I waded out into the creek, scooped out a place under some rocks, and put the picture into the hole. Mama screamed and yelled, wanting to know where her picture was. Her picture of her dear dead Daisy. No one knew. It had disappeared from the face of the earth. A week later, I got to missing it and went to dig it up. It was gone. Even the silver frame.

The Devil smiles and kisses her.

Doors

"IS SOMETHING WRONG WITH YOUR SISTER-IN-LAW?" DELMORE Ricketts asks Hektor who is at the sink washing the glasses.

"She may have had a little too much bourbon. I think she'll be all right for the rosary, though. I've never seen her do this before."

"Grief. We all handle it in our own way. Facing mortality's closed doors."

"I guess so." Hektor dries the glasses and puts them on the counter. "I'd recommend a walk on the beach, but a jubilee really messes it up for several days. There's no telling what condition it's in."

"I think I'll go down and see," Father Audubon says. "All sorts of birds should be down there feasting. You don't want to come?"

"No, thanks. My brother should be here soon. May might like to go, though. I think she's out front."

"I'll see. Do you know not long ago I saw two bald eagles at Hurricane Lake? We see them every now and then. The odd thing was that these two were actually diving into the water fishing. And I didn't have my camera with me." He pulls one from his pocket. "I learned my lesson."

"Good luck," Hektor says. My God, he thinks, Mariel was right. He does look like a priest.

Reese comes in carrying a plate as Father Audubon leaves.

"More ham," he says. "What's that priest doing here?"

"He's a friend of Artie's from San Francisco. He lives in Mississippi now and came over for the funeral."

"Knew he was a priest." Reese places the ham on the counter. "What you want me to do with all those daylilies?"

"Just stick them anywhere. Take some home. I told Mariel she could have all she wants."

"I wet them down. There's no hurry."

"Thanks."

Reese pulls out a chair and sits down at the kitchen table. Hektor does likewise.

"Well," Reese says.

"Well," Hektor says.

"What you reckon Dolly's going to do?"

"I have no idea. If she wants, I'll buy the house. May and I could come over here on weekends and during the summer."

"She ought to live here," Reese says.

"There's not much for young people in Harlow, Reese."

"Everything there is."

"That's what my father used to say. And the important things, sure. But Dolly likes that children's theater group in Atlanta. I doubt she'll want to give that up. And she needs to be where she can meet some young men, too."

Reese nods. "I keep seeing Artie, Hektor. I saw her out by the pecan tree while ago. I waved and she waved back. She looked good. And happy."

"That's the way it was when Mama and Papa died. I kept seeing them. Especially Mama. Sitting at the top of the beach steps. I never told anybody that before."

"Who knows," Reese says.

"Who knows," Hektor says.

The two men sit quietly for a few minutes, each thinking. They hear Father Audubon calling for May and May's answer. "He's going to the beach to look for birds," Hektor says.

"The beach stinks."

"He'll find that out."

"You know what, Hektor? I know when Artie decided to be cremated."

"When was that?"

"Last jubilee. Back in June. She managed to make it down to the beach and watched me burning all the stuff that had washed up. She took some of the ashes and wrote her name on the sand with it. Wore her out, but there was her name, plain as day."

"Could be," Hektor says. "I wouldn't want it for me, but I can sort of understand Artie wanting it. Back to the elements, one with nature." He pauses. "I guess."

"Donnie's gonna sprinkle the ashes in the bay?"

"I think so. She said for him to do it on a day that was perfect. That's a strange thing to say, isn't it?"

"I don't know. There's lots of perfect days around here. You take October. Seventy-five degrees and a breeze from the north and the sun shining like it never thought of doing anything else. That's pretty perfect."

"Or April."

"May when the gardenias are blooming."

"We sound like a damn Chamber of Commerce brochure," Hektor says.

"Just don't mention hurricanes. Hurricane Frederick nearly scared me to death. You know Artie and I stayed here. Lord, Lord! Last time I'll do that."

"You would if Artie did."

Reese smiles. "Most probably. She was scared as I was, though. She said, 'Reese, I told you to leave. You die, it's not my fault.' I told her I wouldn't hold it against her. She said Irene would. She said I ought to be up in Atmore safe with my wife. I told her we both ought to be. Lord, what a time that was!" Reese shakes his head, remembering. "And now, look."

"But just think. You saw her a while ago sitting under the pecan tree."

"God's truth."

The phone rings but neither man moves. Someone will pick it up. It will not be anything of importance. And even if it is, the sun will dip into the bay in a couple of hours and the moon will rise and the earth will continue its journey somewhere.

"I was in an earthquake once," Hektor says. "Talk about being scared!"

But he knows that was not when he was most scared.

TWENTY-SIX

Unexpected Things

DELMORE RICKETTS, IN SPITE OF LIVING SO CLOSE TO MOBILE Bay, has never seen it. He is amazed at the gnarled live oak trees, the magnolias, and the pines that soar a hundred feet into the air. The beach is not wide, and the sand is pinkish, unlike any he has ever seen. Birds are everywhere, still enjoying the bounty from the jubilee. They move aside impatiently as he and May approach, and then they come right back to their meal. Some gulls actually refuse to move. Delmore Ricketts could reach over and pick them up. Probably he would be pecked for his impertinence. He does, however, touch one lightly on the back to see if it will fly away. It doesn't, merely squawks a warning.

"Tell me what kind of birds they all are," May says. "I know the gulls and the sandpipers. And those two big ones over there are great blue herons. They were Aunt Artie's pets."

"Over there in that tidal pool?"

May nods. "They look gray to me."

"If they fly off, you'll see they look blue. At least the bigger one will. He's the male."

"They're here at the same time every day," May says. "If they were late, Aunt Artie would worry about them."

"They're beautiful." Father Audubon hands May a small pair of binoculars. "Look at them through these."

"Wow! They must have a million feathers."

"Probably," Father Audubon agrees. "That's what gets them into trouble during oil spills. They try to clean their feathers and they swallow a lot of oil."

"We don't have any oil around here to spill."

"Hmmm," says Father Audubon, looking out across the bay.

"Let me show you where the creek comes in," May says, taking his hand. "There's lots of birds there. I'm not supposed to go up the creek, though. Snakes, I reckon. Maybe alligators."

Father Audubon wipes his sweating forehead with the back of his hand. "How far is it?"

"Right up there where the beach ends. It just looks like it's ending. It's really a creek. Kind of like a swamp that comes right down on the beach. It's nice and cool."

"Well, I'm all for that," Father Audubon says. "You know, May, this is strange terrain. Cliffs and swamps right together."

"There's probably some of them in the creek, too."

"What?"

"Terrains. They like to get up on the logs when the sun's shining."

"Most probably." Father Audubon nods. "Let's be as quiet as we can so if any birds are fishing in the creek we won't scare them away."

"Okay." May tiptoes over the sand.

The mouth of the creek, Father Audubon decides as they get closer, is probably a rather permanent tidal pool. The large live oaks and palmettos, however, suggest bayou.

"Look," May whispers, pointing upward. A large flock of birds in a loose V are soaring over the bay.

"Brown pelicans," Father Audubon says. "They were almost gone for a while."

"Gone where?"

"Extinct. Killed off mainly by pesticides. They're coming back, though."

"That's good."

"There's hope." Father Audubon counts eighteen pelicans in the v. He does this automatically.

Their feet are miring down as if in quicksand. "Ouch," May exclaims, stepping on something sharp.

A loud cry and a burst of wings. A huge white bird flies right toward them, so close they have to duck. "Kewrooh!" it screams, "Kewrooh!" It sails over them and out over the water.

"Lord God!" May says, holding her hands against her racing heart.

"My God! My God!" Father Audubon grabs his binoculars and gets the bird in the sight. "Look at that. Oh, my sweet Jesus, would you look at that!" He runs down the beach. "Come back! Come back, you angel, you gift of God!"

May can still hear the huge bird's strange scream. The bird itself, however, is becoming just a pinpoint against the blue sky. She checks to see if her foot is bleeding, and limps down the beach toward Father Audubon who is now jumping up and down in a sort of rhythmical dance. "May, May," he says, grabbing both her hands, dancing in a circle.

"My God," he says suddenly, letting go of the child's hands and sitting on the beach. He leans his head over between his knees. "May," he says, "we have just seen a whooping crane."

"That white bird? That thing nearly scared me to death."

Father Audubon lifts his head up and looks at the sky. "Thank you, God," he says.

"It was special?"

"So special that not many people have ever seen one. You remember that, May. You've seen a whooping crane. That makes you special, too." He sits for a few minutes looking in the direction that the bird disappeared. Then he jumps up. "I've got to go make a phone call," he says. "Right now."

"I'll come up in a few minutes," May says.

"Okay." Father Audubon starts running down the beach. "Remember!" he shouts back.

May takes the slices of bread she has brought with her and walks toward the water. She tears the bread into pieces and throws it to the two herons. They grab it before it ever touches the sand. They bump into each other, squabble. May laughs. "You're special, too," she says.

Mariel answers the phone. The ringing awakens Dolly who can tell by the angle of the sun across the floor that it's late afternoon. She's sitting on the edge of the bed when her mother comes in.

"It's Bobby," Mariel says. "I told him you weren't feeling good and I didn't know if you were awake or not. You want to take it?"

"I'll take it." Dolly reaches over to the nightstand and picks up the phone. "Bobby?"

Mariel hesitates for a moment and then leaves. She still doesn't know what the relationship is now between Dolly and Bobby. All she knows is she's got a hurt child in there and by damn, that Bobby Hamrick better not hurt her any more.

"Hey, Dolly. I was out of town and just got your message about Artie. I'm so sorry. You okay?"

"I've been better."

"Your mother said you were sick."

"Sinus. I'm okay."

"When's the funeral? I'm coming down."

Dolly's chest is hurting. She sits up straight, pushes her shoulders back, and tries to breathe deeply. "No, Bobby."

"I won't bother you. I swear, Dolly. I just want to say goodbye to Artie."

"It's too late, Bobby."

"The good Catholic family?"

"Something like that."

There is silence for a moment and then Bobby asks, "And you, Dolly? Would you welcome me? I'm straight and have been for two months."

Tears are streaming down Dolly's cheeks. "Don't come, Bobby," she says and gently replaces the receiver on its cradle.

She goes into the bathroom and splashes her face with cold water. She shivers; she must still have fever. A glance in the mirror is not reassuring. She puts on her robe and stretches out on the bed again.

Mariel sticks her head in the door. "How're you feeling?"

"I'm not sure. Bobby said he was coming to the funeral tomorrow. I told him no. He still may come, though."

"I hope he's got enough sense not to." Mariel lays her hand on Dolly's forehead. "I'll get you a cold wash-rag," she says, "and some ginger ale with lots of ice. Dave Horton called while you were asleep and said for you not to try to go to the rosary if you still have fever. But he said if your fever has broken, you can go to the funeral and he'll see you there."

Dolly catches and holds her mother's hand. It's cool and dry. "Mama," she says, "why are you having the funeral when Artie didn't want one?"

"You know, I decided this afternoon I wouldn't. I was up in Artie's studio and thought if she doesn't want a funeral it's her business. I even told Father Carroll we weren't going to have one, but he came barreling over here to see what was wrong, poor old fellow barely able to get around, wanting to know what was wrong. And God help me, I told him it was all a mistake, that, of course, we were having a funeral. I think he thought I'd lost my mind." Mariel slips her hand away from Dolly's. "So don't ask me why, Dolly. I don't know."

"It's okay, Mama."

"I don't know whether it is or not." Mariel goes to the bathroom for the washrag; she comes back holding it against her own forehead. "But I know this. It's not that I'm all that religious or anything. It's just that when people die, you need to have funerals for them. And Artie should have given us some warning. She should have at least told Donnie."

She hands the wet washrag to Dolly. "I'm babbling. I've had several drinks of bourbon over the course of the last hour and I feel it."

Dolly takes the cloth and lays it across her forehead. "Why do you think she wanted to be cremated, Mama?"

"Lord knows. I never knew what made Artie tick."

Dolly smiles. "Yes, you did. She was an artist."

"Huh. A lot of sense that makes. Artists are just folks who think they can get away with more than the rest of us." Mariel sits on the bed and adjusts the cloth on Dolly's forehead. "I was always jealous of you and Artie, you know." Mariel is surprised by the confession, but Dolly isn't.

"I know. I needed you both, though."

"I was jealous of her and your father, too." What is this? The bourbon?

"He needed you both, too."

"I suppose so." Mariel looks down the beach where she sees two figures she thinks are Delmore Ricketts and May walking at the edge of the water.

"Artie was jealous of you, too," Dolly says.

"No. She didn't like me very much, but it wasn't jealousy."

"Sure it was. She would have Reese and me help her clean up the house before you'd get here, and she'd change clothes."

Mariel thinks of some of the outfits she has seen Artie in and wonders what in the world she had changed from.

"Things weren't always great for her, Mama."

"I know that. But she gave the impression they were. The paintings and the traveling and the fame. It seemed easy. And then, of course, she had my husband for her twin and you for her daughter when she wanted you."

"A surrogate daughter."

"I suppose so."

Dolly folds the cloth across her forehead. "Mama, don't be so hard on yourself."

"That's what my psychiatrist says." Mariel looks at Dolly and sees nothing of herself. "I'll get you some more aspirin, honey," she says. She starts toward the bathroom door and turns. "I love you, Dolly."

"I love you, Mama." Dolly turns and burrows her

face into the pillow that smells of Artie's almond sachet.

Bobby.

Lying on the bed where, though she does not know it, her father and Artie were conceived (Hektor was conceived on the beach after a midnight swim), she allows herself a whole memory of Bobby, of loving him.

They had gone to Stone Mountain and taken a picnic lunch. It was October, and the trees were beginning to turn. The sky was as clear blue as if someone had Windexed it, and Bobby was wearing a blue shirt. When he kissed her, he had tasted like apples.

This is what she will remember of Bobby, she decides. None of the bad things. Just a day colorful as patchwork and a kiss that tasted like crisp fall apples.

She is young.

TWENTY-SEVEN

Thomas and Sarah Sullivan, August 5, 1946

THERE IS A MOMENT EACH AUGUST WHEN THE WORLD TILTS toward fall. Its signal may be a certain slant of light or the fall of the first acorn. Usually it has nothing to do with the weather which is always hot and humid with late afternoon thunderstorms. The moment is discernible, though not the same for everyone. Which proved Einstein's theory, Thomas thought, looking out of the bedroom window at the day which, for him, had suddenly shifted toward fall.

His eyes felt heavy, clogged with sleep. He rubbed them. He was not an afternoon nap man and yet he had slept for two hours so hard he had been confused when he awakened, thinking it was morning.

The fan drew strips of coolness against his bare back as it oscillated in the afternoon stillness. Where was everyone, he wondered. Then he remembered the twins had said they were going to a swimming party. Hektor was probably at the pier fishing. But how had

Sarah managed to leave the bed without awakening him?

"Come," she had said, taking his hand after lunch. And they had gone upstairs, and she had locked the door and made love to him. She had been the aggressor and his body had responded to her as always.

"Thomas," she said. "Thomas, I love you." And he had known it was true. It had always been true.

He put on his shirt and went down to the kitchen. It was empty. He poured himself some iced tea and walked out into the yard. Sarah, dressed in white shorts and a blue shirt, was sitting in the swing. She was not swinging, just moving slightly, making patterns in the sand with her sandals. Her hair, always lighter in summer, hung across her shoulders; her face was in shadow.

"What are you doing?" Thomas asked.

Sarah looked up and smiled. "Swinging."

"Lazy man's swinging." Thomas sat down by the tree. Sarah went back to her pattern-making.

"Something's going to happen," she said finally.

"What?"

Sarah shrugged. "Just got the feeling in my bones."

Thomas got up and began to swing her gently. "Nothing's going to happen we don't want to."

"A lot has already." Sarah suddenly jumped from the swing and fell forward on her knees.

"You okay?" Thomas helped her up.

"Sure." She brushed the sand from her knees. "Let's go sailing, Thomas."

"Right now?"

"Right now."

"Well, let me go get some shoes on."

"Don't bother. Let's just go."

"The sand'll burn my feet."

"Okay. But hurry. I'll wait for you on the beach."
Thomas watched her as she disappeared around the house. She moved like a girl, the same girl from Montgomery who had captured him and never let him go.

He went inside, put on a shirt, and slipped his feet into his boat shoes. By the time he joined Sarah on the dune, he was sweating.

"It's too hot to go sailing," he complained.

"That's when you go sailing," Sarah said. "To cool off."

"We'll just sit there in the hot boat not moving."

"Nonsense." Sarah ran down the dune toward the boat, Thomas following. "There's a breeze. Feel it?"

"No." But Sarah was already pushing the boat into the water.

"Get in!"

Sarah was right. There was more of a breeze than Thomas had realized. As they moved out into the bay, they saw Hektor on the pier and waved.

"I hope he'll be all right," Sarah said, watching their son hold up a large fish for them to admire. "He's too sensitive."

Thomas smiled. "Haven't you noticed? The girls are already lining up to watch after him." He thought for a moment. "If you want to worry, Sarah, worry about Artie."

"I'm not going to worry about any of them." Sarah stood up. "I'm going swimming." And she dived off the side of the boat in her clothes. By the time Thomas had tacked around, she was swimming hard toward the open gulf.

"Come on, Sarah," he said, maneuvering as close as he could.

Her answer was to sink under the water. "Sarah!" Thomas called. But there was no sign of her. She was gone as if she had never been there. Not even a ripple of waves marked where she had disappeared. "Sarah!" Thomas screamed. But she was gone.

He didn't dive in after her. The thought never occurred to him. He just sat in the boat while the afternoon sun beat against him.

"I'm here," she said. She had surfaced as quietly as she had gone under. Her hands were grasping the boat's side.

"Yes." Thomas helped her in. He wrapped her in a towel, held her against him; his breath came in short gasps.

"I wanted to keep swimming."

"I know."

"But I saw the boat up here. And you." She leaned against him. "I'm so tired, Thomas."

"So am I, Sarah."

They stayed like this for a long time, drifting; perhaps they slept. A sudden gust of wind made Thomas look up. A thundercloud towered over the western bay. It was moving swiftly. As he watched, lightning arced from water to sky. "One and two and three and four," he said as thunder rolled over them. "We have to hurry," he said, moving Sarah from his arms, reaching for the sails.

"No," she said. "Please, Thomas." She turned and looked directly at him. "Let's ride it out. You and me."

Thomas looked toward Harlow, toward the house already shadowed by the cloud. "The children," he said.

Sarah leaned forward. "You and me, Thomas. Just us."

Her eyes were the greenish gold that bordered the thundercloud. Thomas looked into them and saw darkness, saw himself reflected in the darkness. "I love you, Sarah," he said.

By the time he decided what to do, the decision was not his to make. The storm roiled over them.

"Thomas," Sarah said, reaching for him. And in that one word was all the love he had ever longed for.

This is what their son, Hektor, believes happened that day. Some of it is true.

TWENTY-EIGHT

One Life to Live

TWO DAYS HAVE PASSED SINCE ARTIE'S DEATH AND THE WORLD goes on as before. The heat of August hovers over Harlow, darting into air-conditioned buildings when doors are opened, collecting in pools in parked cars. The breeze from the bay has given up; Spanish moss hangs limply.

The beach has been cleaned as much as possible. Still, swimmers avoid the water; dead fish can still be spotted floating on its surface. Flies and birds are having a field day; tourists leave.

Along the main street of businesses, nothing much is happening. Two ladies sit on stools in Elmore's looking at patterns for school clothes. Five dollars for a pattern. Whoever heard of such. They are trying to decide if it wouldn't be cheaper to go to the new Wal-Mart on 98. Mr. Patterson in the Harlow Pharmacy fills the prescriptions people bring in from Dr. Horton. Nothing serious. Days like this, he wishes he still had the soda fountain. There would have been people to talk to. He can't remember exactly why he decided to do away with it. It seems it was his wife's idea. He thinks of the people congregated at the Dairy Queen and resents his wife. Sure, help was hard to find, but anybody could make a banana split. She could help him out instead of playing bridge all the time. "Chicken salad again," she always says. "And no cards. I think I had two face cards all day." And he thinks *Big Deal* and opens the *Mobile Register* to read about the California gangs that are selling dope in Alabama now. Turn on TV, it's just as bad. His wife has talked him into getting a gun to keep behind the cash register. Just knowing it's there gives him the creeps. He has bought a small TV to put on the counter and has become hooked on *One Life to Live.*

Next door to the drugstore was once a movie theater. Now part of it is a dance studio. Every afternoon a few little girls in leotards are dropped off by their mothers for Miss Angie Jemison to turn into ballerinas. Never mind that Miss Angie is batting zero. She was Miss Alabama 1946 and was in the top ten in Atlantic City doing an interpretative dance. No one is sure what she was interpreting as this was before the days of television, but a certain glory still attaches itself to her. Miss Angie wears wine-colored leotards with skirts to hide her belly and her sagging butt. She swears all her competition in Atlantic City was padded. "You could stick a hat pin in their derriere and they wouldn't even flinch," she tells each group of aspiring ballerinas who also yearn to be Miss America. On Tuesday and Thursday nights, she teaches ballroom dancing to the junior high school crowd. "One, two, cha, cha cha," she chants, nudging reluctant boys into place with a surprisingly painful yardstick.

At the Cash and Carry, Bear Barganier has just helped stack a load of lumber into the yard. Now he sits in his office, sweating, a nitroglycerine tablet under his tongue. He feels the pain in his chest begin to ease, but his head begins to pound. He thinks he will be the next one to be buried in the Harlow cemetery. He is wrong; it is one of the reluctant ballroom dancers who will hit the sandy shoulder of the road on his way home, lose control of his motorcycle, and sail headlong into a live oak tree.

Father Carroll is having an early, cold supper, tuna salad and fruit, and a large glass of iced tea. He wishes he hadn't drunk the bourbon earlier. He would have liked a glass of white wine but knows, usually, when he's had enough.

Mothers are calling children in to clean up for supper. The commuters from Mobile are beginning to line up at the stop sign. On the bay a few sailboats sit, waiting for a breeze to move them. Many of these people will be at the rosary service tonight or at the funeral tomorrow in spite of hearing the services are to be private. In Harlow they assume that means nobody from Mobile unless they are invited.

Donnie Sullivan drives down Main Street on his way to Artie's. Beside him, on the front seat, is the plastic container with Artie in it. He hadn't wanted to leave her in Mobile by herself on his mantel. The container's presence, however, has made him nervous. He doesn't know what to do with it. Artie is trapped inside it like a genie. At the stop sign, he should open it, let her come smoking out, granting wishes. "I want it to be the summer of 1948," he will say and just like that he and Artie will be having a banana split that Len Patterson has fixed for them at Hawkins Drugstore. Mr. Hawkins will be watching Len to see he doesn't give Artie extra nuts and whipped cream. But Len will sneak some extra in, anyhow, hopeful for one of Artie's beaming smiles. Her brothers knew her smiles well. There were three that she practiced before the mirror: the slight smell of shit smile (Hektor's name for it) which she would demonstrate to her brothers by slightly curling her lips, the butter is melting smile with the tip of her tongue run across her bottom lip, and the beam. Each had been known to throw the boys of Harlow into semi-catatonic states. Even Donnie and Hektor weren't immune, though they knew exactly what she was doing. Her slight smell of shit smile would send them scurrying to find out what they had done wrong. And her beam would make their day. She wouldn't have to say anything, just brush her reddish blonde bangs to the side (also practiced) and smile.

Donnie and Hektor were both in awe of her. She was so tiny, each of them could easily have picked her up with one hand. And yet, there was never any question after their parents died as to who the leader was. Hektor, who helped out at Dr. Barnes's veterinary clinic after school, announced to Donnie that the loudest female was always the leader of the pack. But Artie wasn't necessarily loud. Only once had she gotten so mad at Donnie that she had screamed at him, "You piss-poor excuse for a bastard's ass!" They both had been so startled they had begun to laugh.

"I think I need to go write that down," Artie said.

They had simply wanted to make her happy, to keep her from being hurt. Each boy knew what her relationship had been with their mother; each knew the vulnerability that was so close to the independent, sometimes aloof exterior. They yearned for her to let them take care of her; they gave her to Carl and then to the world with a sense of loss, knowing she would have been incensed at the idea of someone "giving" her at all.

Donnie stops for the sign, waves at old Mrs. Hawkins, and wonders once more why Mariel has always been overwhelmed by Artie. By his whole family, even his dead mother. Mariel's brothers and sisters, with a couple of exceptions, have turned out to be perfectly nice people, hardworking, good company. Her mother is one of Donnie's favorite people. And yet, Mariel has always been preoccupied with Sarah Sullivan. "Your mother would have done it this way," she tells Donnie when decorating a room or planning a party. But Donnie knows good and damn well that his mother would have been walking along the beach with the job turned over to someone like Mariel. "Do it your way, honey," he tells Mariel.

And yet, he can imagine what it had been like for Mariel to be taken under his mother's wing. Mariel saw her when she was at her best, giving parties, attending church. The dark side was never evident then. What Mariel saw was a secure, beautiful woman who knew the social graces, who was charming and kind. That was the memory the town had of her. Thomas Sullivan they saw as the absentminded professor who had in some inexplicable way captured a radiant, beautiful wife.

Donnie turns onto the shell road and sees Hektor's pickup and Mariel's car in Artie's driveway. No one else is there, and he's glad. His stomach is still unsettled, and he wants to take Artie's ashes into the house.

The house. Donnie loves Artie's house with a passion. He loves the way the closet under the stairs smells of mothballs, the way pecans falling on the roof would wake them up when they were children, signifying the season's change. Sometimes he still catches the scent of his father's Prince Albert tobacco, of his mother's L'Aire du Temps. He wants nothing to happen to this house. He wants Dolly to live here and put the Christmas tree in the parlor and tie pine boughs along the banisters. He wants his grandchildren's stockings hung by the chimney with care.

Maybe he and Mariel could move out here. He could ease out of the company. They could sit on the porch and listen to the creak of the swing.

And kill each other they would be so bored. Still, it wasn't an unreasonable thought. It was only a forty-minute drive to Mobile.

"Donnie?" Mariel is sitting in the den looking through a *New Yorker*.

"It's me."

Mariel sees Donnie's package. "Artie?"

"Yes." He goes over and puts it on the mantel. His hand feels very empty.

Mariel gets up and hugs him. She needs to know how he is. She needs to know about the trip. "I'm glad you're back," she says.

"I'm glad to be back." He lets himself rest against her for a moment, his cheek against her hair that smells of shampoo and perspiration. He moves his hands against the familiar back, the rib cage that sinks to the knobby spine. How frail, he thinks. How frail. And he holds her closer.

"We are all armadillos," he hears Hektor say. But armadillos have armor. We have nothing but these thin bones.

Mariel, her head pressed against Donnie's chest, is looking at the package on the mantel. This is it, she thinks. This is all there is. The body. Such a little thing to make such a big fuss over.

"I don't understand a damn thing," she says.

"I don't either."

They move apart and smile at each other.

"How's Dolly?"

"Miserable." Mariel sits back down, closing the magazine and putting it on the table.

"You sounded funny on the phone," Donnie says.

"Two—well, actually, three—big bourbons chugalugged. They hit me."

"You okay now?"

"Better. I was so loopy at one point, I decided the funeral thing was stupid and called Father Carroll and told him it was off. I just told him part of the truth, not that Artie was cremated. Anyway, he came barreling out here to find out what was going on. But by that time, I'd already decided I was right to begin with, that we ought to go ahead with the funeral. Other than thinking I was crazy and more than a little hysterical, he didn't suspect anything."

Donnie sits beside her on the couch. "Honey, having the funeral is fine. In fact, I've been thinking you're right. I've done what Artie wanted done with her body. The funeral is for us."

Dear God, Mariel thinks. She eyes the package on the mantel. It is quiet which surprises her. "Tell you what, Donnie," she says. "We've got an hour or so before the rosary. Why don't you stretch out here for about twenty minutes and I'll fix you something to eat."

"Something light," Donnie says.

Mariel plumps the pillow and helps Donnie pull off his shoes.

"Something light," she agrees, spreading the summer afghan over him. But his eyes are already closing.

Hektor is lying in his old bedroom right above the kitchen when he hears his mother and father talking. The voices are faint, but so familiar, that he gets out of bed, kneels, and puts his ear to the vent.

"The potato salad is delicious," he hears Mariel say.

"I had some," Father Audubon answers. "Peach pie, too."

"Shit," Hektor mumbles. What on God's earth had he been thinking of? His knees creak as he gets up and walks a little stiffly back to bed.

The voices follow him. Unable to distinguish words, he can still detect tone, rise, and inflection. It was the music of his childhood, soothing, comforting, his mother's laugh and the deepness of his father's voice. It was what he had fallen asleep to, imagining them sitting at the kitchen table drinking coffee. And on nights when the music was missing, or was discordant, he would pull his pillow over his head and remember the nice sounds.

Hektor sits on the side of the bed and thinks about the voices, how none of them had known what to expect from one day to another. There would be days on end when their mother would lock herself in her room. And then, one morning, they would awake to the smell of blueberry pancakes and bacon, and everything would be fine. There would be days of partying, of walks on the beach. And then one day, their mother would start criticizing Artie, the way she looked, walked, ate. Everything about her. Sometimes Sarah would leave home. Once she was gone for almost six weeks. His father had found her, somehow, in New Orleans and had gone to get her. When she came home, she had brought them presents and they had awakened the next morning to the smell of bacon. She had brought Hektor a kite that was shaped like a dragon. It was red and gold, and it snapped and curled in the wind like a live thing. They had sat down and eaten breakfast as if nothing had happened. Except for Artie. She had taken an apple and walked down the beach. When Hektor went to fly his kite, he had seen her sitting against the dune, her head down on her knees. Running down the beach with the dragon soaring into the air behind him, he had felt guilty for being so happy his mother was home. For Hektor there was always the beach to run to, the water to swim and fish in, and the bicycle to jump on and whirl away down the shell road. Donnie, he knew, felt the same way. But Donnie was more caught between their mother and Artie.

Hektor has often wondered if the good times outweighed the bad for their father. It had seemed so to the child Hektor. He had seen Thomas's hand reaching for Sarah's in church. He had seen him standing in the dining room looking at the table his mother had readied for a party. "Come look, son," he had said. "Have you ever seen prettier flowers?" And Hektor knew he never had. Nor had he ever seen shinier silver or a whiter tablecloth. His father's hand had reached out and touched the lavender and yellow flowers. "Your mother is an artist," he said.

"Artie is, too," Hektor said. "She can draw anything."

"I know she is," Thomas Sullivan agreed. "Your mother knows it, too. They're a lot alike, you know."

"Mama and Artie?" Hektor didn't think they were alike at all.

"More than they realize." And his father had taken Hektor into the kitchen where they both tasted some of the tomato biscuits and cheese puffs Sarah had fixed for the company. "Mmmm. Good," they agreed.

"Mess it up, I'll wring both your necks," Sarah had said, standing in the kitchen doorway, smiling at them. In Hektor's memory, she is always dressed in a black velvet dress. High-necked, proper in front, it was cut extremely low in the back, ending in a white taffeta bow. Her back was lightly freckled, smooth. Hektor has always thought it the most beautiful dress he ever saw. Someday, he wants May to have one just like it. When she is thirty years old. No use tempting fate.

He hears Father Audubon laughing in the kitchen. He's glad he found him. Delmore Ricketts. God. Worse than Hektor Sullivan for sure. What will he do with him now he's here, though? Why did it seem such an imperative thing to have a priest who knew Artie was cremated, who would accept all of them as they were? Who would say a funeral mass over her ashes? He, Hektor, hadn't thought the logistics out. Should they take the ashes out to the beach or on the front porch? Would Donnie then take them out to sprinkle them on the bay?

Hektor hears Father Audubon laugh again. It doesn't matter, Hektor thinks. We need him to bless us. Bless us all.

"Papa?"

"What, sweetheart?"

"Father Audubon and I saw a whopping crane on the beach." May climbs up on the bed beside him. "He says there are only a few in the world. He nearly had a fit."

"A whopping crane?"

"It was real big."

"You mean a whooping crane?"

"I guess."

"That's wonderful. I'll bet he did nearly have a fit."

"He did a dance. Like this." May gets off the bed and does the Watusi-type jump Father Audubon had executed on the beach. Her chunky short legs hit the floor solidly. For a moment, in the late afternoon sun's shadows, Hektor sees a woman with black hair, whirling, dancing. Ana? But the image disappears.

"He must have been very happy."

"He was. He went to call somebody to tell them."

"Whopping crane headquarters," Hektor says.

But May knows he is teasing. "No," she says, frowning at Hektor.

Hektor is sufficiently chastised. He changes the subject quickly. "Your blue dress ironed?"

"Didn't need it. Aunt Mariel looked at it." May sits down again. "Uncle Donnie's back."

"I know. I heard him drive in."

"He has Aunt Artie in a package but he said it wasn't her."

"Well, why would he say that?"

"Because I'm a child." She examines a mosquito bite on her leg, decides to scratch it vigorously.

Hektor catches her hand. "You're going to make it bleed."

"No, I'm not."

"Yes, you are. Now quit that."

May gives him her frown.

"Have you had any supper?" Hektor asks.

"No."

"Well, let's go get some. We have to get ready soon." He sits up and realizes how tired he is. "You need a mother," he says.

"Because I scratch my legs?"

"Absolutely."

"A mother couldn't stop me."

"No, but she could help me worry. I'm going to start investigating the possibilities as soon as we get back to New Orleans."

"Well, I'll tell you what," May says. "Don't marry that old Marny Naftel or I'll run away from home."

"I'll give you the last say-so. Okay?"

"Okay." May thinks for a moment. "I like Kelly Stuart," she says. "She's letting me read all her old *Nancy Drew*s."

"But I thought she was taken."

"I'll find out for sure," May says. "I'll ask her tonight."

"Thanks."

"You're welcome."

Donnie is drooling on the sofa cushion. He sits up, blinking, wiping the side of his face when Mariel pats his shoulder.

"Here," she says. "Eat some of this. You'll feel better."

Donnie takes the plate and stares at it.

"Drink the tea. That will wake you up."

He reaches for the tea obediently. For a moment, he had thought she was Artie waking him to go to school. Things click back into place.

"I'm going to go on and get ready."

"Okay." Donnie looks at the food. He doesn't think he can eat. But he takes a bite of fruit salad, and suddenly he's starving. He eats everything, sopping his roll in the poppy seed dressing. He finishes the tea, gets up, stretches, and walks to the window. Late August sun is making everything shimmer, blur like a ghost image on TV.

"Mama said you were back." In shorts and ponytail and no makeup, Dolly is his child. She comes to hug him. "Did it go all right?"

"Okay." He feels how hot she is. "I'm sorry you're sick."

"So am I. I don't think I'd better try the rosary. I

hope I can go to the funeral tomorrow, though." She sees the package on the mantel. "Artie?"

Donnie nods.

Dolly goes over to it. "Not much, is it?"

"You and I'll take her out on the bay, maybe tomorrow, and sprinkle the ashes."

"She said on the day you deemed perfect."

"Maybe every day is perfect."

Dolly smiles. "You are becoming a philosopher in your old age."

"Dangerous, isn't it?"

"Well, different, anyway." Dolly touches the package.

But Donnie stays at the window, looking out at the sun, the beach, and the golden-green water of the bay.

TWENTY-NINE

Hektor and the Devil

I KNEW THE DEVIL WHEN HE WALKED IN THE CHURCH THAT Sunday. I was only six years old, but I recognized him right off. He came down the aisle like any man would and sat across from us. He had blond hair and a reddish, freckled face. He looked right at me with eyes yellow and quick as Susie's, Artie's cat. I hid behind Papa.

"Papa," I whispered, "the Devil is here. What's he doing at mass?"

"Shhh," Papa said. I peeped around him at the Devil. The Devil smiled at me. It scared me so bad, I put my face against Papa's arm. The material in his suit scratched; he smelled like Prince Albert tobacco and soap. I must have gone to sleep, because the next thing I remember is being led down the aisle and seeing Father Carroll shaking hands with the Devil. Then he was introducing him to everyone.

"Sarah and Thomas Sullivan, Zeke Pardue. Our new neighbor. Just bought the Simonton place."

Mama and Papa shook hands with the Devil. So did Artie and Donnie. But I ran and got in the car.

On the way home I asked Donnie if the hand was hot or cold but he acted like he didn't know what I was talking about. He had a game he played where he'd lean out of the car far as Mama would let him and count buzzards. That's what he was doing.

"The Devil's hand. Was it hot or cold?"

Artie said it was hot, burning-up hot.

"I knew it!" But then I saw Donnie and Artie were laughing.

Mama wanted to know what I was talking about.

"The Devil. I wanted to know if his hand was hot or cold."

Papa said there was no such thing as the Devil.

"Then why does Father Carroll say there is?"

"Well, everyone is capable of doing evil things. That's what the Devil is," Mama said, "the part of us that isn't good, that makes us misbehave. That's what Father is warning us about."

Artie kicked me and said it was the Devil made me throw rocks at school and hit Jenny Walker.

But Papa told her for goodness sakes not to tell me that, that I'd use it as an excuse, that the Devil would be causing all sorts of problems and I wouldn't be to blame at all. And they all laughed. That was when I decided not to tell them about Zeke Pardue.

We didn't see him again until the next Sunday. I kept thinking about those yellow eyes, though, and knew they would be right where they were, looking at me like we had a big secret together. Which we did. Again, after mass, I ran and got in the car. But this time Mama and Papa stayed longer talking. And when we started home, Papa said Mr. Pardue had invited us out to his place that afternoon, that he had two buffa-loes, real buffaloes he was thinking about raising. Lord knows he'd do better with Herefords. But it would be fun seeing them.

I didn't want to see a buffalo. Besides, I knew who would be there.

The Devil was waiting for us, looking at me with those yellow eyes. I tried to stay behind Papa but he pulled me away from his leg wanting to know what on God's earth I was doing. Zeke Pardue smiled at me. He had big teeth, white, shiny.

"Come on, I'll show you Bill and Sadie," the Devil said. "I hope you brought your camera."

Mama had it slung over her shoulder, said we didn't want to miss a thing.

We all got into Zeke Pardue's pickup, Mama, Papa, and the Devil in the front and Artie, Donnie, and me in the back. We headed down a road that was full of mud holes. The Devil would hit one of them and nearly throw us out of the truck. I held on to the sides hard as I could. Artie and Donnie were laughing like crazy.

Blackberries were blooming everywhere along the road. I remember this. I knew there must be thousands of snakes there. Snakes love blackberry patches. I took my hands off the sides and just let myself be bounced up and down. And then we were at the pasture.

"Ho, Bill! Sadie!" Zeke Pardue called. But nothing happened. "Ho, Bill!"

We waited for a few minutes by the gate while he kept hollering.

"Let's go on in," he said. "We'll find them."

Mama started to get back in the truck, but Zeke Pardue stopped her. "We'll just walk. The truck's probably scared them off. They can't be far."

Mama looked around at us three kids, looked at each one of us like she was measuring us. I remember that. Then she asked if it was safe.

"Sure," said the Devil.

And that is how I almost got killed by a buffalo. We were partway across the pasture and Zeke Pardue was calling, "Ho, Bill! Ho, Sadie!" when they came charging out of a pine thicket. They were huge and coming straight toward me. I dropped Papa's hand and started running. I knew they were behind me, though. I could hear them catching up. I could feel their breath.

And then I was in the air and the Devil was holding me there and was laughing. And Mama and Papa and Artie and Donnie were laughing. The buffaloes were standing by them and Artie was patting one of them on its head.

I looked down at Zeke Pardue, way down into those yellow eyes, so deep I could see flames flickering.

"I know who you are," I said.

"So you do." And he threw me into the air and caught me, laughing. "Now go back to your mama."

And I did. I even have a picture made of me sitting on Bill. I am not smiling in this picture. I am looking toward something out of the camera's range. It is the palm of Zeke Pardue's hand pressed against my mother's thigh.

THIRTY

What Naomi Cates
Will Never Tell Dolly

YOUR AUNT ARTIE KNEW HER MAMA. YES, SHE DID. BOTH MY
girls thought Sarah Sullivan was handed down. They'd
go to her house to help with those parties she was
always giving and come home saying "Mrs. Sullivan
says this" or "Mrs. Sullivan does that." The china was
just so and the silver, and Mrs. Sullivan wore such and
such a dress. And I wouldn't say a thing, just think
that's how much you know about Sarah Sullivan, little
girls. Quite a lady, she is, over at the hotel. I'm the
one changes the sheets. I know.

I knew Thomas Sullivan couldn't afford all that en-
tertaining she did. He was a teacher with mouths to
feed and bills to pay. I said as much one day, and
Mariel jumped right in. "It's her money, Mama. Left
her by her daddy. She can do what she wants with it."
And I thought if it was her money she was using, I
knew where it was coming from and it wasn't her
daddy. Unless her daddy was named Zeke Pardue.

Thomas and the children had to know it. I'd see Thomas at mass not just on Sundays but sometimes at early mass during the week. I guess he still thought God was going to straighten everything out for him. I'd watch him lighting his candles and kneeling and I'd think, Don't hold your breath, Thomas. But I felt for him. The early morning sun showed how thin his hair was getting, how dark the circles were under his eyes. And I wanted to reach out, put my arms around that good, sweet man. Feel his arms around me. But he belonged to Sarah like a fish caught in a net, like she'd cast a spell over him.

And then he would drive to Mobile to work, and I'd clean the sanctuary. That's what I was doing there. Father Carroll kept thinking the smell of incense and those candles flickering would reach out and grab me. I knew that was why he hired me. But if I'd looked up and seen the Blessed Mother herself crying real tears I would've just handed her a rag to blow her nose on. I might have said, "I know how you feel. God treated you bad, too." But I wouldn't have hollered, "Miracle! The statue is crying!" Give the woman her privacy. Besides, Father Carroll would have given God credit for it.

"Listen, God," I said the night Toy was dying. "Let her live and I'll do anything you want. I'll walk on my knees to New Orleans. I'll praise and serve you every day." I couldn't think of anything else, but all he would've had to do was ask. Instead he took Toy away from me.

The doctor came and stood in the doorway. Didn't say a thing. I knew. Father Carroll got up and went to talk to him and then came touching me on the shoulder. "Naomi."

I looked around the room. It was empty except for us. God had gone.

"Let us pray for Toy's soul," Father Carroll said, kneeling by me. But I got up and left him there on his knees. I walked outside where traffic was going back and forth even in the middle of the night.

"Naomi," Father Carroll said, following me. "We can't begin to know the reason these things happen."

"God," I said.

"There is a purpose—" he began. But I walked away into the park across the street.

"Naomi!" But I kept on walking. Somewhere I lost the priest. When I got to the river, I was by myself. The stars were falling into the water. Ping. Ping. Ping. I sat and watched them and didn't feel sad, just empty. I watched the stars and thought that was the way of it. God was too busy for Naomi Cates. No use fooling with him.

I wrapped Toy's blanket around me. It smelled like her. I sat there with the blanket over my head until it began to get daylight. Then I threw it into the river and walked to the bus station to go back to Harlow.

There's one thing needs to be straight. I never threw Will Cates out like most people thought. He took himself out a little at a time. Finally he wasn't there at all, and, sure enough, here comes the priest saying, "Naomi, Will's killing himself with grief."

"He's killing himself with whiskey," I said. "Has been for a long time. You going to tell me it wasn't his fault he passed out and left Toy in the sun? You going to tell me ants weren't already after that burned baby's skin when I found her? Ants, Father."

"He needs some help," Father Carroll said.

"Then get him some." I was busy. It was my day

off and I was boiling clothes in the wash pot. "You're the priest. Pray for him."

Father Carroll slammed the door to his car and started off. Then he backed up and yelled, "He's your husband, damn it!" And before I even had the wash hung, here he was, coming back down the road with Will.

A pitiful sight Will was, too. I took him inside and pulled all his clothes off and put him in the washtub. Scrubbed him like I scrubbed the clothes. Spread a quilt on the floor and rolled him up in it. He was red-splotched and droopy-eyed, lying there like a cocoon. But I knew he could hear me.

"Old man," I said. "I got no quarrel with you." He didn't say anything. Just looked at me with those eyes about half-open but seeing me. "You and me have the same enemy."

He still didn't say a thing. I took his clothes out to wash and when I came back in he was asleep.

"Will," I said. "Will." And I fixed him some milk toast and woke him up to eat it. He was so weak, I had to feed it to him.

When the children came in, I had him in bed. "Your father's here," I said. But not a one went in to see him. Not a one. And he was gone again next day, soon as his clothes got dry.

THIRTY-ONE

A Letter to Dolly, Never Mailed

MAKE NO MISTAKE ABOUT IT, DOLLY, WE CATESES WERE PINEY woods trash, still are to the folks in Harlow regardless of what we do or who we marry.

You could have sliced that town right down the middle. The nice people lived on the bluff and the ladies played bridge and ate at the Grand Hotel at least once a week. Their husbands worked in Mobile, and on weekends they played golf or went out on their boats.

The white trash's houses, sometimes just shacks, were scattered around in the woods, some near the bay but never on it. Our fathers worked in garages or on fishing boats or on the grounds at the Grand Hotel. Or not at all. My father, your grandfather, Will Cates, worked at the boat dock and drank. Your grandmother Nomie was a maid at the hotel.

Of course my sister Elizabeth and I were impressed with Sarah Sullivan when we were teenagers. And I know, God knows my analysts have told me enough, that the things we admired so like the china and silver and Mrs. Sullivan's clothes were superficial. But there was more to it than that. When we studied that poem in school about a woman walking in beauty, I thought that poem could have been written about Sarah Sullivan.

I know what they say about her, about her mental illness and her affairs. I know how she hurt her husband and children. But she walked in beauty. Dolly, your grandmother Sarah walked in beauty.

Mama would say, "Beauty is as beauty does." And I realize now how hard it must have been for her, having us come in bragging so much on Sarah Sullivan and her parties and Mama struggling to keep food on the table for us. So many of us needing things, pulling at her from all directions, and the child she loved best, Toy, dead and buried long ago.

Toy came about three weeks early and caught Mama by surprise. There were a couple of doctors staying at the hotel who were called, so Mama probably got better care than she had for any of the rest of us. Anyway, they put her on a cot in a storage room behind the gift shop, and Toy was born before the second doctor could get off the golf course. Mama named her Dorothy, but everybody called her Toy right from the beginning because the gift shop lady said she looked like a toy. A little doll.

Toy. My sister you are named for, Dolly. My first real memory.

"Sit on the floor, Mariel," and Mama putting her into my arms. The warmth, the sweet, milky breath. She opened her eyes and looked at me.

I didn't want Elizabeth to have a turn holding her. Toy was my baby. I'd lean over Mama's lap while she nursed her, rub my hand over her head, feel the soft spot where her pulse beat, the spot Mama said we must be very careful of. Her hair felt like silk. It was black, not like the rest of us, but Mama said it would fall out and come back blond like ours had done. Every day I'd look to see if she was bald yet.

How old was I? Four years old? Look at Mariel playing in the dirt yard the day Toy dies. The day Papa caused her to die. Gather on the porch and grieve for Naomi and even Will who has to live with his guilt. But Mariel, Elizabeth, Harry, Jacob, Steve, Ben. They're children. They play in the yard, their world going on. What do they know about death? Come have some cake, children.

And we did. And I told myself that Toy was inside, sleeping in the dresser drawer. Once I even heard her cry. How is it I remember this? I said to Jacob, "Toy's crying."

"No, Mariel. Papa left her in the sun too long until she got blisters all over and died."

But I knew the sun couldn't make you die. I pulled off my shirt and sat in the yard and waited. And what I thought was right. I didn't die.

"Better come in now, Mariel." Father Carroll's hand was cool against my hot shoulder. He picked me up and carried me inside and washed my face and hands.

"Is Toy really dead?" I asked him.

"Yes. Gone to heaven to live with Jesus."

"Does Jesus know not to touch her soft spot?"

"Yes."

"She won't come back?"

"No. She'll wait for us, though." He carried me to the bed where Elizabeth was already sleeping. "Try and get a nap now."

But I couldn't sleep. Mama was on the other side of the wall. I got up and opened the door to her room. She was leaning over the washbowl. I could see the steam rising from the cloth she held against her breasts.

"Mama?" She turned. "Mama?" I said again, this time not sure. This woman's face was swollen and gray.

"Come here," she said. The cloth dropped from her breasts. She picked me up and sat in the rocking chair.

"Toy," she said. And I did what I had wanted to do while I watched Toy nursing. I took Mama's breast into my mouth. And while she held me close, I drank.

The pieces came together, how Papa had put Toy on a quilt on the porch and, drunk, had gone to sleep and left her there all afternoon. How was it that he was left alone with her? Where were Mrs. Potts and the rest of us? Were we swimming in the bay or playing at Mrs. Potts's sister's house while Toy was burning up?

Mama, coming home from work, found her, already blistered, already unconscious. She ran with her to the hotel, and Mr. Graham, the manager, took them to Mobile to the hospital.

But she was gone before the sun came up. "Gone to Jesus," Father Carroll assured us. "Gone to Jesus," he told Mama who sat with her beads in her hands turning them over and over. "Gone to Jesus," he told Papa who sat out by the live oak tree not saying anything.

"Take your papa some food," Grandmama said. And we did. But what we had taken him earlier was still there covered in ants.

Jacob told us years later that Father Carroll had told Mama and Grandmama that he was afraid Papa might commit suicide, and they should watch him.

"He's doing it anyway," Grandmama said. "Might as well get it over with before he takes somebody else with him."

But Mama didn't say anything. The day after the

funeral she went back to work. Mrs. Potts came as usual and Grandmama went home. Papa left the live oak. We could hear him chopping wood all morning. I kept hearing Toy cry and I'd run in the house calling for her. Once she was there, lying in her dresser drawer bed, her arms reaching up for me. But I wasn't allowed to pick her up. "You're okay," I said. "You're okay." How is it that I remember this?

Papa fixed himself a pallet in the woodshed and slept there in the summer. I'm not sure what he did in the winter. Jacob said he thought he had a room in Mobile. Sometimes he was home; sometimes not. For a while we missed him.

I have this memory, though, that comes skittering up sometimes when I'm not thinking about Papa at all. It likes to catch me by surprise. We are going to the bay swimming, all six of us kids. We walk down the shell road and cut through the Sullivans' yard.

As we start over the dune, Jacob says, "Whoa!" We stop and he scrambles down to what looks like a partially clothed body that had been washed up against the dune right on the path.

"It's okay," he says. "He's just asleep." And we walk down the path, stepping over our father who is lying face-down in the sand. The sun has already turned his bare back red; a whiskey bottle is clutched in his hand.

By the time we finish our swim, a long one, and start home, he is gone.

THIRTY-TWO

Sunrise, Sunset

MARIEL HAS CALLED HER MOTHER TO TELL HER THE ROSARY IS
still on. Now she and Donnie are driving along the
beach road to pick her up. The sun, above the horizon
as they started toward Naomi Cates's house, dips, a
giant orange, into the bay. One can almost hear the
sizzle as it touches the water. In five minutes, it is
gone. Mariel is convinced it falls faster as it nears the
horizon. She doesn't mention this to Donnie who is
thinking the same thing.

"Someone has been dumping trash on Mama's road
again," she says. "Do you think we can get Reese to
come clean it up?"

"The county ought to do it."

"But it takes forever. Last time I called them it took
six weeks."

"We can ask him. I'm sure he will. He thinks your
mother is handed down."

"I know. They'll probably just sit on the porch and
watch soap operas."

"He'll get it done eventually."

Mariel takes off her sunglasses and rubs her eyes which feel heavy, swollen. "I wonder what he's going to do now."

"Stay on at the house as usual. Regardless. What I wonder is what Dolly will do."

"She'll go back to Atlanta, I expect. There's not much for her here."

"Maybe." Donnie turns on his left turn signal. Habit. No one else is on the road. "I hope she makes the right decisions."

"So do I. Bobby called this afternoon. He may come to the funeral tomorrow, she said."

"She still won't talk about the divorce, will she?"

"Not really. I think she talked to Artie some." Mariel grabs Donnie's arm. "There's the garbage. See?" Someone has added a stained mattress to the pile since she was there earlier in the day. Well, her mother couldn't be blamed for that. "It just makes me furious."

"We'll get it cleaned up," Donnie says. "Hektor and I can come down here tomorrow with his truck."

"Why do people do that, though? Dump garbage on people's property?"

"I don't know, honey. But don't worry about it. I'll get it up."

"Don't patronize me," Mariel says. "I'll get it up myself. I'll go get that lazy pinheaded Junior Morgan out here and make him do his job. That's what he gets paid for."

"Mariel," Donnie says, "are we talking about garbage?"

"What do you mean?"

"I told you the rosary and funeral are okay. I meant it."

"No, you didn't. Besides, just telling me they're okay is patronizing." She looks over at Donnie. He looks more rested since his nap and food. "I don't like you, Donnie," she says.

"Yes, you do." He reaches over to pat her hand.

"I do not. You patronize me. Just like Artie did."

He takes her hand into his. "I'm sorry," he says. "I really don't intend to."

Mariel sighs.

Naomi Cates is standing in her yard waiting for them. She has on the black dress she has worn to funerals for thirty years and yellow flip-flops.

"I couldn't find my good black shoes," she explains. "I'll just tell everyone these are my rosary thongs. Artie would have loved it."

"Mama, you can't do that," Mariel says. "Where all did you look?"

"Everywhere." She gives Donnie a hug. "How you doing, baby?"

"I'm okay."

"Mariel told me about your trip to Birmingham. I'm glad you decided to go on and have the funeral, though."

"So am I." He looks over Naomi's head straight into Mariel's eyes. I mean it.

"I'm going to go look in your closet again." Mariel says.

"Won't do any good, but thanks."

"I think you're right. Artie would love the flip-flops," Donnie is saying as Mariel goes through the door.

"They are rather arty, aren't they?" Naomi grins. "My Lord, that was an awful pun, wasn't it?"

"Awful," Donnie agrees. He is thinking how much he loves Naomi Cates.

"Well, let's sit down here on the steps for a minute. She's not going to find them, but you know Mariel."

"She says I patronize her," Donnie says, sitting beside his mother-in-law.

"You do. I'm glad to hear she's recognizing it."

"You really think so?"

"Of course. Mariel tries too hard. It makes her a perfect target."

"But I don't mean to hurt her."

"Neither do I." Naomi wiggles red painted toenails and sighs. "Days you have to worry are when you can't feel your feet."

"You don't have any feeling in your feet sometimes?"

"Not often. I'm okay. That's what happens when you're eighty."

"Who says?"

"Me. I'm the expert."

They sit silently for a moment. "Tell her you love her more," Naomi says.

"Yes," Donnie agrees.

"Is Dolly going to get to come to the rosary?"

"She's still got fever. I think she'll make it tomorrow, though."

"How did she take Artie's wanting to be cremated?"

"Well, it was a shock to all of us. I think she's okay with it, though."

"And you?"

Tears flood Donnie's eyes. "I'm not okay with anything right now, Nomie."

The back door slams. "Here they are," Mariel says triumphantly. "They were under the sofa on the porch."

"Lord, I wonder how they got there?"

"Here are some stockings, too. Can you put them on in the car, Mama?"

"Panty hose in the car? No way. It takes a whole

room and several pieces of furniture for me to accomplish that."

"Well, hurry. We need to be there soon."

Naomi groans and gets up. "We'll be there soon enough," she says.

"Do you think she's okay?" Mariel watches her mother shuffle into the house.

"She's fine. Here." Donnie pats the step. "Sit down."

Mariel brushes off the step. "I don't want to mess up my dress."

They sit quietly for a few minutes looking over the bay. Then Donnie says, "Tell you what. Let's buy the house from Dolly. Move out here. Just shack up together on the beach. How about that?"

"Don't make me think about another thing right now, Donnie."

"We could, you know."

Mariel puts her face down into her hands. "Don't tell me this now."

"Why?"

"Because it's bullshit."

"Did I just hear what I think I heard?" Naomi stands in the doorway, shoes and stockings on.

"I'm afraid so," Donnie says. "You should have taught her better."

"She learned it at home." Naomi takes Donnie's hand. "Let's go."

The group on the community pier is applauding the sunset as Hektor, May, and Father Audubon drive by.

"It's a town custom," Hektor explains. "Everyone in Harlow thinks they have to clap for the sun's performance."

"Encourage it to come back tomorrow," Father Audubon says.

"Something like that. Truthfully, more of an excuse for a shot of bourbon or whatever."

"It's fun," May says. "I like to go to the pier for sunset."

"Sunrise, sunset," Hektor sings. "Sunrise, sunset."

"Swiftly fly the years," Father Audubon joins in. Neither can remember the next words so they end up humming the tune. They come to the stop sign and turn right toward the funeral home.

"I can't believe we're doing this," Hektor says. "Having a rosary over an empty coffin."

"Think of it this way. All funerals are over empty coffins."

"Spoken like a true priest, Del."

"Just trying to help."

"I know." Hektor waves at a boy on a motorcycle. Sunrise. Sunset.

"I believe in God," May says. "I believe Aunt Artie is in heaven sitting at the right hand of God Almighty. From thence she shall come to judge the quick and the dead."

"That's good, honey. I hope she's the one gets to judge us."

"She will be." May straightens the skirt of her blue dress.

"Jesus used to live at the North Pole," Hektor tells Father Audubon.

"When did he move?" Father Audubon asks.

"Y'all are teasing me," May says.

Hektor hugs her. "Not really."

They turn into the parking lot of Bay Chapel East. Several other cars are already there. Hektor recognizes

Dorothy Jenkins going in the door. "That's Artie's sister-in-law," he says.

"I forgot she was married."

"She wasn't for long. Carl was killed in Korea. She was a widow at twenty-two."

"And never remarried."

"I don't think she even came close. There were men, of course, lots of them. But there was only one Carl. I lived with them when they were first married. Good fellow."

"Is he buried here?"

"No. He was reported missing and finally they declared him dead. I'm not sure Artie ever gave him up." Hektor pulls into a parking space. "Our parents are here, though. They drowned in the bay in a sailing accident when we were teenagers."

"I lost my parents when I was a child," Father Audubon says. "My aunt brought me up."

"I don't have a mama," May says. Both men laugh at her tone of voice. "Well, I don't! I'm going to talk to Kelly Stuart though."

"She's too young for me," Hektor says.

"We'll let her decide that." May slides out of the truck into Father Audubon's arms.

"Yes ma'am, Miss May," Hektor says. They walk to the heavy front doors. Just as they get there, Donnie, Mariel, and Naomi Cates pull into the drive.

"I'll wait and come in with them," May says.

"Okay, sweetheart. Just remember, Mr. Ricketts is a friend of Aunt Artie's from San Francisco."

"Isn't he?"

"Of course he is." The two men watch the child run across the parking lot. Her white socks flash in the late light.

"You are a lucky man, Hektor Sullivan," Father Audubon says.

"I think 'blessed' may be the adjective."

They step into the coolness and artificial light of the funeral parlor. Mr. Griffin is standing just inside the door talking to Dorothy Jenkins.

"Mr. Sullivan," he says.

Hektor introduces Delmore Ricketts to both Mr. Griffin and Dorothy Jenkins.

"We're having the rosary in the chapel," Mr. Griffin says. "I know it's supposed to be a private service, but you know Harlow."

"That's fine."

"Father Carroll is already in there." Mr. Griffin points vaguely toward the chapel.

"The rest of the family is coming in. We'll wait on them."

Dorothy excuses herself and goes into the chapel. She looks old, Hektor thinks. It seems to him that women either balloon or shrink as they age. Dorothy is shrinking. He remembers her leading cheers in high school, plump, golden. Damn. Damn. Sunrise. Sunset.

THIRTY-THREE

A Fine Rosary

FATHER CARROLL COMES OUT OF THE CHAPEL. HANDSHAKES, hugs. The introduction of Delmore Ricketts. The door opens, closes. Neighbors, friends. They finally go into the chapel where the closed gray casket is in an alcove at the front. Each person, even Donnie, sees Artie in it in her yellow dress.

"My friends," Father Carroll says. "Our sympathy is extended to the family of Artemis Sullivan Jenkins. She was a very special presence on this earth and she will be missed. We welcome you to this service in her memory. May we pray:

> *"Lord Jesus,*
> *our Redeemer,*
> *you willingly gave yourself up to death*
> *so that all people might be saved*
> *and pass from death into a new life."*

She's gone, Donnie thinks. She's gone, thinks Ma-

riel, and Hektor, May and Mrs. Cates, Delmore
Ricketts.

> *"Listen to our prayers,*
> *look with love on your people*
> *who mourn and pray for their dead sister.*
> *Lord Jesus, you alone are holy and compassionate:*
> *Forgive our sister her sins."*

She really wasn't all that bad, Mariel thinks. She
had her problems, too. I was too judgmental.

"I hate God," Hektor hears Artie say, opening the
telegram from the War Department. She didn't mean
it, God. You know she didn't. Forgive her. Forgive her
for everything else, too. Please. And Donnie and me,
too.

> *"Do not let our sister be parted from you,*
> *but by your glorious power*
> *give her light, joy, and peace in heaven.*
> *Amen."*

"Amen."

Father Carroll clears his throat. Purses open; beads
click. Crucifixes are held. "I believe in God, the Father Almighty . . ."

Donnie's fingers touch the beads, so familiar from
his childhood. He is surprised that he remembers them
perfectly, at how easily the words come. He feels the
tenseness relax in his shoulders. "Pray for us, O Holy
Mother of God, that we may be made worthy of the
promises of Christ. Amen."

Ghosts sit by everyone in the chapel. They walk
the aisles, young, vibrant. Carl Jenkins, dressed in his

wedding suit, a rose in his buttonhole, smiles at his sister. He stands at the altar, shifting nervously from one foot to the other. He is chewing gum. Oh, Carl, for God's sake. Dorothy Jenkins chews mightily; he gets the message and swallows, guiltily. The music changes. Artie on Donnie's arm. A child. All of them children. Be happy, children.

The ghosts push their way between people. Mariel moves over to make room for her father who insists on sitting between her and her mother. Thomas and Sarah Sullivan's beads click.

"Hail! Holy Queen, Mother of mercy,
our life, our sweetness, and our hope.
To you do we cry,
poor banished children of Eve."

Ana touches May's black hair. Hektor puts his arm around May and pulls her toward him. But May has felt the touch on her head; she looks up and sees her father scowling. She pats his hand. It's all right.

"Turn then, most gracious advocate,
your eyes of mercy towards us;
show unto us the blessed fruit of your womb,
Jesus, O sweet virgin Mary!"

Artie throws Dorothy Jenkins her bouquet of gardenias. She kneels beside Donnie, embracing him. Her hair spills, golden and smelling of Halo shampoo, across his arm. She touches Father Audubon on the shoulder and ignores Zeke Pardue who sits in the back row, grinning.

"Eternal rest grant unto them O Lord
and may your perpetual light
shine on them forever."

"Grant it O Lord."

"And may all the souls of the faithfully departed
through the mercy of God rest in peace.
Amen."

Father Carroll casually pushes his way through the ghosts to shake hands with the family. He's an old hand at this.

"Thank you, Father."

The crowd moves into the parlor. Outside it is night.

"I remember her wedding dress," Dorothy Jenkins tells Mariel. "It had seed pearls all over the bodice. I always meant to ask her if it was her mother's."

"It wasn't mine," Sarah Sullivan says. "Actually I got married in a pink dress. Shocked everyone in Montgomery. They thought I was admitting I wasn't a virgin."

"No," Mariel tells Dorothy. "It wasn't her mother's."

"I wonder what happened to it."

"I'm sure it's stored somewhere at the house. Why? Do you think Cindy could use it?"

"Heavens no. All my girls make two of Artie. I was just thinking about it. You know how things pop into your head. What did you bury her in?"

"A yellow dress. Linen."

"I know she looked nice."

Mariel sees the package on the mantel. "Yes. She didn't want the casket open, though."

"I don't either when my time comes. People standing around looking and you not able to say a thing. Where's Dolly?"

"She's got a sinus infection and fever. I took her to Dave Horton this afternoon. I think she'll be able to be at the funeral tomorrow."

"You give her my love."

"I will. Thanks."

"Mariel." Father Carroll comes up. "That friend of Artie's from San Francisco seems very nice. He must have thought a lot of her to come all this way."

"Yes. Hektor tracked him down."

"I have to be going," Dorothy says. "I'll see you tomorrow."

"Fine, Dorothy. Thanks."

Carl is waiting for Dorothy in the car. "Sister," he says. They drive home, the smell of gardenias strong as a wall between them.

THIRTY-FOUR

Something in Particular

AT THE HOUSE, DOLLY IS WANDERING FROM ROOM TO ROOM.
She opens closet doors, cabinets. Uncle Hektor must
take some things for May. Their grandmother's china
or silver. Something in particular of Artie's that says
Family. The cameo that had belonged to their great-
grandmother. The vase with the embossed roses. How
strange to think that these things cherished by genera-
tions are now hers, hers to take care of and cherish.

She feels dizzy when she moves too quickly. Nevertheless, she can't stay in bed. She fixes a cup of spiced
tea. It smells like fall, like cloves and cinnamon and
orange zest. She looks at Artie's almost nonexistent collection of cookbooks and opens one entitled *Jubilee.*
Published by the Mobile Junior League, it must have
belonged to Sarah Sullivan. Recipes are written in bold
handwriting on all the flyleaves; notes crowd the mar-
gins. *Cook five minutes less. Doubled will serve twenty.*
Pies and cakes have the most notations. It seems to
Dolly that she must have come by her sweet tooth nat-
urally. One recipe that catches her eye is for spoon

bread. When she feels better, she'll try it. *Delicious,* her grandmother has written beside it.

Dolly takes her tea and continues her wandering. She's looking for something. "Cold," says the living room. "Warmer, warmer," says the hall.

She should be at Artie's rosary. She sits on the steps and thinks of the service. "Hail, Mary, full of grace," she begins and then realizes how her voice is echoing in the empty house. She drinks the tea and listens to the hum of the air conditioner. Hot and cold. She gets up and continues wandering.

She turns on the light and steps into the small bedroom that Artie had used for the last few months when the steps had gotten too hard for her to climb. It's the first time Dolly has been in this room since she got home and, with the exception of a small antique desk Artie had had brought down from her bedroom, it looks like the familiar guest room that Dolly has known all her life. Mrs. Randolph has thrown all the medicines into a plastic garbage bag, washed the linens, Lysoled. Death was just a transient visitor.

The bedspread is blue and white checked. Matching curtains hang at the windows. They were ordered from Penney's. Artie had let Dolly choose them and she had pored over the catalog for days before finally deciding. It had been a good choice, she realizes now, sitting on the bed, feeling the coziness of the room. One of Artie's paintings of Dolly, a child running down the beach with a blue bucket, hangs above the white wrought-iron bed. Beneath the bed, Dolly knows, are empty boxes, Christmas boxes that are taken out, dusted off, and used again and again. There's a sack of bows under there, too.

Dolly reaches over and opens the nightstand drawer. It yields nothing more dramatic than a telephone book and a couple of old photographs. One is of Dolly and Kelly Stuart building a sandcastle. They look to be about nine. Hardened glue on the back shows it has fallen from an album. Dolly tries to remember when it was taken, but there were so many days like that. Neither child knows the picture is being taken; they are too absorbed in their work. They have been at it a long time. There are turrets and moats, and both girls have sand in their hair and on their foreheads. Dolly puts the picture on the bed to show to Kelly.

The other picture is wonderful. It's her Uncle Hektor perched on the back of a buffalo. He's tiny, and someone is holding him on the buffalo. You can see a man's hands. But it's the expression on Hektor's face that makes it so perfect. He's looking straight at the camera which has captured not just fear and anger, but the whole indignity of being a child. Dolly puts it on top of the bed, too.

The small desk has always sat in the upstairs hall, a catchall for extra Gem clips, for pieces of stationery without envelopes. Old canceled checks. The junk desk. For some reason Artie had had it moved down here, though. Dolly goes to it and opens the top drawer.

Here are old income tax returns on which Dolly recognizes her father's handwriting. He would come out and do Artie's taxes for her. Artie's theatrics over the amount owed and what could be claimed as an expense were one of the highlights of Dolly's year. "But the trip was *necessary!* And those lunches were with potential buyers, for God's sake!" Artie would pace the floor and wring her hands. "I didn't make a *dime* last year and you want me to support the government single-handed!"

"Get real, Artie. You made a bundle." And Donnie would show her the figures.

"But I had so many expenses!"

"Too many," Donnie would agree, "and how many times have I told you clothes aren't a legitimate expense?"

"They are if they're necessary. Carol Burnett and Julie Andrews get to deduct their clothes."

"They're considered costumes, Artie."

"So are my clothes. Don't you think so, Dolly?"

"Absolutely." Dolly loved this ritual. She recognized some theme being played out. The artist and the businessman. The brother and sister. *This is my role; that is yours.*

But eventually things would be settled and they would sit in the kitchen and eat Baskin-Robbins Pralines and Cream ice cream. It was Artie's favorite. "Enjoy," she would say. "After today I won't be able to buy any more." And they would enjoy, the three of them, sitting around the kitchen table. Mariel never came with them to do the taxes. She wouldn't have eaten the ice cream anyway, Dolly thinks. She was always on a diet. Not for the first time, it occurs to Dolly how unfair the competition had been between Artie and Mariel. She feels her mother's hands holding the cool cloth against her forehead this afternoon. She suddenly wants to see her, tell her it's all right that she won't eat Pralines and Cream. She probably would think that she, Dolly, had lost her mind. On the other hand, she just might understand. Mariel has surprised Dolly several times these last two days. Even her determination and subterfuge about the funeral have been surprising.

In the next drawer are some bundles of letters with rubber bands around them. The first packet Dolly picks up are from Carl to Artie. She opens the top one. *My darling,* it begins. *Don't worry about me, sweetheart.* She closes it and puts the rubber band back. Maybe later.

How young they had been. Artie had been a widow six years when she was Dolly's age.

Suddenly Dolly realizes that surely Artie had had other loves. Carl was a small-town boy who never had a chance to grow up, to live. You can't have experienced the only love of your life by the time you are twenty-two. Especially if you're someone as passionate as Artie. Somewhere there must have been a mature love. Not just an affair—a love. Dolly is surprised she hasn't understood this before. But if it were true, why had no one ever mentioned it? Strange.

Another packet of letters turns out to be from Thomas Sullivan to Sarah. *My darling,* the first one begins, just as Carl's had. Dolly reads this one. Her grandparents, dead before she was born, have always fascinated her.

> *I received a letter from your mother today. She says you are improving every day. I am so happy to hear this and hope you will be back with us soon. The children are fine and send their love. Hektor has started a salamander farm in the garage. He says he will sell them and get rich. I can't imagine much market for them. I have determined, however, that the little creatures aren't suffering, so will let him continue.*
>
> *Artie says to tell you she has been elected a junior cheerleader. She seems inordinately pleased about this in spite of her brothers' teasing. She has to have an outfit, but Mrs. Tibbet is making all of them so it is no problem.*
>
> *We are not whole without you. Come back soon.*
>
> > *I love you,*
> > *Tom*

We are not whole without you. Dolly sees her grandfather trying to keep his family together, trying to deal with her grandmother's illness. How hard it must have been to see the dynamic, beautiful Sarah spiraling into her own hell. How much of them she must have taken with her again and again. Dolly folds the letter and puts it back. She will read these later, too.

Dolly still feels that somewhere in the house there is a message for her, a magic potion, maybe, that says, "Dolly, drink me." And she will drink and understand the people who have lived in this house. Her family. Her place in the family. She wanders to the window in Artie's room. One strip of orange still glows at the horizon; the other side of the world where Carl Jenkins died is lightening. Across the bay in Mobile, lights are on. People are eating dinner, arguing, making love. And like Artie, Carl, Thomas, and Sarah, they are creating stories that no one will ever be able to tell correctly, not even the ones making them.

She picks up the pictures from the bed. She picks up the telephone book to put it back in the nightstand and a scrap of blue paper falls out. On it is written in unfamiliar handwriting, *I scarce know which part may greater be / what I keep of you or you rob from me.*

Dolly sits back on the bed and studies the words. *I keep of you; you rob from me.* On the back of the paper, in Artie's handwriting, is *Fruit-Gathering, Tagore. The purifying process of fire. Transformation. (Donnie)*

Her head is too fuzzy from the antihistamines to try and think it out now. She slips the piece of paper and the two pictures into her pocket. Then she goes to the kitchen and looks in the freezer. It's there, Pralines and Cream. She doesn't bother to get a bowl. She eats it right out of the carton.

THIRTY-FIVE

Perseus

"A SHOOTING STAR!" MAY EXCLAIMS AS THEY WALK ACROSS THE parking lot. She, Hektor, and Father Audubon watch the bright green meteor streak across the sky. "Maybe it's Aunt Artie telling us goodbye."

Both men are thinking the same thing.

"Tonight is the Perseid shower," Father Audubon says. "Around midnight the sky will be full of falling stars. It happens every year."

"What's a Perseid?"

"Well, Perseus is a constellation, a group of stars named for one of Zeus's sons. The meteors seem to come from that direction, so they call them the Perseid meteors. You know what meteors are, don't you?"

"Star junk," May says.

"Good answer," Father Audubon declares.

"Know who Zeus was?" Hektor asks.

"Oh, Papa!"

"Do you know who Perseus was, Hektor?"

"Zeus's son."

"He was the one who killed Medusa."

"Who was Medusa, Papa?"

"A Greek lady."

"Why did he kill her?"

"Because he didn't like her." Hektor slams the door. "Okay, Del, you started it, you finish it."

Father Audubon laughs. "It's all mythology, May. Just stories. Tell you what, when we get back to the house, we'll walk out on the bluff and see some more meteors. Okay?"

"Great. But why didn't he like her?"

"Go on, Audubon. Tell her," Hektor grins.

"She was so ugly that anyone who looked at her would turn to stone."

May thinks about this a moment. "That's pretty ugly."

"And she had poisonous snakes for hair."

May is delighted with this information. "You're kidding! Rattlesnakes?"

"Coral snakes."

"How come they didn't bite her?"

"Because she was so ugly."

Everyone is satisfied with this answer, and they ride in silence for a few minutes. "It was a nice service," Father Audubon says.

"Yes."

"Do you know what I think I miss most about the Church? The incense. You'd think it would be the music or the Communion or the prayers. But tonight, I realized it's the incense."

"You can buy all the incense you want at Pier One," May says. "The sticks smell real strong, don't they, Papa?"

"I love you, May," Hektor says.

"I love you, too." She pats Father Audubon's hand. "Go to Pier One."

"I'll do that. Thanks, May."

"You're welcome." May turns toward Hektor. "Kelly can't marry you, Papa."

"Why not? I'm only twice her age, and I have most of my teeth and hair. What's wrong with that girl?"

"I told her you had money, too. She said that was interesting, but it was too late."

"We'll just have to keep looking."

"She's already getting married."

"Well, I'm glad to hear there's some legitimate excuse for her to turn us down."

"I have a sister who's not married," Father Audubon says.

"Wash your mouth out with soap, Del."

"Nothing ventured."

"Nothing gained." Hektor takes May's hand. "Honey, I promise you, when we get back home, I'll seriously think about it. Okay?"

"You've never been married, Hektor?" Father Audubon asks.

"Once. Didn't last long. I was gone so much we never had a chance to get settled. Ever since, I've kept thinking I'd get around to it later." Hektor pauses. "Guess it's later, isn't it?"

"Kelly says it's too late," May adds.

"Well, what does she know? We'll find us the perfect wife and mama in New Orleans."

"I'll help you," May sighs. "I think I need a mama."

For the first time, Hektor realizes how serious May is. He wants to pull the truck over and hug her, tell her everything will be okay. "We'll get you one, baby," he promises. "Soon."

"A good Catholic widow would be nice," Father Audubon says.

Hektor relents. "Okay, Del. Tell me about your sister."

Donnie, Mariel, and Naomi Cates also see the falling star.

"Would you look at that!" Naomi exclaims. "Bright green. I don't think I've ever seen one like that before."

They stand looking up at the sky for a moment, but nothing else happens. Donnie opens the car door for his mother-in-law. He is so tired, he feels the weight of the door.

"Why don't you spend the night with me tonight?" Naomi asks. "I hate for you to drive back to Mobile and have to drive right back in the morning."

"We don't have any clothes with us, Mama."

"You can borrow one of my nightgowns, and what you have on is fine for the funeral."

"Thanks, but we'd better not."

"Okay. Just be careful. I know how exhausted both of you must be."

"I'm fine," Donnie lies. His eyes feel like they have grit in them. All of the lights are haloed.

"It went well," Naomi says.

"It was fine." It really was, Donnie thinks. He was surprised at how at ease he had felt, how comforting the familiar words had been.

They let Naomi out at her house. Mariel sees her in and turns on the lights for her.

"Quit babying me, honey. I'm fine," Naomi protests. But when Mariel hugs her, Naomi leans into her for a moment.

Donnie's eyes are closed when Mariel gets back to the car. "You want me to drive?" she asks.

"Please."

Mariel is astonished. Never, in all the years they've

been married, has Donnie ever relinquished the driving to her. It scares her. "You want me to drive?" has always been a rhetorical question. But now he moves over, and she gets behind the wheel, adjusting the seat.

"You okay?" she asks.

"Tired."

Mariel turns the car around. Having Donnie as a passenger makes her nervous.

"Nothing hurts you?"

"I'm okay. Just tired."

Don't let him have a heart attack, God. Please. Don't pay any attention to my bitching about him. I can't live without Donnie. Please, God. Don't let him have a stroke, or cancer. Please, God.

"You're sure nothing hurts you? You're not short of breath or anything?"

"Mariel, for God's sake. I'm tired. My eyes hurt. Okay?"

"You're not just saying that? You know how you are."

Donnie laughs. "Thought you were going to quit me."

"I want you well for the divorce proceedings."

"Then just let me close my eyes while you drive us safely home."

"We can spend the night with Mama."

"Mariel!"

"Okay." She hesitates. "You will tell me if anything's wrong, though, won't you, Donnie?"

"I promise." She's really frightened, he realizes. "And you do the same for me. Don't hide anything from me."

Tears flood Mariel's eyes. She brushes them away with her arm. "I promise." We will grow old together. We will have grandchildren we will both adore. We'll die together peacefully in our sleep. The furnace will mess up and carbon monoxide will get us. That's supposed to be a very peaceful death. We'll both see a great light at the end of a tunnel and we'll be holding hands. And everybody we ever loved will be there, glad to see us, welcoming us.

Mariel brushes her tears away again. The shell road makes a swishing sound that is hypnotic. By the time she turns onto the main highway, Donnie is asleep.

They cross Jubilee Parkway. Traffic is light. She's grateful it's not night before last when word of the jubilee was spreading. Everyone in Mobile would have been trying to get to the bay to fill their freezers. She wonders if it's true that this is the only place in the world where jubilees happen. Sounds like something the Chamber of Commerce would put out. She wonders if the fish see a great light and head toward it. We should have spent the night with Mama, she thinks, hearing Donnie's light snoring. Keep breathing, my love. I'll get you home.

At the house in Harlow, the phone rings, startling Dolly who is drifting toward sleep.

"Dolly? How are you feeling?"

"Better," she tells Dave Horton. She pushes herself up on the pillows and realizes it's true. "You won't believe this, Dave. I just ate about a half gallon of Pralines and Cream ice cream."

"Good. Did you take your medicine?"

"Yes, Dr. Horton," she lies. Wandering over the house, reading the old letters, she had forgotten it.

"Well, I just wanted to check on you."

"Thanks, Dave. I appreciate your calling."

"You're welcome." For a moment there is silence

and then he says, "You wouldn't believe how the stars are falling tonight, Dolly."

"The Perseid shower."

"Do you remember Alisha Goodwin? Her folks had a swimming pool? A meteor actually fell in that pool. Scared them to death."

"I remember that." Dolly lies back and lets Dave's words flow over her.

Stories.

THIRTY-SIX

A Cut-Glass Pickle Dish

THE RESIDENTS OF MOBILE ARE INTO AIR-CONDITIONING. THEY consider it the greatest invention of the twentieth century with television a close second. Consequently, ninety-five percent of them will miss the Perseid meteor shower. They also missed, in April, the red glow laced with white streaks that was the aurora borealis making a rare appearance in South Alabama. They won't see the first star of Orion lift from the water or know the exact moment when the sun and moon face each other across the bay. But they are cool, comfortable, and entertained. No small accomplishment.

In the more affluent neighborhoods, Chem-lawn keeps the yards green, the flowers blooming. Some people say this is one reason for the increase in jubilees, but their voices are muted by the lushness of vegetation. It's difficult to be strident in Mobile. Crimes of passion erupt, startling everyone with their violence, but there is little organized crime. "Mobile" and "organization" have never been synonymous. Even Mardi Gras parades occasionally end up going down the wrong streets. The spectators simply determine the new route and move. Or stay where they are if they're having a good time. There'll be more parades along later, more gold coins, beads, and Moon Pies to catch.

Outsiders often mistake this joie de vivre for laziness. Mariel Sullivan is thinking about this as she drives down the deserted streets. Well, let them freeze in North Dakota, or fall into the ocean in California. She wouldn't want to live anywhere but right here. Especially since air-conditioning.

On the beach in Harlow, Hektor is thinking the same thing. He, May, and Father Audubon have come to watch the shooting stars and have found Reese sitting on the bluff.

"Watching the falling stars," Reese says.

"I saw one I thought was Aunt Artie," May says. "It was a great big one. Bright green. I think it was her going to heaven."

"I saw that one. Probably was," Reese agrees.

Hektor leans back and looks at the sky. "Father," he asks, "could we have the mass now?"

"Sure. It'll take me about five minutes to get ready. I think it's a great idea with the stars and all. Mythical." Audubon gets up and starts toward the house. "Hey, listen," he says, turning back. "I know your brother is going to scatter the ashes on the bay, but I really need something to pray over. Something to bury." In the light from the porch, Father Audubon looks embarrassed.

"Would part of them do?" Hektor asks.

"Sure."

"Okay. Go get ready."

"What are you gonna do, Hektor?" Reese asks.

"Just get part of Artie off the mantel. Donnie won't care."

"Lord. Lord."

"It'll be okay, Reese. We're blessing her."

"You just blessing part of her."

"It's all symbolic anyway. Just wait on us here."

"Just none of it makes sense, May," Reese says as Hektor leaves. "None of it. I feel like I'm whirling around like those stars."

The child reaches for his hand.

But Hektor, in the living room, is beginning to feel like Reese. He hasn't looked in the package. Now he does and sees a plastic container. How is he going to get part of the ashes out? This is Artie, his sister, his flesh and blood. Or was. He can't just stick his hand in and get some ashes. He feels goose bumps just holding the package. He could go in the kitchen and get a bowl and pour a few ashes in it. But you can't scoop your sister's ashes out like cereal or soup. He tries to remember where he can find a fancy bowl or cup. Something he could call a chalice. Something dignified. What pops into his mind is a small cut-glass bowl his mother used for watermelon rind pickles every holiday. He goes into the dining room and looks in the china cabinet. There is so much of his life here, he realizes. The dishes with the green and gold border, the turkey platter, the pink Christmas dish shaped like a poinsettia. And the pickle dish. He takes it and goes back to the den.

There he faces the problem of opening the plastic container and pouring some of the ashes into the bowl. He doesn't think he can do it; his hands are shaking.

"You need some help, Hektor?" Father Audubon asks. He stands at the door in purple vestments. Hektor is amazed at the change in his appearance. Delmore Ricketts is every inch a priest.

Hektor nods yes. Father Audubon comes over and

takes the package from the mantel. He takes the plastic bowl out, opens it, and pours a small amount of the ashes into the pickle dish. Chalice, Hektor reminds himself.

"There." Father Audubon closes the plastic container. "We'll need some candles."

"Any special kind?"

"No. In fact one candle will do. We'll need some light on the beach, though."

"Okay." Hektor goes to the table in the front hall where candles are always kept for emergencies. He gets several half-burned tapers and a fat white candle for Father Audubon. "Anything else?" he asks the priest.

"A flashlight."

"What?"

"For light."

"Oh. Okay."

"And a white napkin."

Back to the dining room. This time into the linen closet. Tablecloths and napkins are stacked in neat rows that smell of detergent and starch. Later, he will be surprised to remember how beautiful Sarah's linens are, what good care Artie has taken of them. But now he simply takes a white napkin from the top of a pile.

"Okay," Father Audubon says. "Let's go." He unfolds the napkin and places it over the pickle dish. "You go first."

"What in the world are y'all doing?" Dolly stands at the top of the steps, her blue and white bathrobe clutched around her.

Hektor looks at Audubon who shrugs.

"We're sort of having a requiem mass for Artie," Hektor says.

"Right now?"

Both men nod.

Dolly turns to Father Audubon. "And you're—?"

"Delmore Ricketts."

"He's Father Audubon, Dolly," Hektor explains. "I went to Mississippi today to get him. May and I did."

"Are you serious?" Dolly points to the napkin-covered dish in the priest's hand. "What's that? Don't tell me it's Artie's ashes."

"Just some of them. I left plenty for Donnie to scatter on the bay."

Dolly comes down the steps, sits on the bottom one, and puts her head in her hands. "This whole family has lost its mind. Papa goes and has Aunt Artie cremated and Mama's having a funeral with an empty casket. And now God knows what you're doing."

Hektor comes over and kneels beside Dolly. "It's okay, honey. Your papa knows what I'm doing and he understands. Your Aunt Artie would understand, too." He hesitates. "It's for me."

Dolly leans over and puts her head on his shoulder. "What are you going to do?"

"We're just going down to the beach and Father Audubon is going to say a few words. That's all. Reese and May are already down there."

"Can I come?"

"If you feel like it."

"I need to go get dressed."

"You're fine," Father Audubon says. "If you two will go and join Reese and May, I'll be there in a moment."

"What do you think he's doing?" Dolly whispers as they go out the front door.

"I don't know."

"You feeling better?" Reese asks Dolly.

"I think I'm hallucinating."

"I think we all are," he says.

"Lord God," May exclaims, jumping to her feet. Reese also rises. Hektor and Dolly turn and see Father Audubon coming toward them in his purple vestments. He has lighted the large white candle which casts shadows on his face. Behind him, the porch light makes him appear to be looming, large, dark.

"The grace and peace of God our Father and the Lord Jesus Christ be with you."

"And also with you," the four people on the bluff answer automatically.

Father Audubon holds out his candle. Hektor hands May, Reese, and Dolly each a taper. He leans over and lights his from Father Audubon's. The others do the same.

"The Lord be with you," Audubon says.

"And also with you."

The priest starts down the steps to the beach. The others follow, their candles flickering in the slight breeze from the bay. Dolly shivers and tries not to trip over her bathrobe.

"Turn on the flashlight, Hektor," Father Audubon says. "I can't see a thing."

"I'm sorry." Hektor shines the flashlight down the steps. Don't fall, Audubon, he thinks. For God's sake don't fall and drop Artie.

Father Audubon begins to chant. "I am the Bread of Life. No one can come to me unless the Father draw him. And I will raise him up on the last day." He reaches the bottom of the steps. "Where, Hektor?"

"The edge of the water?"

"Is that Aunt Artie under that napkin?" May whispers.

"Don't ask me," Reese mumbles. "I wish I'd gone home with Irene."

"Yes," Dolly says. "It's Aunt Artie."

They follow Father Audubon across the beach. "His skirt's going to get wet," May whispers.

"Shhh."

But Father Audubon stops about ten feet from the water, puts down the napkin-covered bowl, and places his candle beside it.

"Let us pray."

Dolly wonders if she is having a vivid fever dream. Stars are falling all around her, and she can hear the music from the Grand Hotel where couples are dancing on Julep Point. And all she had done was to come downstairs to take her antibiotic.

"Lord God," the priest says. "Since our sister Artemis believed in the mystery of our own resurrection, let her share the joys and blessings of the life to come. We ask this through Christ our Lord. Amen."

"Amen."

God, Hektor pleads, please let her in. We all messed up.

"Let us pray with confidence to God who gives life to all things, that he will raise this mortal body to the perfection and company of the saints."

Reese begins to sob. "Artie won't get along with any of those saints two minutes." May puts her arm around him. Audubon pauses for a moment and then continues more forcefully.

"May God give her a merciful judgment and forgive all her sins. And may she be happy forever with all the saints in the presence of the eternal King."

Hektor recognizes the song they are playing at the Grand Hotel. It's an old one from World War II, "It's Been a Long, Long Time." His mother used to sing it. His mother in that beautiful black dress.

"Welcome our sister to paradise and help us to

comfort each other until we all meet in Christ to be with you and with our sister forever. We ask this through Christ our Lord. Amen."

"Amen."

"Hektor?"

Hektor is imagining paradise. He's hoping it will be better than Artie anticipated. He jumps. "What?"

"This is where we bury her."

"Oh." He looks at May and Dolly who look back solemnly. Reese's face is buried in his arm. "What do I do?"

"Dig a hole."

Hektor kneels down and scoops out a small hole. Father Audubon hands him the bowl. For a moment, Hektor wonders if he is supposed to bury the whole thing, but decides not. He takes the napkin off and sprinkles the ashes into the hole.

"Tide'll get her before morning," Reese says, wiping his nose on his shirtsleeve.

Hektor covers the tiny grave. Father Audubon kneels beside Hektor and bows his head. Dolly, May, and Reese kneel also. Their candles form a perfect circle of light. Father Audubon places the fat white candle on the sand. "We commit Artemis's body to the earth from which it was made. May the Lord receive her into his peace and raise up her body on the last day. Amen."

"Amen."

"Repeat after me: Give her eternal rest, O Lord."

"Give her eternal rest, O Lord."

"And may your light shine on her forever."

"And may your light shine on her forever."

The five remain kneeling in the candlelight. Above them meteors crisscross the sky. Tiny waves stir against the beach.

"Is that all?" Dolly finally asks. She is thinking how

Artie would have loved this, the falling stars, the five of them with their candles, the pickle dish which Dolly has recognized, the orchestra at the Grand Hotel which is now playing "Blue Bayou."

"Yes." Father Audubon picks up his candle.

"I hope it works," Reese says. "I hope all of her gets there."

"She will," the priest assures him.

Follow those angels into paradise, Artie, Hektor is thinking. Give the place a chance.

Father Audubon holds out the empty pickle dish to Hektor who backs away.

"I'll take it," Dolly says. She carries it to the edge of the water and rinses it out.

"Lord, Lord," Reese says, tears running down his cheeks. "Just seems like everything's either shit or sugar, don't it?"

Seeds

THOMAS SULLIVAN ALWAYS THOUGHT OF MOBILE AND THE Mobile Bay area as a woman. No wonder. She was plump, ripe, juicy; she wore too much makeup, too much perfume. And she was fertile. Seeds planted in her rich soil sprouted recklessly. The fish in the bay swam to the beaches. All Thomas had to do was reach down and gather them in.

He had heard about jubilees while he and Sarah were living in the apartment in Mobile. The first one he witnessed was right after they moved into the house at Harlow.

Sarah had been having trouble sleeping, but since they had moved, she had slept like a child. Even the twins crying for a bottle wouldn't wake her up. Thomas gladly got up and heated bottles, a baby on each hip. He was happy to see Sarah lying there peacefully.

The night of his first jubilee, he was dreaming his mother was calling him. "What?" he said. "What?" Sarah stirred beside him and he realized he had spoken out loud. He also realized there were calls from the beach. He got up and looked out the window to a sight he would never forget. A full moon cut a path across the water and lights danced all over the beach.

Then, "Jubiliee!" he heard. "Jubilee!"

He shook Sarah. "It's a jubilee, honey. You want to see it?"

"No, thank you," she said formally. He knew she was not really awake. He looked at the clock. It would be an hour or two before the twins woke up for their bottles. He pulled on some old pants and slipped his feet into some tennis shoes.

The scene at the foot of the dune was amazing. People were running along the edge of the water with crab nets and buckets scooping up fish, crabs, shrimp. And Thomas, stopping at the edge, saw that what looked like a dark wave moving toward the beach was alive—twisting, jumping. He moved back as a large fish slapped against his leg. The beach was silvering with the bodies.

"That you, Thomas?" his neighbor, Buck Stuart, asked, holding up his lantern. "Where's your buckets, man?"

"I'll have to go back and get them."

"This is something. Right?"

"I've never seen anything like it."

"Don't happen anywhere else. Well, get busy. Hey, look at that crab!" Buck scooped up a huge crab and dropped it into an already heavy bucket. "Better than a circus!" he declared, continuing down the beach. "Jubilee!" Thomas heard him shout.

"Jubilee! Jubilee!" The shout rose and fell like a wave.

Thomas picked his way through the squirming bodies on the beach, climbed the dune, and got a bucket and lantern. For the next hour, he picked up what he considered the choicest fish and crabs. They would make a huge gumbo, he thought. Fry the fish.

"Hey, Thomas. How you doing?" People he had just met greeted him from the circle of their lanterns. It was a giant party. "Jubilee!" someone shouted. "Jubilee!" Thomas echoed as the wave came down the beach.

By the time he got his heavy bucket up the dune and into the sink, the twins had already awakened, cried, decided no one was coming to feed them tonight, and had gone back to sleep.

Thomas went into the backyard, stripped, and turned the hose on himself. Then, naked, he went and crawled in beside his sleeping wife. The next thing he heard was Sarah screaming, "Thomas! Come look in this sink! Where on God's earth did all this come from?"

"It was a jubilee," he called. "I picked it up."

"Well, you just come here and get it out of the way. I can't even fix the coffee."

Thomas smiled. He heard Artie and Donnie begin to whimper. Let Sarah get them. He turned over and went back to sleep.

His job at the university had not turned out like it was supposed to. A dropping enrollment had meant that Thomas was required to teach two history classes as well as the Greek, Latin, and ancient literature he had been hired to teach. This suited Thomas fine, though. The day the head of the department had called him in, he was sure his contract was not being renewed. So when he was informed of the added history classes, he was relieved. And the truth was, he enjoyed them. Even more than the languages.

Many of the students who signed up for the classical languages, particularly Greek, were planning on entering the ministry. Premed students were required to take Latin. They hated it. Their hatred was so intense and so universal, Thomas began to wonder how it was he had been captured by these ancient languages, how it was he considered them beautiful. Was it something his teacher had done that he, Thomas, was totally neglecting to do? Or was it the fact that outside Mobile Bay shimmered, cool, inviting, and the oscillating fan mounted above the blackboard did nothing but stir the warm air and hum hypnotically? Sometimes he would turn from the blackboard and be startled by the sight of the bay, its sailboats and barges. In February, azaleas were already banked in full bloom around the live oak trees. Spanish moss hung from the trees.

"Would you look at that!" he might exclaim. And the students would look dutifully at the scenery they had known all their lives. "I've seen snow banked against the windows in Massachusetts this time of year."

It would have surprised him to know how many of these South Alabama students yearned to see snow. Just a few flakes. Snow up to the window was beyond their imagination.

"Well," he would say. "Back to Odysseus." And heads would bend back over textbooks. Such nice young people, Thomas thought, not realizing that many of them were still watching snow drift down.

Mobile, Sarah, the children, and the classes were a long way from Salem and the priesthood Thomas had considered.

"Consistency," Dean Huffstutler said one day in an address to the faculty, "is the key to good teaching. Imagine if you never knew when you turned your steering wheel if your automobile were going to the right or left. It would drive you crazy, wouldn't it? Well, that's how students feel when we aren't consistent."

And Thomas thought how he had been headed for the church and New England and celibacy and here he was, far from all. He even knew when his steering wheel turned toward the left when he, with the help of his parents, was turning it right.

It was the Summer of Celia. He loved the alliteration and had always thought of it as that, though he had never spoken to anyone about it, not even a priest. It had started when Celia, the Grangers' niece, had come to spend the summer in Salem. The Granger house was next door to the Sullivans' and like the Sullivans' was a two-storied Victorian, too large for the lot it was built on. This meant the Sullivans and Grangers could easily converse through their open windows. It also meant if the shades weren't drawn, each could see right into the other's house. Which never bothered anyone until the Summer of Celia.

She appeared in June, blonde, peachy, at nineteen a year older than Thomas. The Sullivans went over after supper to meet her.

"Pretty girl," Mr. Sullivan said.

"Lovely," his wife agreed.

Their son didn't say a word. Words had failed him. He went to bed thinking of her pink-golden skin, the way her dress curved. And while he lay there in the dark, a light came on in the Granger bedroom opposite his. He sat up and saw Celia unbuttoning her dress. She was no more than ten feet away. He should say something. At least lie down. Instead, he knelt by his window in the shadows and watched. She stepped out of her dress, her petticoat. Wearing only a flesh-colored silk teddy, she began to dance around the room, holding her arms out as to a partner. Finally, she opened a dresser drawer and took out a nightgown. Turning toward the window, she lowered the straps of the teddy and stretched. Thomas felt he could reach out and cup his hands around her breasts. He was having trouble breathing; he was afraid Celia could hear him wheezing.

The teddy shimmered to the floor and she stood before the window naked. Thomas could see the dark V of her pubic hair, the way her upper legs bowed slightly. That was all it took. Thomas sinned mightily on the worn Persian rug that had always been on his bedroom floor. When he opened his eyes, Celia was pulling the nightgown over her head. In a few minutes, she turned out the light.

Thomas crawled into his bed, spent, happy, confused. Even ashamed. Tomorrow he must figure out a way to tell her how close their rooms were.

But he never did. The same thing happened the next night. And the next. The only difference was that Thomas kept a towel under his bed. And felt more guilty, if possible. It wasn't until several years later that he realized that Celia had known exactly where he was and exactly what he was doing. By that time, Celia was married and a mother, and Thomas's thoughts of becoming a priest were in the distant past, as blurred as the memory of Celia's firm young body was still clear.

He had no ties left with Salem. His father had dropped dead while he and Thomas were bringing a trunk down from the attic to pack Thomas's mother's clothes in for the church's charity work.

"Wait," he said, quietly, the trunk between them on the stairs. He sat down. Thomas stood at the top of the steps holding the trunk by its strap for a full minute before he realized something was wrong. He had had to pull the trunk back to the attic before he could get to his father who had slumped against the banisters.

There were three days between Thomas's parents' deaths. "A blessing," the priest said. And Thomas knew it was so. They had been married twenty years before Thomas put in his appearance, startling everyone. And they had been good parents, loving, thoughtful. But, as Thomas admitted to Sarah once, he had always felt like a guest in their house. A beloved guest, but a guest, nevertheless. It was best that they had gone together.

He shipped the furniture to Mobile and sold the house to a Granger niece (not Celia) and her husband. The hardware store his father had owned was eagerly bought out by a partner. Everything was over so quickly, he felt disoriented as he got on the train leaving Salem. The snow his students loved to hear about was covering the two new graves in the cemetery. Somehow, he knew he would never be back.

Driving up the shell road to his house on Mobile Bay, he considered how his life had veered from the path he always thought lay before him. He also thought how lucky he was. He had a job, money saved back from his parents' estate that he had not told Sarah about. His conscience hurt him slightly about this, but not too much. Sarah had never seemed to grasp what the Depression was all about even though her own brothers and sisters had lost houses and businesses and been forced into bankruptcy. Thomas was just protecting his own family. A family which was about to be increased. Sarah was expecting another baby in a month's time. The twins were almost five. But Sarah had had such a hard time after they were born that neither she nor Thomas had been anxious to have another child soon. Actually, they had been very surprised when Sarah got pregnant. "Hey," Sarah had told Thomas before they were married. "The Church stops at our bedroom door. Okay?"

And so it had. The twins had been planned. But this baby had defied the odds. And so far, Sarah was okay. Tired, big, but not unhappy like she had been when the twins were born.

Thomas pulled into the yard and saw Bo Peep, Willie Mae's daughter, swinging Artie and Donnie. Thomas had built an extra-wide swing with a back on it and had hung it from a pecan limb. That way both children could swing at once.

"Papa! Papa!" Artie jumped from the swing and lost her balance. Bo Peep grabbed the swing to keep it from hitting Artie in the head. In the process, she fell and Donnie was slung from the swing. All three children started crying.

Thomas had piled soft sand beneath the swing. He knew they were just startled.

"Anybody bleeding?" he asked.

The children examined their knees and elbows carefully. Artie discovered an old mosquito bite with a tiny scab on it. She picked it off. "I am," she said proudly when a red drop appeared.

"She just did that, Dr. Sullivan," Bo Peep said indignantly. "Nothing's wrong with her. It's all her fault anyway. I was swinging them good."

Thomas picked Artie up under one arm and Donnie under the other. "I know you were, Bo Peep. Come on. Let's go see if your mama has some lemonade for us."

"I'm bleeding!" Artie wailed. "I'm bleeding, Papa!"

"If it doesn't stop in an hour, we'll go get you a transfusion."

"What's a transfusion, Papa?" Donnie asked.

"It's where they take somebody else's blood and put it in you."

"It's about to quit," Artie said.

Thomas put them down inside the kitchen.

"Hey, Dr. Sullivan," Willie Mae said. "You early?"

"Got to thinking about lemonade."

"Good thought. How about I fix us some?"

"Great." Thomas put the children down. Artie limped to a chair.

"What's the matter, baby?" Willie Mae asked.

"Bo Peep made me fall out of the swing."

"Oooooh, Mama! No! I never did!"

Artie sighed. "Then it was Donnie."

"Someone's papa saw someone jump out of the swing and almost cause everybody to get hurt," Thomas said. "Someone is telling fibs."

"Donnie," Artie said.

Donnie screamed and lunged for her. Thomas caught him. "Welcome home, Papa," Thomas said. "We're so glad to see you."

"Welcome home, Papa. Would you like some cookies with your lemonade?" Artie frowned at the wriggling, red-faced Donnie. "Donnie, if you're good, Willie Mae might give you some too."

Thomas held Donnie high in the air. "We'll all have cookies. Lots of cookies." The little boy squirmed in delight.

"A tea party on the porch. Come on, Bo Peep. Donnie. We'll use palmetto leaves for plates." Artie led the other two out. Thomas and Willie Mae smiled at each other.

"That one's a pistol ball," Willie Mae declared.

"How's her mama today?"

"Fair to middlin'. Might still be napping."

"Well, fix the tea party. I'll go see about her."

"I'm fat," Sarah exclaimed as Thomas walked into the bedroom. "I'm hot. I'm ugly." She was lying on the bed crying. Thomas sat down and gathered her to him. She sobbed against his shirt. Welcome home, Thomas, he thought, smoothing her hair and looking out at the water that glittered in the afternoon sun.

THIRTY-EIGHT

Artie on Her Thirty-second Birthday

I NEVER INTENDED TO MARRY CARL. I DID, THOUGH. JUST LIKE everybody expected me to. White dress, veil, the works. Sweet Carl. I still see him standing at the altar waiting for me. He has on a tux too large for his skinny neck and his long forehead is shining in the light from the stained glass window.

"I'm marrying Fred Astaire," I whispered to Donnie. But he didn't hear me which was just as well. We both would have started giggling.

For years I would close my eyes and see Carl waiting for me. It was as if my mind snapped a picture of him, knowing I would need it later. I even remembered how he smelled when he leaned to kiss me. Mainly like Old Spice but also like Ivory soap and Juicy Fruit gum. And little boy sweat.

Carl. I loved him.

"I want us to have a baby," he said. But I wasn't

sure. I wasn't sure of anything at the time. I was eighteen when I married Carl.

"Soon as you get back from Korea." Why did I feel safe saying this? As if I had given him a talisman. You have to come home so we can make a child.

Carl. Sometimes he still comes back and we dance on the bluff at Harlow. Carl Jenkins smelling of Ivory soap and Juicy Fruit gum.

"Don't leave me," I say.

Right after he died, he was everywhere. He sat at supper with Hektor and me. He followed me to bed. He held my hand while I tried to paint. So one day, I took down a suitcase and said, "Carl, I have to go away. Please don't follow me." He turned and walked down the stairs. I watched him go over the bluff and to the beach.

I had never been farther north than Lynchburg to visit some of my mother's family. But I drove right through Virginia, all the way to Salem. I saw where Papa had grown up. I saw where my grandparents were buried. I saw Carl standing by a gravestone.

"Go back to Harlow, Carl," I said. And he turned and walked away. No one else was in the cemetery. I wondered where the Salem witches were buried. I didn't ask, though. Whatever it was I was looking for wasn't there. I left the same day.

I drove to New York and sold my car. People kept asking me, "What? What?" when I talked to them. You would have thought I was from a foreign country. I found a place to live and a job filing in an insurance office. Mama would have died. There were roaches at both places.

I felt better than I had in a long time, though. I bought some canvases and started to paint again, signed up for a class at the Y.

"Come with me to Europe," Jerry Whitley, the instructor said. "You won't believe the light in Greece."

"I don't have any money."

"I do."

So I packed my suitcases again. We rented a little house overlooking the Aegean and Jerry was right about the light. It was so clear, you could see the colors that it was made of. Some days there would be more yellow, or blue. You could see it.

Jerry was principally an abstract artist. He seemed to be playing with color, throwing it against the canvas. But the most beautiful pictures evolved. It was amazing, intimidating. I worked on the porch, trying to capture the way the sun reflected from the water. In other words, doing what I'd always done, beach scenes.

"What is that?" Jerry asked one day, pointing to one of my canvases.

"A barge."

"No. The green at the edge."

"A live oak tree."

He laughed. "Get real, Artie."

I am real, I thought. I looked out at the Aegean and then back at my painting. Mobile Bay.

I stayed with Jerry three years. They were learning years, but we also cared for each other. We knew when the time came to say goodbye. Jerry wanted to go back to New York; I was still looking for something.

The night before he left, I made a pot of Mobile gumbo. "We need jubilees here," I said.

"What's a jubilee?" Jerry wanted to know. I couldn't believe I hadn't told him about them, how exciting it was to have the fish and crabs come swimming up on the beach.

"You're homesick," he said when I got through telling him, showing him how you had to carry the heavy buckets, describing the fun, the parties.

"I'll go back," I said. And I knew it was true. But not yet.

"Hey, Artie!" I was walking down the street in Rome and couldn't believe I had just heard an Alabama voice. "Artie!"

I looked around and saw a large, redheaded man coming toward me, grinning.

"I can't believe I actually ran into you," he said, enveloping me in a hug.

I pulled away and looked up at him. He looked familiar, but I wasn't sure who he was.

"Hey, you don't recognize me, do you? It's me. Bo. Your cousin, dummy."

"Little Bo?"

He laughed. "They had to drop the 'little' part."

"Bo?" I hugged him and jumped up and down at the same time. Here was Bo, my Aunt Mary's Bo, right here in Rome.

"What are you doing here? And what about Aunt Mary and Uncle Bo and Ione? Are they okay? And have you heard anything from Harlow? Donnie? You know he got married. And Hektor? You seen any of them?"

"Hey, wait up." He looked around and spotted an empty table at a sidewalk cafe. "Let's go get some coffee. I'll tell you everything I know." We got to the table just as another couple did. "Excuse me," Bo said politely, sliding the chair around for me as the other woman dived for it.

"That was a neat trick," I laughed. And he grinned.

"The last time I saw you, you had braces," I said. "Is it really you?"

He chomped his straight, even teeth together. "One

and the same. Now it's your turn to say, 'My, how you have grown, Bo.' "

"My, how you have grown, Bo."

"You too, Artie. Do you know the last time I saw you was at Grandmama's funeral? How old were you? Sixteen?"

"I guess so." The waiter came and we ordered coffee. "What are you doing here, Bo?"

"Putting space between me and Huntsville mainly. Mama's decided it's time for me to settle down. Picked out the girl and everything. Nice girl. But God!" He stretched and looked around. "I like it here."

"But are you working or anything?"

"I work for Daddy. They gave me a trip to Europe when I graduated and I didn't take it then. Said to give me a rain check. Well, when Merry Calhoun started showing up for supper every night, I decided it was time to cash the check. Swore I would call on every potential customer for Hardemond Mills. So far, I've seen two." Bo smiled at me. "I was sort of hoping I might find you, too. I had your last address."

"I moved."

"I know."

"I'll show you around."

"Great." He reached over and took my hand. "I knew I would find you."

"Tell me about Ione," I said. But I didn't move my hand. It was warm and comfortable enveloped in Bo's.

What is this, I thought. What is this? I drank the strong coffee; I smelled the diesel fumes from the cars that darted by just inches from us. I listened to Bo and knew I had been waiting for this. Waiting for my cousin Bo, for the reddish blonde hairs curling on the back of his hand. For the sound of his voice.

The first time we made love was as if we had always been together. "Artie?" Bo was staying with me. Visiting cousin.

"Artie?" He had just come in and I was in the bathtub.

"Lord!" he said, standing in the doorway. And then he was out of his clothes and in the tub with me, one of those deep tubs you have in Europe that you have to climb out of. My head hit the faucet. Clunk.

"Are we sinning?" I asked.

"Probably." And we were rolling in the tub, splashing water, laughing. The next day we each had bruises. But we stayed in that tub a long time, adding hot water when we got cold. When we finally got out, there wasn't much we didn't know about each other.

"I didn't expect that," Bo said, toweling me dry. "I hope to hell you aren't pregnant."

"Not to worry," I said, "I have my diaphragm in."

"Witch! Seducer!" He popped me on the behind with the towel. I ran for the bed.

"Harlot! Scarlet woman!" He dived on top of me.

"Lover," I said, my face pushed into the pillow.

He rolled me over. "What did you say?" He loomed over me like something I had dreamed.

"Lover."

He sighed and stretched out beside me. I pulled up the quilt and we slept. We got up and ate supper, made love again, and went back to sleep. Sometime during the night, I felt him restless against me. I turned and held him. "Donnie," I whispered, startling myself by saying my twin's name.

If Bo heard what I had said, he never mentioned it. But I stayed awake the rest of the night remembering that it was my birthday, mine and Donnie's. We were thirty-two years old.

THIRTY-NINE

The Devil's Grave

AS PROMISED, THE LADIES OF THE CHURCH BRING LUNCH AFTER the funeral. Food fills the dining room table, and other dishes are in the kitchen waiting to be brought out when space opens up. Mrs. Randolph is kept busy handing out freezer tape. "Put your name on your dishes. Be sure and put your name on your dishes." Jerry, the cat, is traumatized by all the commotion. He is hiding under Artie's bed. When May comes looking for him, he slides behind some empty Christmas boxes that have a layer of dust on them.

Dolly, who has gone to the funeral, brings Naomi a plate of food to the porch. Naomi is sitting in one of the wicker rockers fanning herself with an envelope.

"Why don't you come inside, Nomie, where it's cool?" Dolly asks.

"Too hard to get up." Naomi takes the plate. "Thanks, sweetheart. What have we got here?"

"A little bit of everything." Dolly hands her grandmother a napkin and a fork and then kneels beside her.

"Have you had anything to eat?" Naomi asks.

"Some congealed salad."

"Good."

"I think the antibiotic's kicking in." Dolly looks out at the bay where a large freighter is heading toward the Mobile docks. Her parents come out and sit on the steps with plates of food.

"You okay?" Mariel asks as they go by Dolly. "Mama, you got everything you need?"

Dolly and Naomi both nod yes.

"Nomie," Dolly says, "I've got a lot of decisions to make."

"I know you do, honey." Naomi takes a bite of squash casserole. It must be Mrs. Daniel's. She's the only person in Harlow who puts sage in squash. The woman's never learned that cornbread dressing's the only place for sage and precious little there. It reminds Naomi: "Whatever happened to that cookbook you were writing, Dolly?"

"I'm still working on it."

"Don't put sage in the squash."

"No ma'am. I won't." Dolly settles into a more comfortable position. "I need to ask you something, Nomie."

Naomi puts her fork down and looks at Dolly. "What is this? You want some advice from me? Some words of wisdom from the elderly?"

"I guess I do."

"Okay, Nomie's words of wisdom for grandchildren: Don't ever take yourself too seriously."

Dolly grins. "I'll try not to."

"And forgive yourself a lot. You're not carrying the world on your shoulders." Naomi looks over at Mariel who is handing a piece of chicken to Donnie. "I don't think I impressed that on your mother enough."

"I've got a specific question, Nomie. If you could do it over again, would you marry Grandpa Will?"

"You thinking about your Bobby?"

"I guess so. He called again this morning. He's been out of rehab for a couple of months and he's clean."

"Dump him." Naomi spears a bite of ham.

Dolly is startled. "But Nomie, you didn't dump Grandpa Will."

"No. I ended up carrying him which was a terrible thing to do to him. To all of us."

"But you had your children, Nomie."

"Yes. I did." Naomi puts the ham into her mouth and chews. "Good ham. I'll bet it's one of those honey-baked ones that's already cut."

Dolly looks at her grandmother. Naomi looks up and smiles. And in that smile, Dolly sees the truth. She rubs her shoulders which suddenly feel lighter.

"You feeling okay, Dolly?" Dave Horton, who has been talked into staying for lunch, stands over the two women with a full plate of food in his hand.

"Much better," Dolly says.

"Then come keep me company. That swing looks mighty comfortable. Can you spare her, Mrs. Cates?"

"Sure. There'll be another grandchild along in a minute. The place is crawling with them." Naomi takes another bite of squash casserole. Now why in the world did Jessie Daniel put that sage in there?

"Have you had any lunch?" Dave asks as they settle in the swing. He's pulled off the jacket he wore to the funeral, and has loosened his tie. Dolly sees how golden the hair on his arms is, the tiny freckles.

"Some salad."

"You need to eat something taking that antibiotic." Dave hands Dolly a roll.

"Yes, Doctor." She takes a small bite and forces it

down. On the steps, her mother appears to be feeding her father. Mariel has on a pale blue dress that Dolly has never seen before. It looks like something Artie would have painted, she realizes.

"We never really know people, do we," she says to Dave Horton.

"Probably not. Not completely."

"Do you know, sometimes I've wondered why my parents married each other. It's always seemed like such a strange relationship to me."

Dave looks at Mariel and Donnie. They have been joined on the steps by their cousin Bo Hardemond who has come from Huntsville for the funeral. "Doesn't look strange to me."

"That's just it. Look at them. It's weirding me out. I asked Papa one time why he married Mama."

"What did he say?"

"He made me mad. He said he married her because she had a great butt."

Dave laughs.

"It's not funny."

"Well, maybe he just found it hard to put into words." Dave puts his plate down between them. "You want some of this chicken?"

Dolly shakes her head no.

Dave nods toward the steps. "Who's the man with them? He looks like he should have been the twin, not Artie."

"Our cousin Bo from Huntsville. His mother, Aunt Mary, was my grandmother's sister. She wasn't able to make the trip." Dolly looks at Bo Hardemond and her father. "They do look a lot alike, don't they? Those Harvey genes are potent."

"They sure are." Dave stretches. "I'm getting full as a tick."

"This is the only place where I've ever heard people say that."

"Makes you homesick, doesn't it?"

"Not exactly."

"Well, I'm sure I could think up some other sayings that might work. How about my telling you that one of my patients is half a bubble out of plumb?"

"Only one? Is that what you wrote as the diagnosis?"

"Sure. Had trouble with the insurance company, though."

"I'll bet." Dolly watches as Donnie hands Mariel something from his plate. "My God, would you look at that. My father's actually feeding my mother stuff. I must be sicker than I thought. I'm hallucinating."

"You know, maybe he doesn't know why he married her," Dave says. "Happens all the time. It seems to have worked out okay, though."

"But it hasn't. My mother stays at her psychiatrist's and Papa's the workaholic of the world. I don't know. I've decided I don't know anything about relationships." Dolly takes a carrot stick from Dave's plate. "Last night I was thinking that Artie was only twenty-two when she was widowed. Twenty-two. Now how could she have had the love of her life by twenty-two? Lots of Artie's men were talked about at our house, believe me. But why do you suppose she didn't marry and have children? She loved children, I know."

"Maybe all her creativity went into her painting."

"Maybe."

"And she had you."

"Which made my mother jealous."

The two of them smile at each other. "Families," Dolly says.

"Families," Dave agrees. "Wait till you hear about mine."

Mrs. Randolph sticks her head out the door. "Dolly, you got a phone call."

"I'll save your place," Dave says.

Mariel tells Donnie that she bets Dolly's call is from Bobby, that he's already called a couple of times.

"I hope she doesn't get messed up in that again," Donnie says.

"I'm scared she will. She says he's straightening up."

"Dolly's husband?" Cousin Bo asks. His arrival this morning had been a nice surprise. When Mariel had called and talked to Merry, his wife, she had said that Aunt Mary's days were numbered and she didn't know if Bo would be able to make it to Artie's funeral or not.

"Hell, all our days are numbered," Bo had told Merry when he came in and heard the news. "I'm going." Then he got in the shower and cried for Artie, his beautiful girl.

"Ex-husband," Mariel says. "They weren't married in the Church, thank the Lord. He was connected somehow with the dance company Dolly works for. A nice enough guy—we all liked Bobby when we met him, didn't we, Donnie? Of course, we didn't know he was screwed up on drugs. What gets me is that Dolly did know it and married him anyway."

"Maybe she thought she could straighten him out," Bo says.

"I suppose." Mariel takes Donnie's hand. "Try not to worry. She's a grown woman."

They sit looking out over the bay. They see Hektor walking along the water's edge.

"Hektor said he had Delmore Ricketts say a mass for Artie last night on the beach," Donnie says.

Bo has been told the truth, but he already knew Artie wanted to be cremated. They had talked about it. "A regular funeral mass?" he asks.

"I don't know how much they followed the ritual, but Hektor said it made him feel better."

"Just like I felt better having the rosary last night and the funeral mass this morning," Mariel adds.

"And I needed to do what she wanted," Donnie says.

"I'm just glad it's over with." Mariel lets go of Donnie's hand and rubs her tense neck. "Too many people knew Artie wasn't in that casket."

"But in a way, it was like she was." Donnie watches Hektor holding out his arms for May who is running down the beach toward him. "I don't think it matters, anyway." He points his fork. "Look at that Hektor. Who would ever have thought he would get so wrapped up in a child."

"I would have," Mariel says. "He didn't surprise me going to get Father Audubon, either. There are depths in Hektor I think you've never give him credit for, Donnie."

"He's my little brother."

"Who could buy and sell you ten times over. And you've always put that down as luck. Well, some of it might have been, but Hektor took his luck and ran with it. He's a shrewd, complicated man, Donnie. And kind."

"Lucky," Donnie says. He watches a barge coming down the waterway.

"I want to live in this house. I've always wanted to live here in this house with Artie." Bo puts his face in his hands and begins to sob.

Surprised, Donnie and Mariel look at each other over Bo's bent head. As tears begin to seep through Bo's fingers, Mariel presses a tissue into his hand.

Long married, Donnie and Mariel need no words for the ensuing conversation.

Donnie, do you think? Bo and Artie?

Don't know. Guess it's possible.

Her first cousin who, incidentally, looks just like you?

Don't read too much into this, Mariel.

But Donnie knows. Oh, my precious girl. My other half.

Hektor and May are trying to locate the tiny mound where Artie's ashes had been placed. As Reese had predicted, the tide had come up during the night and erased all signs of it.

"That's as it should be," Hektor says. "Earth to earth."

"I think it's nice," May agrees. "We got her up to heaven."

The early afternoon sun is blistering hot. "We better go in," Hektor says. He and May wave at the barge that blows its horn in reply. "Would you like to live here, pumpkin?"

"Sure," May agrees. "Just find me a mama."

"Nag. Nag." He takes her hand and they walk to the bluff steps.

"Did you eat lunch?" Hektor asks.

"I ate a whole lot. I never saw so much food in my life."

"That's the way the Harlow people do when people are in trouble. They come bringing food. They're saying, 'Let us help you.' It does, too. Help."

"Mrs. Randolph said she'd pack some in a cooler for us to take home. Are we going this afternoon, Papa?"

"Well, I don't know of anything else we can do here. And I need to get back to work. And Audubon needs to get back to his fishing. We can come over any time Donnie or Dolly needs us. Okay?"

"Okay."

Hektor turns to look at the beach again. He sees Artie setting off with her crabbing nets. Wait for me. Thomas and Sarah set out for a sail. Wait for me. Wait for me. I love you.

"Go get your things together," he tells May. "And find Father Audubon and tell him we'll leave in about an hour. I think I'll walk down the beach a few minutes." The child runs by her Uncle Donnie and Aunt Mariel and the cousin sitting on the steps.

"Whoa," Mariel says. "Give us a hug."

May hugs them hard and goes on into the house, unaware that her father is standing at the foot of the bluff crying. Sunrise, sunset.

There's one more thing Hektor needs to do before he can go back to New Orleans. He wipes his eyes and starts walking down the beach. He's not surprised when his mother, Sarah, joins him in her black dress, nor when his father, Thomas, in his blue seersucker suit appears beside Sarah. Artie in her peach dress smiles and takes Hektor's hand. This is not a surprise. What is a surprise is when Donnie takes his place beside Artie.

"You okay, Hektor?"

"They're here with us, Donnie."

"I know."

"Artie has on her peach-colored dress. She was a pretty girl, wasn't she, Donnie?"

"Not beautiful like Mama, but cute and pretty."

"What did you think of Mama, Donnie?"

"Like I said, beautiful. But I felt sorry for her and I'd get mad at her." He pauses. "And I loved her."

"Me, too." They walk in silence for a few minutes, the tiny waves slapping at their feet.

"Tell me the truth," Hektor says. "What do you think happened the day Mama and Papa died?"

"I think Papa sank the boat. I think he did it out of love and that it took a hell of a lot of courage."

"I think it was an accident."

Donnie nods. "Just telling you what I thought."

"True." Hektor stops and says he's going up Logan Creek. "You want to go?"

"I think it's past time we did."

They turn and walk along the slippery creek bank. "Watch for snakes," Donnie warns Hektor.

After a few minutes, Hektor and Donnie agree that nothing looks familiar.

"There was a big water oak that used to be right about here. We dug the grave between the tree and the creek because the ground was soft there." Donnie looks around, trying to get his bearings.

"Guess Hurricane Frederick got it. Probably got Zeke Pardue's body, too."

"I hope so."

"Did we wrap him in anything? I don't remember."

"You weren't but ten and you were pretty upset. Artie got a tarp from the garage."

The brothers sit on a log and look up and down the creek.

"Does it still bother you, Donnie?"

"Always will."

"I've often wondered what he was doing on the beach anyway. Like he knew we were coming and what we'd do."

"You thought he was the Devil."

"I'm still not sure he wasn't."

"He fell off a boat, managed to make it to the beach."

Both men see Artie running to the figure at the edge of the water. "Zeke Pardue," she calls back to them.

"Is he dead?" The brothers rush forward.

Artie pokes the body with her foot. Zeke Pardue gives a strangled cough, opens his eyes.

"Remember how yellow his eyes were?" Hektor asks Donnie as they sit on the log.

"His liver. All that whiskey."

"It was Artie's idea, wasn't it?"

"Yeah, but when she said, 'Help me hold him under' we didn't argue."

"I sat on him."

"And I tried to hold his head under the water. He was still pretty strong. I remember blaming him for everything that had gone wrong with Mama and Papa and just thinking, 'Die, you bastard.' "

"Do you remember the sound his head made, Donnie?"

"Like dropping a ripe melon. God! Who would have thought Artie was that strong?"

"And where did she find that piece of pipe on the beach?"

"Lord knows. We had a mess on our hands, didn't we?"

"Did you ever confess it, Donnie?"

"No. And I'm sure Artie didn't."

"I told Father Audubon that the three of us had committed a mortal sin when we were children. He said he'd say some extra prayers for Artie. But Donnie, maybe it's something we ought to start thinking about. We'd be forgiven, and it would stay in the confessional."

"Hektor, do what you want. I know you've always thought there's some Supreme Being out there keeping tabs, and that you don't deserve the good things that happen to you, like May. Maybe it would be best for you."

"What about you?"

"If Artie's in hell, Hektor, that's where I want to be."

The log they are sitting on moves slightly. Beneath them, another bone breaks off the Devil's hand.

After Dolly hangs up the phone, she goes out the back door and sits under the pecan tree. Dave Horton finds her there in a few minutes.

"It's too hot out here for you," he says. "Are you okay?"

Dolly surprises herself by bursting into tears. "I want to live here, Dave," she sobs. "I want to live here and have a dozen children and make everything turn out right."

Dave kneels and wipes her face. "All right."

Reese, sitting in the shade of Hektor's truck, listening, thinks she just might do it.

FORTY

The Wishbone

AFTER HEKTOR, MAY, AND DELMORE RICKETTS DRIVE AWAY IN the truck, the house seems empty. Mrs. Randolph finishes cleaning the kitchen and goes home, carrying supper to her husband. She has neglected him and her house long enough, she thinks. Tomorrow she will get him started on those bannisters on the front porch that he has been promising for weeks to repair. All he does when she isn't there is sit around and drink beer and watch TV.

But Mr. Randolph will enjoy the supper and not worry about the bannisters. Kelly Stuart has already called and left word for Mrs. Randolph to call her. He knows what she wants; he's heard old Mrs. Stuart's health is failing. He greets his wife and her offering of food happily.

Dolly drives Naomi home and then runs by the Harlow library. In her pocket is the scrap of blue paper that fell out of Artie's telephone book. The words may be just some casual jotting, but Donnie's name in parentheses beside "Fruit-Gathering" seems important to Dolly.

It's a new library, not the old house that had been the library when Dolly was a child. The librarian is the same, though, Mrs. Tallulah Smith, who is curved with osteoporosis and who says, "Oh, honey, I'm so sorry about your Aunt Artie. Bless her heart. I wish I could have been at the funeral this morning. And how's your daddy doing?"

"He's doing pretty good, Miss Tallulah. Thank you." Dolly takes out the note that had fallen from Artie's telephone book. "Miss Tallulah, I'm looking for something called 'Fruit-Gathering.' I think the author is Tagore. I don't know if it's a poem or what."

"Well, let's look in *Grangers Index*."

Mrs. Smith leads Dolly across the shiny new floor to the small reference department. "Here you go." She points to a large book from the shelf. "They're listed by author, title, first and last lines. If we don't have the book it's listed in, we can borrow it from Mobile."

"Thanks." Dolly takes the book down and sits at a table while Mrs. Smith returns to the circulation counter saying, "Holler if you need some help."

Dolly turns to "Tagore." Nothing. "Fruit-Gathering." Nothing. Then she looks up "What I keep of you, or you rob from me." And it's listed as the last line of a poem by George Santayana entitled "To W.P." She goes to the computer and clicks on "Author—Search." The Harlow library doesn't have a copy of Santayana's poetry, but Mobile does. She writes the title down. Next she looks up Tagore and finds a long list by Rabindranath Tagore. No "Fruit-Gathering" is listed. It must be a smaller piece in one of the many books. And how would that be indexed?

None of his books are in the Harlow library. She is listing the ones that Mobile has when Mrs. Smith comes over with a thin dark blue book.

"Artie checked this book out and renewed it and then had Reese check it out on his card and renew it. I think she got a lot of comfort from it. You might, too, Dolly."

Dolly takes the book. Its title is *A Humanist Funeral Service*. The author is Corliss Lamont.

"I know your family's Catholic and Artie had a regular Catholic service, but I thought you might like to see what she was reading." Mrs. Smith shakes her head. "The title scares a lot of people off, but it's a nice book."

Dolly knows what she will find when she opens the pages. She thanks Mrs. Smith and takes it to a table. And there it is on page twenty-four, a reading from "Fruit-Gathering" by Sir Rabindranath Tagore.

Oh Fire, my brother, I sing victory to you.
You are the bright red image of fearful freedom.
You swing your arms in the sky, you sweep your
impetuous fingers across the harp-string,
your dance music is beautiful. . . .
My body will be one with you, my heart will be
caught in the whirls of your frenzy,
and the burning heat that was my life will flash up and
mingle itself in your flame.

On the next page is the poem "To W.P." by Santayana.

Dolly wipes her eyes with the back of her hands, then goes to the counter to check the book out. She thinks the book smells like almonds.

With the shades drawn against the August sun, Mariel and Donnie lie in Donnie's old room after making love quietly and unhurriedly. Mariel is dreaming she is walking through a field of daylilies. Suddenly she sees a blue one. At first she is excited, but when she gets closer, she sees it's a silk flower. She jerks it from the ground. Someone is playing a trick on her. She turns on her side away from Donnie.

He has closed his eyes to a slide show. Artie on the pier as they brought their parents' bodies in. Artie at eighteen marrying Carl. Artie in the front hall with her suitcases packed. "I have to leave. I have to. You and Hektor take care of things." "Where are you going?" "I'm not sure. I'll call you, though." Watching her drive away, running toward the road to catch a last glimpse of her '50 Ford. Be safe, Artie. Be safe, sister.

"Why did you let her go?" Hektor is standing inside the screen door. He looks as if he will cry. "Where is she?"

"This is something Artie had to do, Hektor. She said for us to take care of things while she was gone. Okay?"

"But where's she going?"

"To slay some dragons, Hektor. She'll call us."

Artie showing them around New York. Her first opening at a gallery. A silver outfit, the skirt so tight she has to lie on the bed while he and Hektor zip her up. "This can't be comfortable. You can't breathe."

"I'm holding my breath tonight anyway, Donnie."

"You're going to be a smash."

"I'm going to be okay, Donnie." Hugging him, the material of the dress rough, like fish scales.

"Yes."

The calls. "I'm going to Europe, Donnie." To Japan. San Francisco.

Be happy, Artie.

"I'm happy, Donnie." It's Christmas and they are putting up the tree in Harlow. He looks at her and sees it's true. She smiles and hands him a string of lights she has just tested.

"Good. Dragons slayed?"

"Sleeping quietly. What about yours?"

"Sleeping."

"Merry Christmas, Donnie."

"Merry Christmas, Artie."

"And to all a good night." She plugs another string of lights into the socket. It shines brightly. "Hey, how about that! You're paying the preacher."

Walking down the beach. "I have lymphoma, Donnie." The sun is warm and sandpipers scurry away from small waves, rush back to scoop up minnows. And the twins sit on the sand holding each other, their arms and legs entwined as they had been in Sarah's womb, their tears the same.

Donnie gets up quietly and dresses.

"You okay?" Mariel mumbles.

"Fine." He goes downstairs and gets the plastic container out of the desk drawer where it has been kept during the funeral. My brother Adonis. The day he deems perfect. Bullshit, Artie. You'd be sitting around in this drawer for a long time.

He puts the container on the coffee table and sits on the sofa looking at it. It's as inanimate as it was yesterday.

"What are you doing?" Dolly stands in the doorway. She has on the wrinkled khaki shorts and yellow shirt she changed into after the company had left.

"Trying to decide what to do." Donnie looks at his child. "How are you feeling?"

"Better than I look." She comes into the room and sees the ashes. "You decide when to sprinkle them?"

"What do you think she meant by the 'day I deemed perfect'?"

"I don't know." Dolly sits down on the sofa beside Donnie. "What do you think?"

"I'm thinking she was trying to tell me something. Something she understood and that I don't know."

"What?"

"Something about living. About each day. I don't know. I'll have to think about it."

"She enjoyed living, I know that."

"Yes, she did."

They are both quiet for a few moments.

"Where's Mama?" Dolly asks.

"Asleep."

"You two are getting along splendidly."

"We always have."

"Don't hand me that."

"And don't you be sassy, young lady."

They grin at each other. "Let's take Artie to the bay," Donnie says.

"Now?"

"Right now. I think that's what she intended for us to do."

"Okay. But first, I've got something I think she wanted you to read." Dolly hands her father the book. She has marked the place with the scrap of blue paper.

"What is it?" he asks.

"The note was in her telephone directory. I found the book at the library. Miss Tallulah said Artie checked it out several times." Dolly stands up. "Tell you what. I'll go get me something to drink while you're reading it."

It's a half hour before Donnie comes to the kitchen door. He has been crying, but he smiles at Dolly. "Like I said, let's take her to the bay."

"You okay?"

"I'm okay."

"Do you want to get the boat or just walk out or what?"

"We'll get the boat."

Mariel hears the car start. She gets up and goes to the window just as they pull out of the driveway. She knows where they are going. Good. Be careful, my darlings.

Because of the bluffs, most of the residents of Harlow keep their boats at a communal dock. The slips hold boats that range from small fishing boats with trolling motors attached to sleek cigar boats used (to the annoyance of the natives) for skimming across the surface of the bay at incredible speeds. Artie's boat is one she has had for as long as Dolly can remember, a blue and white outboard with GRAVY on the side. It is kept in the same slip that had once wintered Thomas and Sarah's sailboat.

"Old *Gravy Boat*," Dolly says affectionately.

"I don't remember when it's been out." Donnie puts the plastic bowl on the pier and unhooks the cover. "Hope it starts."

"We can always row."

"Old *Gravy*'s made me do that quite a few times." Donnie jumps into the boat and unhooks the cover from the other side. "Come on," he tells Dolly.

She hands him Artie's ashes which he puts on the floor of the boat. Then he holds her hand while she steps onto the seat. The boat rocks gently as they settle in.

"Keep your fingers crossed," Donnie says. He turns the key in the switch. *Gravy* coughs and sputters before settling into a steady rhythm.

"Good girl," Dolly says.

"This is no girl," her father says. "This is an old lady."

"Well, she's still got some get-up-and-go."

"Old folks will surprise you every now and then."

They back out of the slip and start slowly toward the open bay. "You need any gas?" Jeff Crenshaw shouts as they round the end of the pier. Donnie waves no. The tank is almost full.

He points *Gravy* toward the middle of the bay, toward the channel. The air, though warm, feels good blowing against them. Then sun is getting low in the sky.

"I love this place," Dolly says.

Donnie nods.

"I see Mama." Dolly points toward the houses on the bluff. Mariel is visible sitting at the top of the steps. Dolly waves to her but Mariel apparently doesn't see them and doesn't wave back. "Daydreaming," Dolly says. "I see Cousin Bo, too. Down on the beach." She waves at him, but he doesn't see them. He has what looks like a stick in his hand, and he's writing in the sand. "Where are we going, Papa?"

"To the center."

There is very little traffic on the bay today, not like there will be tomorrow and Sunday when the sailors and fishermen are out from Mobile. Even the Grand Hotel at Point Clear seems somnolent. No one is on the grounds and the beach seems deserted. Tomorrow it will be a different story.

"How will we know we are in the middle?" Dolly asks.

"I'll deem it." They smile at each other. Dolly leans back and closes her eyes. The heat and the sound of *Gravy's* motor are making her drowsy again. "Almond cream pie," she says to Artie who has taken her to Sunday dinner at the Grand Hotel. "Almond cream pie."

"What did you say?" her father asks.

"I said 'Almond cream pie.' I was thinking about the Grand Hotel."

"I used to dream about it when I was away from here. I swear I think that's why Artie liked the smell of almonds so."

"I never thought of that. I can remember her laying away a couple of pieces at a time, though."

"And never gaining an ounce. It killed your mama."

"Artie as a sister-in-law must have been pretty formidable. Do you know, I don't think I really thought about that much until this week."

"Your mama can be pretty formidable in her own way."

"I've been thinking about that, too. It must have made your life complicated at times."

"Certainly interesting. What drove me the craziest, though, was how much they were alike, deep down. And I seemed to be the only one who could see it."

"I can't see it," Dolly says.

"Nobody else can, honey. But they are. They're both strong women; take my word for it. That's why they never could get along with each other."

"Do you think if Carl had lived, Artie would have stayed here?"

"Harlow was always her security."

"You were her security."

"And she was mine." Which, of course, Dolly knows has always been the contention between Artie and Mariel.

Dolly holds her hand out and catches some spray. "Do you think Artie ever had another great love? I've been thinking about that, too. Besides Carl, I mean."

"Yes."

"Who was he?"

"I don't know, honey."

He's lying, but Dolly doesn't mind. She rubs her wet hand against her shorts and asks, "Have you ever heard, Papa, that psychologists say we marry ourselves?"

"And you look at your mama and me and wonder about it?"

"Well, yours is the only marriage I have to go by. Do you think it's true?"

Donnie thinks for a moment. "Probably. I think your mama and I are opposite sides of the same coin with the edges beginning to blur."

And Bobby? Dolly feels the familiar rush of pain. There were no dividing lines, Bobby. What you did to yourself, you did to me.

"Everything will turn out fine," her father says, reading her thoughts. Dolly reaches over and pats him on the leg.

They are now in the ship channel with no barge or large boat in sight. The few sailboats and small fishing boats are clustered near the beach. Donnie cuts the engine down. "Here?" he asks. Dolly nods.

Donnie turns off the motor and they drift. Waves slap against the boat; seagulls squawk above them.

"The current here will take her to the gulf," Donnie says. Dolly nods.

Donnie picks up the plastic bowl and takes the top off. I scarce know which greater be, what I keep of you, or you rob of me. You are robbing me, Artie. "Do you want to say anything?" he asks Dolly. She says no. "Do you want to sprinkle some of the ashes?" Dolly again shakes her head.

"Then I better get to it. I'll need you to move, though, so I can put some on that side." Dolly sits on the back of the seat.

"I commend my sister to you, Lord," Donnie says. "I loved her. We all did. We ask that you be merciful to her and grant her eternal rest. May your light shine on her forever. Amen."

"Amen," Dolly says through tears.

Donnie holds the container over the side of the boat and lets some of the ashes fall into the water. Then a few more. Finally, he shakes the bowl. Dolly hears a noise that sounds like a fish feeding. Then he moves to her side of the boat and does the same, this time holding the container upside down and finally dipping it into the water to rinse it out.

"Look," Donnie says. "Look, Dolly."

Dolly looks behind them. The drifting ashes have formed a wishbone that is gleaming golden in the last rays of the sun. Artie would have loved this, she thinks. The light. It was what she was always trying to get on canvas. Now she's part of it. Goodbye. Goodbye.

They sit quietly for a few minutes watching the wishbone widen, change shapes, get caught in ripples.

"Let's go home now," Donnie says.

"Not yet. Let's wait for the sun to go down. It's almost to the horizon."

At that moment a breeze springs up and the wishbone's forward motion quickens toward the light. The hot, cold, dangerous, forgiving light.

"Lord!" Dolly stands up and shouts. "Lord! Here comes Artie!"

They drift until the last chord of sun disappears and Dolly says, "Okay, Papa. We can go home now."

And they do.

FORTY-ONE

Waiting for Artie

"I DECLARE I LOVE THIS TIME OF THE DAY," SARAH SULLIVAN says. She is sitting in a yellow canvas chair at the end of the community pier. The setting sun is making her hair golden.

"Anybody else want this last tomato sandwich?" Thomas Sullivan asks.

"I'll half it with you," Carl Jenkins says.

"Okay. Will, lend me your knife."

Will Cates fumbles in his overall pockets for his knife and hands it to Thomas.

Sarah leans back and closes her eyes. "When the breeze comes up like this, it makes you feel like you're floating."

Thomas reaches over her to give Carl his half of the sandwich. "Ana," he says to the dark-haired girl sitting on the pier with her feet dangling in the water, "did you have enough?"

"Plenty." She splashes the water slightly; her toenails are painted bright red.

"It sure is taking Artie a long time," Carl says.

Sarah laughs. "She's pulling herself together."

Ana laughs, too. "That Hektor is crazy. He got half of her blessed and buried."

"I think it was sweet." Sarah turns to Will. "Don't you want me to hold Toy a while?"

"No. She's asleep. She's fine."

"That's a beautiful christening dress, Will," Ana says. "I think it's prettier than the one May had."

"Thank you." Will rocks back and forth in his blue canvas chair, holding the baby against his chest.

"The ladies of the church made it in one day. Amazing." Sarah reaches for her glass of iced tea.

Thomas leans forward. "I see a boat coming in. It's probably Donnie and Dolly."

Sarah looks toward the boat. "I hope so. Dolly doesn't need to get chilled." She turns to Carl. "I think she's going to stay here and marry the doctor."

But Carl isn't paying any attention to his mother-in-law. He's listening to the music from the Grand Hotel. They're playing "Sweet Caroline." When Artie gets here, they'll dance. He hasn't danced in a long time. Which is all right. It's pleasant here.

"Who knows?" Thomas says.

But Sarah insists. "She'll marry the doctor and have a dozen children. We'll be great-grandparents, Thomas."

"So will I," Will says.

"I keep forgetting that." Sarah smiles and sips her tea. What does it matter?

"That's my favorite dress, Sarah," Thomas says. It is, of course, the black velvet dress without a back that Hektor remembers so well.

"I know."

Carl gets up and walks to the edge of the pier. "I wish Artie would get here."

A man in a white dinner jacket is walking down the beach.

"Have patience." Ana stretches. "Listen to the music."

Sarah looks at Carl's uniform. "You know," she says, "it's amazing how those Korean uniforms still look good. Still stylish."

A teenage boy joins the group and sits beside Thomas. "What's going on?" he asks him.

"We're waiting for my daughter. What's going on with you?"

"Don't know. I was just riding my motorcycle."

Thomas nods. "It happens."

"You want to fish?" Will asks the boy. "I've got an extra pole."

"Might as well. It's nice out here this evening."

"Always is," Ana says.

"There's tea and almond pie," Sarah offers. "The tomato sandwiches are gone. We can get some more, though."

The boy shakes his head no.

"Hush, little baby, don't say a word," Will sings to Toy who has begun to stir.

"It's them," Thomas says as the boat pulls closer to the pier. "It's *Gravy Boat*. Artie will be here soon."

"It's nice out here," the boy repeats.

"What's your name, son?" Thomas asks.

"Joe Murray."

"You Eugene Murray's grandson?"

"Yessir. He's going to be wondering where I am. My whole family is."

"No, he's not. Go on and cast. See what you catch."

"Papa's gonna buy you a mockingbird," Will sings softly.

Donnie brings *Gravy Boat* into her berth. He and Dolly get out and tie the boat up.

"Dolly's going to be fine," Sarah says. "Look how much she looks like me."

"May's going to be fine, too," Ana says.

The lights come on on the pier. A slight eastern breeze stirs the banners on the boats. The boy pulls in a five-pound catfish.

Sarah reaches over and takes Thomas's hand. "It's a lovely evening."

"I wonder where Artie is," Carl says.

Thomas smiles at him. "She's be here in a little while, Carl. We've got all the time in the world."